UNDER COVER *in* HIGH HEELS

GEMMA HALLIDAY

JAICO PUBLISHING HOUSE
Ahmedabad Bangalore Bhopal Bhubaneswar Chennai
Delhi Hyderabad Kolkata Lucknow Mumbai

Published by Jaico Publishing House
A-2 Jash Chambers, 7-A Sir Phirozshah Mehta Road
Fort, Mumbai - 400 001
jaicopub@jaicobooks.com
www.jaicobooks.com

UNDERCOVER IN HIGH HEELS
ISBN 978-81-8495-495-1

First Jaico Impression: 2013

Printed by
Snehesh Printers
320-A, Shah & Nahar Ind. Est. A-1
Lower Parel, Mumbai - 400 013

For my favorite leading man, Nicky.

CHAPTER ONE

"Wait, Chad, don't leave. I... I have something to tell you."

"After all your lies and deception, there's nothing you can possibly say to make me stay now, Ashley."

"Chad, please! You know I love you. I only did what I had to to keep us together. Besides, you can't go now... I'm carrying your baby!"

I gasped, grabbing another handful of popcorn as the TV switched to a commercial for deodorant.

"Oh my freaking God, the baby is the gardener's?" my best friend Dana shouted from the sofa beside me. "Her husband is gonna freaking flip."

"Don't worry," I said, taking a sip of Diet Coke. "He's still in that coma, remember? He'll never know."

"Oh, right. I missed that episode. So, does that mean the lady that hit him with the car went to jail?"

I shook my head. "No, her husband blackmailed the D.A. to get the charges dropped, but only if she checked herself into rehab. But instead of going to rehab, she shacked up with her sister's husband at his place on the lake."

"Oooooooh," Dana said, drawing out the word. "So that's why the sister is poisoning the husband."

I nodded. "Shhh, it's back on."

Dana and I went silent, our eyes glued to the screen as Chad and Ashley fell into a passionate embrace. I'm not ashamed to admit it. I was seriously hooked on this show. *Magnolia Lane* was the hottest prime time soap to hit the air waves since Brandon and Brenda moved to the 90210, and I was powerless against its junk TV spell.

My cell rang from my purse.

"You're ringing," Dana said.

I waved it off. "Commercial," I mumbled around a bite of popcorn, my eyes glued to the screen as Chad asked Ashley just how sure she was the baby was his and not her comatose husband's. While, of course, Ashley's nosey neighbor listened at the bedroom door, catching the whole conversation.

Just as they switched to a shot of Ashley's husband in the coma ward, my purse rang again.

"You sure you shouldn't get that?" Dana asked.

I shook my head. "Are you kidding? Ashley's husband is about to wake up."

I ignored the William Tell Overture trilling from the region of my Kate Spade, instead grabbing another handful of popcorn as Nurse Nan leaned over the comatose Preston Francis Barton the third. Considering she was his wife's secret evil twin sister, I figured we were in for two options: she was either going to smother him or pull the plug.

She leaned in closer. Her hands reached for the plug.

Dana and I did a collective gasp.

Then the screen went to a life insurance commercial featuring a baby boomer in leather pants air-guitaring a Jimi Hendrix song.

"I hate it when they do that!" Dana said, throwing a piece of popcorn at the screen. Hers, of course, was minus the butter, oil, fat, salt, and flavor. Dana was an aerobics instructor slash wanna-be actress with the kind of curves that caused car crashes on the PCH. Her body was a temple. Mine, on the other hand, required regular sacrifices from the natives of double stuffed Oreos, cheeseburgers, and popcorn with lots of bright yellow butter flavoring made of things I couldn't pronounce. My theory? As long as my favorite Cavalli jeans still fit, I was doing okay. (Fine, so they were a little snug around the waist lately, but I could still zip them up!)

While Dana tossed another kernel of popcorn at the television, I reached into my purse and checked my cell readout. Two missed calls. Both from the same number, one that had me doing a little happy squirm in my seat. Ramirez.

Detective Jack Ramirez was not only the LAPD's hottest cop, but as of last fall he was also mine. All mine.

Okay, so he hadn't exactly officially said that I was his girlfriend yet, but I'm pretty sure that just last week he used the words "girl" and "friend" in the same sentence. Which was a start. Ramirez wasn't exactly your typical Happily Ever After material. He was a homicide detective with a very large gun, a very large tattoo and some very dangerous moves in the bedroom. More of a bad-boy Russell Crow than a home-and-hearth Ward Cleaver. Not, mind you, that I was complaining. (See bedroom reference above.)

We were supposed to meet for "drinks or something" later after he got off shift. Me, I was wearing a black lace Vicky's Secret thong under my Capris in hopes of the "or something."

I keyed in my pin number and waited for my messages while the *Magnolia Lane* theme song played and credits rolled over a backdrop of manicured lawns and a picture-perfect neighborhood.

"Hey, Maddie, it's me," came Ramirez's voice. "Listen, something came up. I've got to meet someone at the Cabana Club, so I can't get together later after all. Sorry. I'll call you tomorrow."

Great.

Ramirez's fatal flaw, as you may have noticed, was his tendency to make and break plans. Or, worse yet, not make them at all. Even though I was seconds away from actual girlfriend status, I hadn't seen Ramirez since last Friday night when a dinner and movie at City Walk had turned into appetizers and me in a cab when he got a call about a gang shooting in Compton. And now, true to form, he was blowing off our "or something" again. I narrowed my eyes at my cell, wondering what kind of *someone* he was meeting instead?

"What's up?" Dana asked, watching my face fall.

"Ramirez. He's canceling on me." Again.

"What, again?" Dana asked, voicing my thoughts.

"I know! He said he has to meet someone. What does that mean?"

Dana shrugged. "I dunno." She popped another piece of popcorn into her mouth.

"I mean, are we talking a work-related-someone or a personal-someone? 'Cause if it's a personal someone, why not just ask them to join us for drinks? Why cancel on me? What, is he ashamed of me? He doesn't want his friends to meet me? That's bad, isn't it? It means something really bad. He's having second thoughts about this whole relationship thing isn't he? I knew it. I knew it wouldn't last. I knew he'd never settle down. I mean, not that I'm asking him to settle down. Oh, God, do you think he thinks I want him to settle down? Is that it? Am I smothering him? Am I too needy? I'm not too needy, am I?"

"Whoa. Take a breath, Gilmore Girl. No wonder he needs a night off."

Dana was right, I was beginning to hyperventilate.

"Look, he's probably just out with the guys or something tonight. You know how those cops are. It's a total boy's club."

"You're right." I took a deep breath. "Right. He probably just needs a night out with the guys. It's not that he *doesn't* want to be with me. I mean, of course he wants to be with me. Why wouldn't he want to be with me? I'm so not smothery." I paused. "But, just in case, how about we go on a double date this weekend?"

Dana shot me a look. "Double date?"

"It's way harder to smother someone on a double date. Beside, it'll be fun. Me and Ramirez, you and..." I paused, unsure which flavor of the month Dana was presently working her way through. As much as I loved my best friend, even I had to admit she had an uncanny ability to pick men destined for short term romances. Case in point, her last boyfriend, Rico, a self-proclaimed Urban Soldier who'd ended up joining a group of mercenaries in Afghanistan searching for the last remnants of the Taliban. Dana was still nursing a sore ego at being dumped for a bunch of dusty caves halfway around the world.

She bit her lip as a little frown settled between her strawberry blonde brows. "Sorry, Maddie, I can't do a double date."

"Please! It's not like I'm asking you to actually have this relationship for me; I just need a buffer."

Dana shook her head. "No, no. It's not that. I can't date. I'm off men."

"Oh, no. Please don't tell me you're trying that lesbian thing again," I said, sipping my Diet Coke.

Dana shook here head. "No, it's not like that. It's… well… I can't have sex." She put her hands on my shoulders, turning me to face her as she put on her serious look. "I have a problem."

"A problem? What, like an STD?"

She shook her head again. "No, Mads. This is worse."

I arched an eyebrow. "Okay, I'll bite, what's worse than an STD?"

"I'm addicted to sex."

I rolled my eyes. "Oh, good. I thought this was something serious." I laid on the sarcasm double stuffed as I grabbed another handful of popcorn.

"This *is* serious!" she protested.

"Dana, you are hot. Men like you. Since when is that a problem?"

"That's not true, Maddie. I'm sick."

"You're lucky is what you are. You know how many push-up bras I own just to have half your cleavage?" A lot. I was pretty sure that Jack Black and I were the only people left in L.A. that still wore B cups.

Dana ignored me. "Sex can be like any other addiction. It's a disease. One I have to accept and learn to manage one day at a time. I'm practicing positive sexual sobriety."

I crunched down hard on a popcorn kernel to keep from laughing. "Positive sexual sobriety?"

Dana nodded. "Uh-huh. Therapist Max says it's the only way to break the cycle of addiction."

I blinked. "Therapist Max? You're seriously taking advice from a guy named 'Therapist Max?'"

Dana nodded again. "Yes, Maddie. We're all first names at SA. Even the therapists."

I knew I was going to regret asking. "SA?"

"Sexaholics Anonymous."

Mental forehead smack. "And I thought *Magnolia Lane* was over the top."

"Oh, Maddie," Dana said, her eyes lighting up, "you should totally come with me to a meeting. There are tons of hot guys there, and they're always super nice to new girls."

I'll bet. "Thanks, but no thanks. Besides, I have a boyfriend. Sort of," I added ruefully, thinking of my Vicky's thong going to waste tonight. "You sure Ramirez isn't blowing me off?"

Dana opened a bottled water and took a long drink. "Positive."

"All right. Then I promise not to freak out about it anymore tonight. I mean, if he wants to go with the boys to the Cabana Club, I'm not going to be one of those whiny kind of girlfriends about it."

Dana's head snapped up, and she did a little cough/choke thing with her water. "The Cabana Club?!"

Uh-oh. "Yeah… why?"

"Maddie, have you ever been there?"

I shook my head. To be honest my idea of a night on the town started with dinner on Ventura and ended with a turn around the Beverly Center and a new pair of pumps. I wasn't exactly a regular on the club circuit.

"Ohmigod, Maddie. It's a total hook-up place. You didn't tell me Ramirez was going *there*!"

Oh, shit. I felt my stomach bottom out, fizzy Diet Coke mixing with fake buttered popcorn mixing with pure dread. "Oh, God. This is it. He's totally dumping me, isn't he? It was all about the chase, wasn't it? Now that he's got me where he wants me, he doesn't want me anymore! I'm stale, Dana. I'm like that day-old bagel no one wants. Oh, God, what am I going to do?"

"I'm sorry, hon." Dana laid a hand on my arm and sent me the same pity look she'd been giving me ever since my mother insisted on giving me a bob with bangs in seventh grade. "Look, I'm sure it's nothing. I'm sure he's just…" She trailed off, unable to come up with an adequate lie.

"Right." I took a big gulp of my Diet Coke, the carbonation burning all the way down my throat. "But just in case, you feel like grabbing a drink?"

* * *

The Cabana Club was a large, brick building on the corner of La Brea and Sunset, painted pink and flanked by flashing neon flamingos. Since it was Friday night there was a line to get in, but luckily Dana knew every bouncer in town (most on a more intimate basis than I knew my gynecologist) and we were inside before you could say "Lindsay Lohan."

As my eyes adjusted to the dimly lit interior, punctuated by pink and green flashing lasers, I realized Dana was right. The placed reeked of hook-up. A crowded dance floor to our right held L.A.'s hottest bodies – actress-slash-waitresses, model-slash-waitresses, a bunch of CW actors, and that girl from *Survivor* that everyone hated – all gyrating together in a way that couldn't even air on HBO. Tables to the left were filled with groupings of men and women doing the heads-bent-together thing and drinking tall cocktails while grabbing each other under the table. The bar straight ahead was two people thick with singles looking to score a martini and a phone number. I squinted through the darkness, praying my boyfriend wasn't one of them.

"This is *so* not a boys night out," I shouted over the techno beat pulsating off the walls.

"This is *so* not the place a recovering sex addict should be spending her Friday night." Dana eyed a guy at the bar wearing leather pants, an unbuttoned shirt and a "how you doin'" smile.

He winked at her.

Dana bit her lip.

"Let's find Ramirez and get out of here fast before I do something I'm going to regret," she said.

Fine by me. We wove our way through the crowd, circling the bar. I got elbowed by an Olsen twin look-alike, and a guy in a cowboy hat spilled a margarita on my Capris, but I didn't care. I was on a mission. I had been patient with Ramirez. I had given him his space. I had even waited a record two months before having sex with him. (Not entirely by choice, but that was beside the point.) I had done everything known to woman to make this relationship work. And what did he do? Blow it all for a night in hook-up heaven. Woman scorned didn't even begin to describe the anger surging through me as I scanned the club.

Then I spotted him. He was sitting at a table near the back, a half empty glass of beer in front of him. I gnashed my teeth together, my vision going red as I stared my worst fear in the face.

Ramirez was sitting next to a woman. A *tall* woman. If there's anything in this world that my 5'1 ½" self hates more than being dumped, it's being dumped for someone tall.

Her legs were almost as long as I was, tucked under the table beneath a barely-there leather mini. And her top didn't cover a whole lot more. A plunging neckline dipped almost to her belly button, showing off cleavage that was obviously man-made. Over her shoulders was a little red shrug jacket, more for fashion effect than actual coverage, and her long black hair was loose, flowing down her back, giving her that dark, exotic look that a blonde Irish/English mutt like myself could never pull off.

And then she put her hand on his thigh.

I felt my nostrils flare, my hands balling into fists at my sides. That's it, police officer or no, I was gonna kill him.

I vaguely heard Dana yelling something along the lines of, "Maddie, wait!" but I couldn't have stopped if I wanted to. My body was moving all on its own as I marched straight toward the happy couple.

"You sonofabitch!" I yelled once I was in earshot.

Ramirez turned around, his dark eyebrows hunching together at the sight of me. Despite my anger, my hormones did that little happy sigh they always did when he was around. Ramirez had perfected the tall, dark and dangerous look - his black hair just a little too long, his dark brown eyes just a little too hard, and a sleek panther tattooed on his arm, just a little too big to hide beneath the sleeve of his black T-shirt. His tan skin was interrupted by a thin white scar running through his left eyebrow and a perpetual dusting of rugged stubble across his chin. The Bad Boy slash Sex God effect of it all was almost enough to stop a girl in her tracks.

Almost.

"I can't believe you blew me off for this!" I yelled, gesturing to his Amazon woman. She gave me a startled look, her eyes darting from side to side as if trying to figure out where I'd come from.

"Maddie, what are you doing here?" Ramirez asked, his eyebrows still drawn together in confusion.

"I could be asking the same question." I poked a finger at Ramirez's chest, coming up against his hard, six-day-a-week-at-the-gym pecs. "Who the hell do you think you are that you can lead me on then just blow me off like this for another woman?"

"Maddie," Ramirez said, his voice low and commanding. "Go home. I'll explain later."

"Oh, right! I'll just go home and let you finish your date with Slut-zilla here." I was yelling loudly enough now that even over the pounding dance music, the couples at the adjacent tables were staring.

"Who is this?" Amazon's eyes ping-ponged between Ramirez and me. "I told you to come alone."

"Maddie," Ramirez said again, his eyes shooting daggers at me. "Don't do this."

"Don't do this? Don't *do* this! I'm sorry, what exactly am I doing? Because it sure as hell isn't dating some abnormally tall chick when you were supposed to be doing 'or something' with me!"

"Ramirez?" the Amazon asked, shifting nervously.

"Maddie," Ramirez warned.

"Jerk!" I yelled.

Then I picked up his half-empty glass and tossed the contents in his face.

"Jesus," he sputtered, jumping from his chair and blinking Budweiser out of his eyes.

"And as for you…" I said, turning on Amazon Woman.

But I didn't get to finish that threat.

She bolted from her chair and before I could register what was going on pulled a gun out from her little red shrug (which, I now realized was clearly not *just* for fashion's sake) and grabbed me by my blonde roots. I let out a strangled cry as she wrapped one arm around my neck, holding me in a vice grip.

"All right, nobody move!" she shouted, commanding the shocked couples at the nearby tables, their mouths hanging open as they watched the scene unfold.

Then Amazon Woman pushed the barrel of the gun against my temple.

"Or blondie dies."

CHAPTER TWO

Holy crap! My first irrational thought as I stared at the barrel of Amazon's gun was that not only was I being dumped for a tall woman, I was being dumped for a psycho! (Hey, I said it was irrational.) The second was pure thankfulness that Ramirez had quick cop reflexes. In a spilt second he had his gun un-holstered and pointed at Amazon in a Mexican standoff.

"Isabel, drop the gun," he commanded, his voice the only calm thing in the room.

As soon as the guns had popped out, people started screaming and scattering. The *Survivor* chick dove under a table, and the CW actors trampled over the Olsen twin look-alike in a mad dash for the front doors. The D.J. stopped spinning music, ducking behind a pair of speakers, and all I could hear now was the sound of glass breaking and a chorus of hysterical voices yelling, "Call 9-1-1." I'm pretty sure I picked one of them out as Dana's.

"Isabel," Ramirez prompted again.

"No way!" she shouted, tightening her grip on me until my vision started going blurry. "No fucking way."

"Isabel, let's just calm down."

"I'm not calming nothing, you pig. This is a setup. I told you no other cops."

"She's not a cop, Isabel," Ramirez ground out through his clenched jaw.

"Honest!" I squeaked. "I never even made it as a Girl Scout."

"Shut up!" she commanded, pushing the barrel into my temple.

I shut up.

"Isabel, listen to me," Ramirez said. He was slowly inching closer to her, his gun straight-armed in front of him. "Just set the gun down, and you can walk out of here right now. No one has to get hurt."

She shook her head, long black hair flapping wildly around her face. "Unh-uh. No way, pal. I know you've got this place surrounded. You've got cops outside waiting for me. You set me up. And quit moving closer!"

I heard Ramirez mutter the word, "Jesus," under his breath and send me another dagger-sharp look. "I didn't set you up. She's not a cop, Isabel. She's my…" He paused.

I held my breath and leaned forward. Date? Lover? *Girlfriend*? Come on, for the love of God, finish the sentence, man!

"… friend," he finally said.

Jerk.

"I don't care who she is," Crazy Isabel responded. "She's coming with me." She shifted her hold on me, grabbing me by the arm with one hand and stuffing the gun into my ribs with the other.

"And don't you try to follow me, pig. I'll kill her. I'll happily splatter her brains all over this room."

I winced. Granted, this entire episode was proving just how very few brains I had (Why, oh why, hadn't I just sat at home neurotically *wondering* what my boyfriend was doing like a normal girl?), but I wanted to keep them right where they were, thank you very much.

I saw the muscles in Ramirez's jaw flinch, but he kept the gun steady on her. "Don't do anything stupid, Isabel."

Isabel ignored him, dancing me backwards as she made her way to the nearest exit sign. Ramirez stood rooted to the spot, his eyes intense, watching the gap between us widen.

This was bad. Seeing Ramirez with another woman wasn't so hot, but this? This was big steaming piles of cow dung bad.

Isabel pushed through the emergency exit, sounding a fire alarm that whipped the panicked crowd into a frenzy again. A bartender yelled, "Fire!" and I saw two girls in halter tops shove Dana out of the way, dashing like linebackers to the front doors. Unfortunately, Dana knocked into Mr. How-You-Doin', sending him teetering backward and colliding with Ramirez. Ramirez staggered back a step. Which was just enough to make his aim waiver. Isabel took that opportunity to bolt.

"Come on, blondie," she said, as the door slammed shut behind us. Keeping her vice grip on my arm, she kicked off her mules and sprinted through the parking lot.

"Where are we going?" I asked as I stumbled after her, breaking a heel and stubbing my toe on the asphalt.

"Shut up!" she said. Then paused, scanning the lot. "I need a car."

I pointed to a green VW bug. "How about that one?" Not that I was actually into helping the crazy lady make a great escape, but I figured the faster she got away from here the smaller the chance I was going to pee in my pants. If there was one thing I hated in life, it was having guns pointed at me.

"A bug? What, do I look like a midget to you?" she asked, whipping her long hair around again.

I narrowed my eyes. Was that a crack about my height?

"Okay, how about that one then?" I gestured to a blue pick-up with a "cowgirl-up" sticker in the back window.

Isabel turned on me. "What about me exactly screams redneck?"

"You know, you're awfully picky for a woman on the run."

"Shut up!" Isabel shoved the gun in my face again.

Chances of peeing my pants just rose astronomically. I clamped my mouth shut.

Isabel looked over my shoulder and apparently found a vehicle to her liking. Her face broke into a grin. "Now that's more like it." She tightened her grip on my arm and dragged me with her, weaving through the rows of parked cars toward a big, black Escalade in the corner. She peeked in the driver's side window. The valet had left the keys in the ignition. "Chumps," she said, through a big creepy smile.

She was jiggling the door handle when the emergency exit flew open again and Ramirez's voice rang out across the parking lot.

"Isabel!"

Without skipping a beat, she spun around, raised her arm and fired in the direction of his voice. A bullet shattered the passenger side window of the VW.

"Shit," I heard Ramirez cry as Isabel popped off three more rounds in the direction of the midget car. "Maddie?" he called.

"I'm okay," I replied. "She just really hates that car."

"Shut up!" Isabel screamed. "What are you, stupid? What don't you understand about 'shut up?!'"

I clamped my lips together and did a zipping-them-up-and-throwing-away-the-key thing.

"Isabel, let's talk about this. We can work something out," Ramirez said from behind the VW. I vaguely heard the sound of sirens in the distance.

Isabel must have heard them too, because her only response was to blow out the VW's back windows. Clearly, Isabel wasn't in the mood to talk.

But there was one good thing about the crazy lady shooting at my boyfriend. The gun wasn't pointed at me anymore.

I took a deep breath and, with my one good heel, stomped down on her bare foot as hard as I could.

"Sonofabitch!" she cried. It stunned her just enough for her to loosen the grip on my arm. That was all I needed. I turned and ran as hard as I could on one broken heel in the opposite direction, diving behind a Ford Festiva just as I heard a bullet rip into its tires.

"You blonde bitch!" Isabel howled, sending a wild spray of bullets through the parking lot.

I ducked, covering my head and praying the Festiva wasn't as cheaply made as it looked. If only I'd ducked behind a Hummer instead.

"Maddie?" Ramirez cried again from the other side of the lot. But I was honestly too paralyzed with fear to respond. I just sat there, my arms wrapped around my head, my knees tucked to my chest, my heart beating faster than when Dana made me crank the Stairmaster up to six.

The gunfire paused for a second, then was immediately followed by the sound of tires squealing. I peeked my head up over the shot out window of the Festiva just in time to see

Isabel's wild hair flying through the driver's side window of the Escalade as it screamed out of the lot.

"Maddie?" Broken glass crunched under Ramirez's feet as he sprinted across the lot to where I was still doing a fetal position.

"I'm okay." Sort of. I looked down. In my dive for cover, I'd skinned both my knees. My big toe on my right foot was bleeding, turning my Passionate Pink pedicure into something out of a horror movie, and my Nina pumps would never be the same again. But, on the up side, I hadn't wet my pants.

"Are you sure?" Ramirez asked, suddenly at my side. He lifted me up and ran his hands quickly over my arms and legs. Too quickly, if you asked me. I wouldn't have minded if he lingered just a little longer in the thigh region. Yep, I had it so bad for Ramirez that even gunfire didn't deter those overactive little hormones of mine. Geeze, maybe I *should* accompany Dana to her next SA meeting.

"I'm fine, really," I said, shaking off the inappropriate thoughts.

Satisfied, he stood back and looked at me. The concern in his dark eyes slowly fading into annoyance. And not the kind of annoyance you feel when telemarketers call at dinner time, but the kind where your insecure *friend* spurs an insane Amazon woman to take her hostage which results in you getting shot at. Yep, that was the level of annoyance making the little blue vein in his neck start to bulge and his jaw set harder than the granite Clinique counters.

I bit my lip and shuffled my heel-less foot. I looked down at his beer-stained shirt. "Um... sorry about the Budweiser."

He just shook his head and muttered another, "Jesus," under his breath.

* * *

Two hours later the Cabana Club parking lot was still swarming with police officers, and Ramirez was still giving me the evil eye. Which, as I sat on the tailgate of an ambulance wrapped in an ugly green blanket waiting for paramedics to give me the all-clear to go home, was kind of unfair. I mean, it's not like I *meant* to get taken hostage. And it's not as if *I* was the one who'd shot at him. In fact, if I'd had *my* way, we'd be at my place, sprawled across my futon going for round two of "or something" by now. So, really, this was all Ramirez's fault. (What can I say? Twelve years of Catholic school had taught me how to reassign guilt with the best of them.)

"Ohmigod, honey, check out the cop at three o'clock," Dana said, standing beside me. After the club had cleared out of panic-stricken singles, Dana had found me in the parking lot watching uniformed officers drape crime scene tape around the remnants of the VW. I was grateful for the hand to hold, since it was clear by the whole evil-eye thing that Ramirez and I wouldn't be holding hands any time soon. But the sight of so many men in uniform was almost too much for Miss Sexual Sobriety.

I turned my head to the right.

"No," Dana said, pointing to the left. "I said three o'clock."

"Why didn't you just say, 'left,' then?" I mumbled, eyeing the object of Dana's ogling. A tall, slim guy with a big nose and dark hair dressed in uniform blues slouched near the rear entrance, questioning the Olsen twin.

"He is delish!" Dana made the kind of yummy sound in her throat that I usually reserved for the tiramisu at Giani's.

"I thought you were off men?"

"Uh-huh. Oh!" she gasped. "Maddie, eleven o'clock. Blond, blue eyes, and biceps to die for!" She was practically licking her chops.

"Dana, how long *has* it been since you've had sex?"

She sighed, watching Mr. Biceps sweep shards of glass into an evidence baggie. "Way too long." She tilted her head as he leaned over the VW, showing off glutes that, I'll admit, had even me staring. "Since Monday. Four whole days."

Oh, brother.

"If I make it a week, I get a chip."

"You do realize I've had hangnails that have lasted longer than a week?"

Dana ignored me. "Uh-oh. Bad news at four o'clock."

I turned my head to the right.

"No." Dana grabbed my chin and tilted my head left. "*Four* o'clock."

Uh-oh was right. Ramirez was picking his way over the broken glass, evidence cones, and shot out car parts, headed right toward us. And by the rigid set of his shoulders this was not going to be a friendly sort of chat.

"Um, maybe I'll just... um... " Dana trailed off, wisely giving Bad Cop a wide berth as she joined the rest of the looky-loos behind the yellow crime scene tape.

Ramirez barely acknowledged her as she passed, his eyes boring down on me, his arms crossed over his chest. He stopped in front of me, shaking his head, his unreadable Bad Cop face reminding me of the one my Irish Catholic grandmother had used when she'd interrogated my five year old self about which "creative" little girl had drawn all over her kitchen walls with a Crayola.

He didn't say anything, just gave me that hard stare. I bit my lip, vowing not to be the one that spoke first. Okay, so I'd kind of mucked up his evening, but he was the one that started it by going out with Crazy Chick in the first place.

I crossed my *own* arms over my *own* chest, narrowed my eyes at him, and prepared to wait him out.

We stood like that for a full five seconds.

One guess who cracked first.

"Okay, so here's the thing; I had this thong, and it was totally cute, and it was going to waste just sitting at home watching TV, and I wouldn't have minded so much, but you were canceling our 'or something,' and unlike Dana, I haven't gotten any 'or something' in over a week — that's long enough to get a chip at SA, you know! And then 'something' came up, and you didn't want me meeting your friends, even though I'm so not smothery, and then you were at a hook-up club. I mean, you could have told me she was carrying a gun, and I so wouldn't have come. Or at least I would have waited outside. So, I'm sorry you got shot at."

Ramirez just shook his head at me, and I wasn't sure if he thought I was pathetic or was just trying to keep from laughing at me.

"Maddie, you seriously thought I was here on a date?"

"Um, well, yeah. I mean, with that message you left and the hook-up bar, what was I supposed to think?"

Ramirez rolled his eyes at me. "Isabel was an informant, Maddie. She's the girlfriend of a major drug distributor, and she was meeting me to give me details about the next shipment coming into his organization. Information that we could have used to get these guys off the streets for good."

I felt myself growing smaller and smaller the more he talked. "Oops."

"Oops?" He raised an eyebrow at me. "Oops?! Seven people injured, thousands of dollars in property damages, one stolen vehicle and three weeks worth of investigative work down the toilet and all you can say is 'oops?'"

If I grew any smaller I'd be looking up at the bottom of my broken heels. "Oops, sorry?"

He narrowed his eyes and made a growling sound deep in his throat.

Suddenly I kind of wished Isabel *had* taken me with her.

"It would be one thing," he said through clenched teeth, "if this were an isolated incident. But this isn't the first time you've butted into a police investigation. What, exactly, do you suggest I tell my superiors?"

I bit my lip again, eating off any remnants of lip gloss. He was right. Unfortunately, this wasn't the first time I'd stuck my nose in his police business. That was actually the way we'd met. He'd been investigating my last boyfriend, Richard, a prominent L.A. attorney, for fraud and, subsequently, murder. I'd sort of inadvertently gotten into the middle of that investigation when I'd popped the real murderer's breast implant and stabbed her in the jugular with a stiletto heel. After that there'd been the incident last fall involving my father, a bunch of drag queens, and the mob, which had ended with me getting kidnapped and Dana blowing a hole through some guy's chest. So, I could see why this was something of a sore spot with him. Not to mention, his superiors.

"Look, Jack, I'm really, really sorry."

He took a deep breath and did some more head shaking. He opened his mouth to say more, but was cut off by the uniformed officer with the cute butt.

"Hey, Ramirez?"

"What?" Ramirez called over his shoulder.

"It's the captain." Buns of Steel held up a cell phone. "He wants to speak to you."

Ramirez shut his eyes in a two-second meditation. "Shit." He turned and grabbed the cell phone, then paused, jabbing a finger my way. "You – go home. We'll talk later."

I nodded meekly. Later was good. Later was after he'd had time to calm down and hopefully gotten that whole bulging-vein thing under control.

After Buns of Steel took my statement (where I relayed the events of the evening the best I could without making it sound like his co-worker was dating a loony) and the paramedics checked me out (scrapes and unattractive bruises, but not much more), Dana bundled me into her Saturn and drove me home. She offered to stay the night with me, but from the way she was frothing at the mouth over every guy we passed (including the greasy haired attendant at the Chevron station), I figured she needed an SA meeting more that I needed a sleep over.

Instead, I climbed the steps to my cozy second story studio alone. "Cozy," of course, being real estate slang for "dinky." My fold-out futon, a drawing table and three dozen pairs of shoes had the place fuller than Paris Hilton's BlackBerry. Still, it was near the ocean, relatively quiet, and most importantly, fell within my *cozy* budget.

As a young girl I had dreamed of being a runway model in Paris. But since, as I may have mentioned, I top out at just below Tom Cruise height, genetics worked against that career plan. Instead, I went to the Academy of Art College and got a degree in fashion design. Namely, designing shoes. Unfortunately, a job which sounds way more glamorous than the paycheck. As an unknown designer the only steady work I'd been able to get so far had come from Tot Trots children's shoe designs. And, thanks to my recent brushes with the law, even those jobs were becoming fewer and further between. Sure I was still working on the Pretty Pretty Princess patent leathers for Easter, but they'd given both the Superman flip flops and the summer line of Disney water shoes to someone else. In hopes of someday moving beyond SpongeBob slippers, I'd lately started doing a little freelancing on the side, for – wonder of wonders – actual adults. Okay, so I'd designed a pair of purple size thirteen sequin covered heels for my father's birthday (Yes, you heard me right. Father. He danced in a Las Vegas all male 'showgirl' revue.), and I'd recently put the finishing touches on my first Maddie originals for myself. Pink pumps with three inch heels, leather ankle straps, and tiny crystal details on the buckles. All in all, I was rather proud of them.

I let myself into my apartment and kicked off my abused heels, then dragged myself into the shower, careful to rinse all the bits of broken auto glass out of my hair. I pulled on an oversized Guns 'n' Roses T-shirt, left over from my college days, and curled up on my futon with my TV remote. Three late-night episodes of *Cheers* later, and I was fast asleep.

* * *

I wasn't sure how long I'd actually been asleep, but I knew it wasn't long enough. My phone was ringing from somewhere deep inside a lovely dream of Ramirez and me doing horizontal acrobatics across my kitchen counter when I cracked one eye open to stare at the digital clock beside my bed. 6:15 AM. Ugh. I'm not exactly what you'd call a morning person. I'm more of a stumble-out-of-bed-at-ten-and-make-a-break-for-the-nearest-Starbucks kind of person. Which may be why my voice sounded like I'd been sucking on sandpaper as I croaked out a, "Hello?" in the vicinity of my phone.

"Maddie! Oh my word, honey, what happened?"

Instinctively, I pulled the phone away from my ear. 6 AM was too early for anyone to be that loud.

"Mom?" I croaked out again. "You don't have to shout, I can hear you."

"Sorry. I'm on a cell phone, sweetie," she yelled.

I felt a headache brewing between my eyes.

"Maddie, what's going on? I was having breakfast with Mrs. Rosenblatt, and we saw a man reading the *L.A. Informer* at the next table. Honey, your picture was on the front page. Were you involved in a shoot-out last night?"

I smacked my palm to my head. Leave it to L.A.'s sleaziest tabloid to sensationalize a simple misunderstanding between a girl and her beau into a wild west showdown at the O.K. corral. "It wasn't a shoot-out, Mom. Just… a misunderstanding." Okay, I admit, saying it out loud, the *Informer*'s version sounded closer to the truth.

"Are you okay? They said you were taken hostage."

I groaned again. "Mom, I'm fine. I promise."

"Oh honey, I'm coming over right now."

"No!" I fairly screamed into the phone. Don't get me wrong; I love my mother. But the last time she was in my apartment she insisted on organizing my underwear drawer, covering my cook top in aluminum foil, and feng shui-ing the entire place by moving my television into the bathroom and my futon next to the refrigerator. "No, I'm fine, Mom, really. Never better." Except for that headache which seemed to be spreading to my temples.

"Now, don't try to be all adult and independent on me, Mads. I know when my baby needs me."

I rolled my eyes. I was facing the big three-o this year. God forbid I should be adult and independent.

"Mom-"

"Nope. No protests."

"But-"

"And no buts."

I rubbed my temple, hoping I still had that travel-sized bottle of aspirin in my purse. "Okay, how about this, Mom. How about I just come down to the salon later? That way you wouldn't have to drive all the way out here, and I could get my pedi fixed at the same time?" I asked, hoping for a compromise that didn't involve rearranging my furniture.

Mom paused, considering this. Luckily, I knew how much she hated to drive the 405. "Well, if you're sure you're okay…"

"Right as rain!" I said doing my best perky cheerleader impression.

"All right. Why don't you meet me at Fernando's after lunch, and you can tell me all about it. Okay?"

I did a silent sigh of relief. "Perfect. I'll see you then."

I hit the end button and flopped back down on my pillows. 6:20 AM, and already one crisis averted. My day was off to a smashing start.

CHAPTER THREE

Fernando's Salon was located on the ultra chic, ultra high rent corner of Beverly and Brighton, one block north of Rodeo and smack in the center of Beverly Hills' Golden Triangle. It was the kind of neighborhood where the champagne was free and the pumps cost more than a small country. My step-father, Ralph (or as I had affectionately dubbed him, Faux Dad), started out in a small strip-mall in Chatsworth, but his mastery of the cut and color soon earned him a place in the hearts and hair-dos of the rich and not-quite-famous. Only, knowing a salon called "Ralph's" wouldn't fit in with the Versaces, Blahniks, and Vuittons of BH, Ralph reinvented himself with a faux Spanish ancestry and twice weekly spray on tans, and thus was born, Fernando, European hair sculptor. When I first met him I was convinced he was gay, but considering he and Mom have been married almost nine months now, I'm almost sure he's not.

In addition to Faux Dad's skills with a blow dryer, he's also quite the interior decorator (Hey, I said I was almost sure.), a fact illustrated by the metamorphosis his salon went through every few months. Today, as I walked through Fernando's polished glass doors, I was treated to a Caribbean theme. The walls were done in watercolor washed turquoise blue with knotted bits of rope hung like swags along the ceiling line. Bright pictures of exotic beaches, along with bits of fishing net, decorated the walls, interspersed with large leafy green plants and bright tropical flowers in artfully chipped planters. The reception desk was paneled in white clapboard with silk flower leis glued to the sides. And, I kid you not, in the corner sat a three foot high birdcage holding a bright green parrot.

He squawked at me as I approached the reception desk. "*Hips don't lie. Squawk*!"

I turned to Marco, Faux Dad's receptionist, who was slim, Hispanic, and probably the only person in the world as addicted to *Project Runway* as I was. "What did he just say?" I asked.

Marco rolled his heavily-lined eyes. "Oh, honey, tell me about it," he drawled in an accent that was pure San Francisco. "The previous owner apparently had a thing for pop music. This damn bird has been singing Shakira all day." Marco shook a finger at the bird. "You stop it, Pablo, you naughty boy."

Pablo The Parrot tilted his head to the side. "*Hips don't lie. Squawk*!!"

"Aye, yai, yai!" Marco clicked his tongue and rolled his eyes again. "We couldn't get a nice quiet goldfish. Nooooo, it had to be a parrot."

"Sorry," I sympathized.

"So…" Marco leaned his elbows across his desk. "I heard about your big shoot-out last night. *Ex-ciiiiii-ting*!" he said, drawing out the word.

My turn to roll my eyes. "It wasn't a shoot-out. It was a simple… misunderstanding." That was my story, and I was sticking to it.

"Do tell, dahling," he prodded me on.

Since Marco practically lived for gossip, and the *Informer* had already beaten me to it anyway, I filled him in on the latest entry in my top ten not-so-finest moments. So un-fine, in fact, that as I related the story I felt worse and worse. Geeze, had I really thought Ramirez was cheating on me? How paranoid was I? To be quite honest, Ramirez had every right to be mad at me. I mean, only *I* would turn a little thing like a canceled date into a shoot-out.

I mean misunderstanding.

True to his Queen of the Beverly Gossip status, Marco hung on my every word, and when I got to the part about Ramirez doing his Bad Cop face at me, Marco did an exaggerated swoon and started fanning himself. "That man is hotter than my mother's chili con carne, honey."

I had to agree. Unfortunately, he had a temper to match. "Yeah, well, I think he's just a wee bit miffed with me at the moment. And speaking of miffed people…" I surveyed the room behind Marco, scanning the hairdresser stations and buzzing blow dryers. "Are Mom and Ralph here?"

"*Fernando*," Marco chided, "is with a client. He's doing a weave for Mrs. Banks." He leaned in close and did a pseudo whisper that could be heard all the way to the Valley. "Tyra's mom."

"Oh." I nodded, appropriately impressed.

"But your mother's in the back doing a pedi." Marco gestured toward the back of the salon where a line of foot tubs flanked the turquoise walls.

"Thanks," I waved as I walked off.

"*Hips don't lie, hips don't lie*!" I heard behind me.

Then Marco mumbling another, "Aye yai yai…"

In keeping with the island paradise theme, the pedicure chairs had been covered with red tropical prints, sporting large, colorful hibiscus flowers. Which completely clashed with the neon green muumuu covering the woman getting the pedi. Though, to be fair, Mrs. Rosenblatt was one of those people that clashed with just about anything. She was a five-time divorcee who weighed three hundred pounds, wore her hair in a shade of Lucille Ball red, and talked to the dead through her spirit guide, Albert. (Yeah, I know. Only in L.A.)

She'd met my mother when, after a particularly depressing Valentine's Day, Mom had gone to Mrs. R for a psychic reading. When Mom met the dark haired stranger Mrs. R had predicted the very next day, Mom was hooked. Never mind that the stranger turned out to be a chocolate Lab named Barney, Mom and Mrs. R had been firm friends ever since.

"Mads!" Mrs. Rosenblatt called as I approached. "I heard about your shoot-out last night. Very impressive!"

I gritted my teeth together. "It wasn't a shoot-out."

Mom looked up from Mrs. R's toes. She dropped a bottle of green polish on the floor and immediately grabbed me in a fierce hug. "Oh, my baby, I'm so glad you're all right!"

"I'm fine, Mom." Which actually came out sounding more like, "I fie ma," considering she was cutting off my air supply.

"I was so worried about you! My poor, poor baby."

"Really," I said, extracting myself from her death grip. "I'm fine. It was just a little… misunderstanding."

Mrs. Rosenblatt nodded sagely, her chins (plural) bobbing up and down. "It's Mercury. Mercury's in retrograde this month. Makes for a whole heap of misunderstanding."

At least someone understood.

"So, did you have a gun during this 'misunderstanding'? You pop anyone?" Mrs. R asked.

I rolled my eyes. "No, I did not pop anyone. No one got popped."

"Bummer," Mrs. R said. "I always wanted to know what it would be like to shoot a gun. My first husband, Ollie, had all kinds of guns. He used to hunt quail with 'em. Never let me shoot one though."

Ollie was a smart man.

"So, what did happen last night?" Mom asked, sitting down and wiping the spilled nail polish on her black skirt. I grimaced. At the nail polish stains, yes. But more at the skirt.

When I was ten, Mom was the hippest mother in my Brownie troop. Unfortunately, she hadn't changed her fashion style since then. Today she wore a lacey black skirt that was about two inches too high for comfort, black mesh leggings, ballet flats, and three different tank tops layered together above about a billion jelly bracelets in every color of the rainbow. A little mole and she'd be the perfect post-menopausal Madonna.

Ignoring the urge to comment on her outfit, I gave Mom a much edited version of the night's events. However, by the end, her plucked eyebrows were still hunched together in concern.

"Maddie, you could have been killed!"

"I'm fine, Mom. Really," I tried to reassure her.

"I think you should think about carrying some protection."

"Protection?"

"What you need is a gun," Mrs. Rosenblatt offered. "I think I might still have one of Ollie's in storage."

"No!" I said a little too loudly. "Look, I've got pepper spray at home. I'll be fine." I didn't add that when I'd gotten it I'd been so scared of accidentally spraying myself with the mini canister of eye scorching stuff that I'd promptly shoved it to the back of my junk drawer, and it hadn't seen the light of day since. My idea of protection was a ribbed Trojan. Carrying actual weapons was a little too Rambo-chick for me.

"I don't know, Maddie…" Mom said, still not convinced.

"Honest, I'm fine. Look, this was just a fluke. A misunderstanding. Isabel is probably in Mexico by now. I'm fine. There's nothing to worry about. Really."

"Wait!" Mrs. Rosenblatt held up a pudgy hand. Then smacked it on my forehead. "I'm getting a vision." She rolled her eyes back into her head until she resembled a *Dawn of the Dead* reject. "I see a woman with long dark hair. She's screaming. And destroying a bug." Mrs. R opened her eyes. "You got a roach problem or something?"

Mental forehead smack.

* * *

After I reassured Mom for the bazillionth time that I was not likely to encounter a bullet anytime soon, I left the salon (to the tune of Pablo still singing Shakira and Marco still threatening to have roast parrot for dinner if he didn't shut up) and hoofed it the two blocks to my Jeep. The first thing I did when I got in was crank on the air conditioning. Even though it was barely the end of March, we were nearing triple digits this week. One of those freak heat waves that seem to hit L.A. more and more often. I blamed global warming. Though, personally, I'd still rather break out the tank tops and flip flops in March than give up my aerosol hair spray and gas guzzling Jeep.

I let the air blast over me as I made my way down the bumper-to-bumper afternoon traffic on Pico, people-watching the Saturday afternoon shoppers, admiring the Lexus dealerships, taking in the latest billboards. I passed one of a man popping out of the page 3D style, carrying a cell phone and advertising something about a long distance carrier. There was another that featured huge Dumbo ears and urged me not to let the magic of Disneyland pass me by. But it was the one on the corner of Pico and Westwood that made me sit up and stare in earnest.

A woman, lying on her stomach, spanned the length of the billboard, clad only in a teeny tiny pair of lacy panties that would make a Playboy Bunny blush. Two big round globes of D D's peeked out between her strategically placed arms. She had one finger seductively touching a glossy red lip, the caption "Like to watch?" underneath her with a web address to view her 24-hour web cam. But the part that almost made me gag was the woman's name. "Sexy Jasmine."

Last year when I'd been involved in the murder investigation that resulted in my meeting Ramirez, Jasmine (or as I was more fond of calling her, Miss PP. As in Plastic Parts. Seriously – you think those kinds of boobs grow naturally?) had, at one time, been my prime suspect. But, instead of offing embezzlers, it turned out Jasmine's biggest sin was moonlighting on a pay-per-play adult website. Apparently, after being fired from her day job as a receptionist, she'd turned her hand to full time cyber whoring. And, by the size of that billboard, it looked like it was paying off.

I shook my head and marveled at the fact I was schlepping through traffic, and Jasmine was now famous. (Or infamous as the case may be.) In New York, you're no one until you've made Page Six. In L.A. you're no one until your face has been plastered on a twenty-foot tall billboard.

By the time I got back to Santa Monica, it was nearing noon, and the smog index was creeping up to that level where you could almost taste the air. The radio DJ advised school children to stay indoors, and the fire marshal declared the Hollywood Hills a high hazard area. Instinctively, I cranked my air up.

As I rounded the corner, pulling off Venice, my apartment came into view.

As did the guy standing outside of it.

His tall, solid frame leaned casually against the side of his black SUV, both arms crossed over his chest. His eyes were unreadable behind a pair of mirrored sunglasses, but if the tension in his stubbled jaw was any indication, they weren't twinkling with glee.

Ramirez.

I paused, warring between apprehension and total lust as I pulled into my drive. Finally lust won out, and I got out of the car.

"Hey," I said tentatively.

Nothing. He didn't move, didn't nod, just kept his cop face on as he stared at me. Yep. He was definitely a little miffed.

"So, uh, have you been waiting long?"

I think I saw his shoulders shrug half an inch. Or it might have just been a smog induced illusion.

"Um… are you going to say something? Anything?" I squeaked out, my voice doing that caught-coloring-on-the-walls falsetto again.

He did a deep breath in, then out, his nostrils flaring. Then he reached up and slowly took off his sunglasses. Yikes. Nope, his dark eyes were a far cry from twinkling. Seething might be appropriate. Or searing, penetrating.

Pissed off.

"Do you have any idea what kind of trouble your stunt last night caused?" he asked, his voice low and strained, a clear undercurrent of dammit-you-really-screwed-up-this-time-Maddie running through it.

I wondered if it was too late to jump back into my car.

"Um, lots?"

He took a step forward. I instinctively took one back, coming up against the driver's side door of my Jeep.

"Thanks to my association with, and I quote, 'that crazed shoe girl,' my captain has reassigned me."

"Reassigned?" I repeated. "Like, demoted?"

Ramirez made a low growling sound deep in his throat.

Yep. Like, demoted.

"Isabel is MIA, her boyfriend got the tip-off that she's been talking to the police, and now he's in the wind, and my captain has busted yours truly down to celebrity bodyguard duty."

Ramirez had been advancing on me as he spoke until his face was just inches from mine, those granite features starting to twitch as if they might crack into a full blown rage at any second. I leaned further back into my car, and I think did a little whimper thing.

"I'm sorry," I squeaked out.

His eyes narrowed, and he placed a hand on either side of my head, barring any ideas of escape. "Sorry?"

I gulped. "Really, really sorry."

He did that low sort of growl in the back of his throat again. I wasn't sure what it meant, but it didn't sound a whole lot like, "I forgive you."

I gulped again. "But a bodyguard isn't all that bad, right? I mean, celebrities can be fun?"

"Oh sure. Tons of fun. Watching a bunch of pampered actresses while they open their fan mail. My idea of a good time."

"You're being sarcastic, aren't you?"

There was that growl again.

"Look, I'm *really,* really sorry. I *so* didn't mean to get you in trouble. And I'll *so* make it up to you."

One eyebrow hitched up. "Make it up to me? I've gone from working homicide to spending 24/7 babysitting a bunch of second rate actors on the *Magnolia Lane* set. How the hell do you think you're going make that up to me?"

"Well, I don't know, I mean, maybe I could talk to your captain, maybe if I just explained this… Wait. Did you say, '*Magnolia Lane*'?"

He nodded, giving me a "yeah so?" look.

"Ohmigod. *The Magnolia Lane*?"

"You've heard of it?"

"Ohmigod, are you freaking kidding? Only daily on *Entertainment Tonight*. It's like the hottest show on TV. These are no minor celebs. The star, Mia Carletto was up for an Emmy last year. Wow, you actually get to meet Mia Carletto. You should be thanking me!"

His eyes narrowed again. Apparently he didn't watch as much TV as I did.

"So, what will you be doing? Will you get to hang out with the cast? Go to parties with them? Ohmigod – are you going to the Emmys?!"

Ramirez muttered a, "Jesus," under his breath, then took a step back and rubbed a hand through his hair until it stood up in little tufts. "No, I'm not going to the Emmys. Miss Carletto has been getting threatening letters, and her publicist just happens to be my captain's daughter-in-law. So, lucky me, I'm supposed to keep an eye on the set until we find out where they're coming from."

"Ohmigod, I heard about those letters on *Access Hollywood.* That is so cool!"

Ramirez gave me a look.

"Well, I mean, not cool that she's getting threatening letters but so cool that you'll get to meet her. Oh, oh – do you think you could get me on the set? Just to get an autograph?"

"No!" Ramirez yelled loudly enough to make my downstairs neighbor peek through her chintz curtains at us. He rubbed another hand through his hair, then spoke through gritted teeth. "No, I don't want you anywhere near that set; do you hear me? I don't want you anywhere near my work. Ever again. Thanks to you, a cranked up felon is tooling around L.A. in a stolen car, and I'm on Hollyweird detail. I want you as far away from me as possible. Got it?"

Ouch. Apparently my boyfriend – wait, *friend* – thought I was a total jinx. A less confident girl might start to take this personally. "I said I was sorry. I mean, really, really sorry. I never meant for this to happen. I just... I mean when I heard your message... I kind of...."

"Freaked out?" he supplied.

I nodded. "Major freak out. I'm so, so sorry," I said again. Honestly meaning it.

Ramirez must have noticed, because his face softened. He reached one hand out and lightly brushed the backs of his knuckles against my cheek. "I have to admit," he said, "the jealous thing? Kind of cute."

I sniffed. "Cute, huh?"

He nodded. "Very. And it's a damn good thing, too, 'cause you're a whole lot of trouble."

"I know. I'm amazingly sorry," I said again. Hoping that if I said it enough times maybe I could make this whole thing just go away.

"I know," he whispered, his eyes starting to do that sexy, glazed over thing as they roved my face.

His hand trailed around to the nape of my neck, his fingers lightly massaging there until I felt myself break out in goose bumps, sending a tingle straight down my spine. He leaned in close. I could smell the scent of Ivory and Tide as his lips brushed mine. The tingle turned into an all out quiver as our tongues touched.

Suddenly my insides were gooier than a Snickers bar in the hands of a first grader.

"So, does this mean I'm forgiven?" I mumbled onto his lips.

He leaned back and raised one dark eyebrow. "Forgiven is a strong word."

"Maybe I can make it up to you?" I said coyly, trailing one finger down the center of his chest.

The other eyebrow shot up. "What did you have in mind?"

"Oh, I don't know…" I slid my hand lower, toying with the top button of his jeans.

He did a small groan.

Then his pager went off.

He did a *large* groan.

He pulled away, glancing at the readout. "Shit. The captain. I've gotta go."

And I swear he looked so dejected that I felt myself pack for that guilt trip again. He really didn't deserve this. As cool as I might think hanging out all day on the *Magnolia Lane* set was, I knew it wasn't Ramirez's gig. Ramirez belonged working homicide. He was a cop who enjoyed all that gritty detective stuff, and he was damn good at it, too.

As he got into his SUV and pulled down the street I vowed that, despite how little faith he might have in my abilities, I *would* make this up to him.

* * *

"Well, it seems clear to me," Dana said, popping a soy nut into her mouth. "Blow job. A little attention to Mr. Winky and I'm sure he'll forgive you."

"Know what? I think maybe you really are a sex addict." I shook my head, blonde hair whipping my cheeks. "No, that's not the kind of 'making it up to him' I mean. I mean I need to make this right. I need to get him reassigned back to homicide."

"I give up. How do you do that?"

I shrugged. "Good question."

We were sitting on my futon, watching last season's DVD of *Magnolia Lane* for inspiration, trying to come up with some way to get Ramirez to not only forgive me, but somehow put back the Humpty Dumpty of his career that I'd shoved off the wall the moment I'd walked into the Cabana Club.

I watched the screen, digging a hand into my own bag of snacks, Keebler fudge cookies. (As far as I was concerned, anything with the word "soy" in its name didn't qualify as a comfort food. And after my encounter with Ramirez, I needed all the chocolate covered comfort I could get.)

"Ashley, your husband will be home any minute."

"Oh, he has no idea about us, the fool. Kiss me, Chad!"

"No, Ashley, it's not right. What if he sees?"

"He's blind to our love, Chad."

"Oh, Ashley, you know I want to. I've wanted to since the moment I saw you. It's just..."

"What, Chad? What's wrong?"

"Oh, come on, just kiss her!" Dana yelled at the TV. Then crunched down hard on a salted soy nut. "Chad is gorgeous. She's absolutely insane if she doesn't kiss him. Who wouldn't want to kiss him? I'd kiss him. In fact, I'd do more than kiss him..." Dana trailed off mumbling to herself.

"Chad, I've never felt this way before."

"Me neither, Ashley. I swear I've cut every woman's lawn on Magnolia Lane, but yours – yours is special."

"Oh, Chad!"

"Oh, Ashley!"

"Oh, for the love of God, kiss him already!" Dana threw a soy nut at the TV.

"Are you okay?" I asked.

"Yeah. Fine. Great. Why?" She crunched down on another nut.

"Um, no reason," I mumbled.

"Kiss me, Chad. Kiss me like you mean it."

Dana leaned forward in her seat.

"I can't wait another second to do just that, Ashley. Come here..."

"Wait – what's that?"

"It sounds like a car door."

"My husband. He's home!"

"Argh!" Dana threw the bag of soy nuts down on the carpet as Chad and Ashley broke apart. Ashley stuffed her would-be lover into the closet as her husband came up the stairs, and Dana mumbled a, "lousy timing," under her breath.

"Um, so did Therapist Max mention anything about the side effects of abstinence?"

Dana paused. "Sorry. I'm a little tense lately."

"You know, maybe celibacy just isn't for you."

Dana shook her head. "No way. Two more days, and I get a chip. I can do this. I am experiencing the joy of positive being as a single, non-physically dependant entity." She picked the bag up and crunched down hard on another nut.

"Oh, yeah. I can feel the joy from here."

Dana ignored me. "So, what are you going to do about Ramirez?"

I blew out a long breath. "I don't know." I watched Mia Carletto, a.k.a. Ashley try to convince her husband that the gardener's boxers really belonged to her. "Maybe I could make it up to him by helping him with his new assignment. He said something about those letters that Mia's been getting. Threatening fan mail."

"Oh, I totally read about that in *People* last week. She's, like, got a stalker or something. Ohmigod – light bulb moment!" Dana popped up off the futon, jostling the soy nuts onto the floor as she started hopping up and down. "We could totally find the stalker for Ramirez! He'd totally forgive you then."

"Dana, Ramirez is a cop. What makes you think we could find a stalker any easier than he could?"

"Uh, hello?" Dana rolled her eyes. "Ramirez doesn't even watch *Magnolia Lane*. We totally know Mia way better than he does. I mean, come on, you watch *Access Hollywood* daily."

She had a point there. I'll admit it, I was a celebrity gossip junkie. I religiously watched every single Barbara Walters interview, I never left the house on the night of the Emmys, Oscars, or SAG awards, and I bought copies of *Star* and *People* on the sly every week. I was even known – on a very rare occasion – to use words like Bennifer, Brangelina, and Tomkat. I know. It's a disease.

Still, I wasn't convinced our knowledge of Mia's latest boy-toy fling could really outweigh a badge and a gun.

"How much could we possibly do without even being on the set of the show?" I reasoned.

Dana waved me off, switching from the hops to a little footwork-in-place thing. "So, we get on the set. How hard can that be? Look, I'll call my agent in the morning and see if he can get me on as an extra or something. And maybe you could see if they need a costume designer or a wardrobe assistant? I'm sure you've got some connections, right?"

I bit my lip. "Well, my college roommate did do wardrobe for that cop drama on FX."

"Perfect! I bet she totally knows someone. Ohmigod, this is going to be so fun. We'll, like, totally be undercover again!"

Dana was referring, of course, to last year when, against my better judgment, I'd let her dress me as a hooker in order to suss out a murder. Unfortunately, that evening had ended in a dead body. Not an experience I was dying to repeat. (Yes, pun intended.)

"I don't know…" I trailed off, picturing Ramirez's face that afternoon. I had a feeling that if I showed up within ten feet of his assignment he'd likely pop a blood vessel. The words "as far away from me as possible" echoed in my head.

Dana started jogging in place, bobbing her knees up and down like little pistons. "Come on, Maddie! We could so do this. You've got a good track record, girl!"

I hesitated to mention that both times I'd ferreted out a killer in the past it was more by accident than sheer brilliance.

On the other hand, this whole "reassignment" thing was all my fault. And sitting on my futon watching *Magnolia Lane* reruns wasn't doing anything to improve my rapidly crumbling love life. If I was going to make it up to Ramirez, I had to do *something*. "All right, I'll call my college roomie."

Dana let out a high pitched squeal and clapped her hands together.

"I said I'd call. No guarantees," I hedged, grabbing my address book. I wasn't sure if I'd put her number under "L" for Lana, "P" for Paulson or "R" for roommate.

"I think we should start by talking to her costars," Dana said, ticking items off on her fingers. "See if anyone has seen a suspicious character around. Second, maybe we should question Mia herself; maybe the stalker is someone from her past, and he's coming back to seek revenge. Ooo – or maybe she had a secret love child that's coming back to haunt her now."

I resisted the urge to roll my eyes. Suspicious characters? Revenge? Secret love child? What was this, *Montel*?

Thankfully, before I could change my mind, I found Lana's number (under "C" for college) and dialed. She picked up on the first ring.

"Hello?"

"Hi, Lana. It's Maddie," I said, with a backward glance at Dana. She was still ticking off possible stalker suspects. I think I heard her mumble something about a political plot to rig the Emmys. I scrunched my eyes shut, hoping I wouldn't live to regret this.

"Say, I was wondering if you know anyone at Sunset Studios?"

CHAPTER FOUR

"This is where we keep Kylie's clothes," Dusty said, gesturing toward a long wardrobe rack of designer suits and blouses.

Dusty was a fresh-faced twenty-two year old, just out of design school, with short purple hair and pierced studs in her nose, eyebrow, and lip. Last season when the head wardrobe consultant for *Magnolia Lane* quit over a SAG award snub, Dusty landed the job because her best friend's ex-boyfriend's mother played canasta with the producer's aunt. Hollywood was the original who-you-know town. Luckily, thanks to my college roomie, I now knew Dusty.

"Kylie plays Tina Rey on the show," Dusty continued. "Blake, Ricky, and Deveroux have their stuff over there." She gestured to the far end of the room where men's wear hung on two rows of clothing racks. "And Mia's are here." She ended by pointing to a row of clothes stuck on dry cleaning hangers and swathed in plastic. "Mia has her own wardrobe person, so you'll mostly just be making sure the others have the right outfits for their scenes and doing a little damage control. You know how to hand sew, right?"

I nodded.

"Great!" Dusty said, tucking a purple lock behind her ear. "Any questions?"

Only about a million. The second Dana and I had walked onto the Sunset Studios lot that morning it had been like entering some alternate reality, and I was still trying to get my bearings.

We'd parked my Jeep off-site in the designated parking garage behind the lot, then hoofed it along with the other cast and crew not-quite-somebody-enough to have their own parking places, to one of the studio's three entrances at the rear of the gated lot. We'd stood in line with women toting wardrobe bags, and a seemingly endless supply of guys with tool belts and little walkie-talkie headsets while the two-hundred-year-old security guard (give or take a year) in coke bottle glasses checked our names against his list. Wonder of wonders, when I got to the front of the line mine was actually there. The guard even gave me a, "Good day, Miss Springer," before passing me through the gates onto the sacred grounds of the Sunset Studios.

The best way I could describe the studio lot was to compare it to a life-sized doll house – every corner dressed within an inch of its life but none of it real. Just beyond the rear entrance lay the Sunset Studios "city", which was basically a maze of city streets with hollow buildings made to look like New York, Boston, San Francisco, and, of course, a generic middle American suburb.

Beyond the "city" were rows of squat warehouses with the names of hit shows painted on the outside. All buzzing with activity. I spied a group of extras and guys in headsets milling around outside stage 3F, where the sign said they shot that new cop drama. Outside stage 4B was a catering truck handing out breakfast burritos and the guy who played Screech digging into a box of morning Krispy Kremes.

I would have loved to do a slow celebrity gawking tour around the rest of the lot, but, since I'd hit snooze about a dozen times that morning (if God wanted people to be awake at 6 AM, he wouldn't have invented late night TV) we were already running ten minutes behind, so instead we'd hightailed it to stage 6G.

The Assistant Director (or AD) quickly ushered Dana to a holding room with the other extras. She'd given me a co-conspiratorial wink as she headed off, which I'd tried not to roll my eyes at. (Okay, fine. I hadn't tried very hard.) And only thirteen minutes late (but who was counting?), I'd made my way into the wardrobe department, where Dusty was currently filling me in on suburbanite fashion, Hollywood style.

"So, basically the outfits will be hung up here for you ahead of time," she pointed to a rack along the wall where outfits were clumped together and tagged, "and all you have to do is make sure the right person is wearing the right thing for the right scene."

"That's it?" And people were going to pay me for this?

Dusty laughed. "It's harder than it sounds. Getting actors through wardrobe is like herding cats. Especially if they aren't happy with what we've picked out for them. Speaking of which, watch out for Margo. She's notorious for adding her own accessories." She did a mock shudder. "Costume stuff and cheap as hell."

"Margo?"

"She plays Nurse Nan on the show. You know, Ashley's evil twin sister who just escaped the mental institution and is secretly living in Ashley's attic?"

"Oh, riiiight. Nurse Nan."

Dusty chuckled again. "You'll get used to calling them by their real names, don't worry. In the meantime, how about we go get some coffee, and I'll introduce you around."

Grateful for a moment to absorb it all, I followed Dusty out of the wardrobe room and down a series of hallways littered with make-up bags, discarded scripts, and lengths of cable. As I picked my way around the landmines, I made a mental note to wear wedges tomorrow. I could just see myself snagging a stiletto on a cable and doing a face plant in front of Mia Carletto.

Finally the hallways opened up to a larger common area just behind the actual soundstage. In the center of the room sat craft service – a large folding table laden with chips, cookies, crackers, soda, water, candy and about a million other fattening, sugar filled treats that made my mouth water. Not the least of which was a large metal carafe of coffee with the Starbucks emblem emblazoned on the side. That was it. I was never leaving.

A mousy looking girl in an oversized T-shirt and jeans stood behind the table, refilling bowls of Chex mix. Around the table two guys in tool belts full of tape, wires, pens, and huge walkie-talkies stood munching on handfuls of cookies, while two waif-thin women with sprayed-in-place hair sipped at water bottles.

Dusty pulled me aside confidentially. "That's Margo there on the left." She pointed to the older of the two women, a tall brunette in a tailored suit with skin pulled so tightly back from her face that her lips were bulging. Obviously a fresh face lift, and an aggressive one at that.

"And her?" I asked, gesturing to the other woman. She was slim, with long blonde hair, and there was something vaguely familiar about her.

"That's Veronika, Mia's stand in."

"Stand in?" I asked.

"The stand in runs through the scene for the technical crew, so they can get the lighting right, block out the camera angles, that sort of thing. She's pretty much the same height, size, and coloring as Mia, and she generally wears the same clothes Mia will be while she's running through the scenes. In fact, that," she said gesturing to Veronika, "is the identical Armani suit that Mia will be wearing in the scene we're shooting today."

No wonder she'd looked familiar. As I took in the light, cream-colored pencil skirt and blazer paired with alligator pumps, I was struck by just how much she did look like Mia. They honestly could have been twins.

"So, how long have you been working in production design?" Dusty asked, pouring herself of cup of coffee.

"Oh, well, uh…" Okay, so here's the thing. I might have exaggerated my resume just a teeny tiny bit when I'd spoken with Dusty on the phone last night. In fact, if you wanted to get technical about it, I might have even lied. A little. But, it was for a very good cause. There was no way I'd be able to help Ramirez get his old job back just sitting at home watching the daily entertainment report. He needed a man on the inside, so to speak. And I was that man.

Even if it meant fudging the truth a little.

"Well, I've been interested in design my whole life," I said, noncommittally as I grabbed a paper cup.

"Yep." Dusty nodded. "Me too. I was always the artistic type. When I was fifteen, I got my first piercing," she gestured to the silver barbell cutting through her heavily lined eyebrow, "and my mom just about freaked. She didn't get my need to express myself, you know?"

"I totally hear you." Okay, so my need to express myself had come through the use of my mother's Visa to buy two hundred dollar pumps when I was fifteen, but same concept.

"Oh, are you pierced?"

"Me?" I asked, dumping cream into my cup and taking a sip. Heaven. "No. Well, my ears, but that's it. My vice is shoes. I'm a total pain chicken. I'm really impressed that you have three."

"Seven."

I coughed, choking on a mouthful of coffee. "Seven?"

"Yep." She nodded. "I started with the eyebrow, then nose, lip, bellybutton, both nipples, and my hood."

I cocked my head to the side. "Hood?"

"Yeah. You know… down there." Dusty pointed down at the crotch of her jeans.

I think I went about fifteen different shades of red. I sipped at my coffee to cover my embarrassment, doing a physical cringe at the thought of needles going… down there.

Luckily, though, I didn't have to come up with a clever reply.

"Uh-oh," Dusty said, glancing to the left.

"Uh-oh?"

She gestured to a doorway. "You're about to meet Hurricane Mia. And it looks like she's a category four today."

I turned just as a tall, slim woman strode through the room making double time. Her long, blonde curls hung loose at her sides, bouncing up and down furiously as she stomped on two inch strappy heels across the cement floor. She had on the same cream-colored pencil skirt as Veronika, paired with a white button-down blouse… open far enough that a lacey push up bra showed beneath, maximizing her D cups. I'd recognize her anywhere. It was Ashley!

I tried not to go all fan-clubby on her, instead containing my excitement to something between open admiration and just plain staring. I had to admit, Ashley (or Mia, as I supposed I would have to get used to calling her) was much prettier in person. Her eyes were a bright green emerald, her alabaster skin perfect even without the effects of airbrushing, and the body stuffed into that pencil skirt wasn't an inch over size two. She looked like she either existed on Tic Tacs or had a personal trainer on twenty-four hour standby. Or maybe both. The only thing marring her perfection was the scowl etched on her face.

Mia strode up to Dusty, bearing down with purpose.

"Dusty!" she barked.

"Yes?" Dusty replied, coolly. Though I could tell by the way her hand had tightened around her coffee cup that she was steeling herself for the worst.

"What did I say yesterday about teal?" Mia narrowed her eyes.

Dusty bit at the inside of her cheek, looking like she hadn't been ready for a pop quiz so early in the morning. "I give up?"

"It makes me look pale!" Mia slammed a hand down on the snack table, making a plate of chocolate chip cookies jump. "I told you I want to wear peach in the neighborhood watch scene. I'm a Spring. Springs wear peach."

Dusty sucked in a slow breath, obviously keeping her composure with much difficulty. "Margo is wearing peach in that scene. You can't both wear peach."

"Screw Margo!" Mia screeched.

I saw Margo's spine straighten, but she didn't say anything.

"I am the star of this show," Mia went on. "People tune in to see me. Let Margo wear the teal and look like a corpse. I will be shot in peach. Got it?"

Dusty opened her mouth to respond, but Mia cut her off, sticking one manicured finger in Dusty's face.

"Or it will be your job. You know how easily I could get you sacked? I'm Mia Carletto. And you? You're expendable." With that Mia slammed her hand down on the table again so hard the cookies hit the floor. Then she turned and stalked out of the room.

Dusty clenched her jaw, her eyes shooting daggers at Mia's back. I joined her. Those looked like they'd been really good cookies.

"And that," Dusty said, still clenching her jaw, "was Mia."

"So I gathered. Is she always that friendly?"

"Oh, this was a good day. You should have seen her during sweeps week."

"Yikes. Remind me to stay on her good side."

"Impossible. Mia doesn't have a good side." Dusty tossed the remains of her cup in the trash can. "Well, apparently I've got to go switch out Mia's outfit for something 'Springy peach,'" she said, doing air quotes with her fingers. "Think you can start rounding up the others and get them dressed for the first scene?"

"No problem," I responded.

Famous last words.

* * *

The trouble with actors, I was soon to learn, was that they lived by the hurry-up-and-wait credo. Depending on the complexity of a scene, the director might spend an hour setting up the shot for fifteen seconds of dialogue. This left the actors with way too much time on their hands and nothing to fill it. Which, as any kindergarten teacher will tell you, just spells trouble.

The *Magnolia Lane* cast had me running from one end of the Sunset Studios lot to the other all day long. First it was fetching Blake, a.k.a Ashley Culver's comatose husband, who was, by the way, not in his trailer but across the lot at the basketball court playing one-on-one with a doc from *E.R.* Then, I had to find Kylie, who played Tina Rey Holmes, the perky newlywed turned high-class call girl who'd moved in next door to Ashley and had the hots for the single electrician across the street, who was being framed by the D.A. for murdering his ex-girlfriend. If last season's cliff hanger was any indication, I suspected Tina Rey would be having an affair with Ashley's husband when he woke up from that coma. (That is, if Nurse Nan didn't off him first. God, I loved this show!) Kylie, of course, was nowhere near her trailer either. Instead, I finally tracked her down smoking a cigarette near the fake Golden Gate Park in the San Francisco section of the Sunset "city." Ricky, who played the show's hunky gardener and everybody's favorite boy toy, Chad, was, predictably, not in his trailer either. (See a trend here?) Instead, I tracked him down outside stage 3E, chatting up two of the briefcase girls from *Deal Or No Deal.* And last, but certainly not least, was Deveroux Strong, the Nordic looking blond who played the hot electrician slash framed murderer, and who, incidentally, all the tabloids suspected was about to come out of the closet any day now. After checking the studio cafeteria, the craft service table, the basketball courts, and the producer's office, I finally found Deveroux, wonder of wonders, in his trailer.

I changed my mind about the wedges. I was wearing running shoes to work tomorrow.

The worst thing about it all was that I hadn't even gotten a chance to talk to Mia. The only thing I'd gathered from the other actors was that they routinely got fan letters, some of which verged on the unbalanced edge. The odd thing about Mia's was that, unlike the usual fan mail, these letters had started showing up in her trailer. Which meant that the writer had somehow gotten onto the set. I thought of the security guard standing sentinel. It didn't seem likely he'd let a crazed fan in, which meant that whoever wrote them either worked on the show or at the studios. A somewhat disconcerting thought. And, unfortunately, one that didn't narrow things down a whole lot. But, I dutifully relayed it all to Dana when I met her for lunch in the studio cafeteria.

"Ohmigod, that means someone on the show is threatening her?" Dana asked, shoveling a spoonful of fat-free yogurt into her mouth.

I shrugged. "Not necessarily. The letters could be coming from outside, and someone on the set is just delivering them."

"I think it's the AD. That guy has totally shifty eyes." Dana illustrated by wagging her eyeballs back and forth like she was watching a ping-pong match.

"Creepy. So, what did you gather in holding?" I asked, digging into my cheeseburger and fries. Hey, all that running around burned a lot of calories. I needed fuel. Thick, greasy, cheese covered fuel.

"Well, there are seven regular extras on the show and a few others that filter in and out," Dana said, nibbling on a carrot stick. "But I think we can eliminate them from the suspects list. That AD watches us like a hawk."

"With his shifty eyes?" I couldn't help adding.

She ignored my sarcasm. "There's no way an extra could wander off without being noticed. The leads, however, are a different story. They're all over the set. One of them could easily slip away to Mia's trailer for a minute without being missed."

I popped a fry in my mouth. "I wish I knew what the letters said. I mean, at least then we'd have a clue what kind of person we're looking for."

"Someone who doesn't like Mia very much."

"From what I gather, she's not exactly popular."

"Have you had a chance to talk to her yet?"

I shook my head. "No. But I'm on it this afternoon."

We finished our meal, topping it off with dessert (Dana's a fat-free bran muffin, mine a chocolate chip brownie with whipped cream) and promised to meet at the back gate after work, before Dana went back to her holding room under the shifty gaze of the Assistant Director.

I took the long way around the studio, picking my way through the maze of warehouses until I found myself in the back of stage 6G. Here six white, portable trailers were lined up in rows, most of them with their blinds shut tight. The first one bore the name of Ricky Montgomery. The next two, a generic "Talent" and the fourth, "Mia Carletto." I paused, squinting up at the windows for any indication of life inside. Nothing.

"Mia?" I called, doing a gentle little tap, tap, tap on the door. Still nothing.

Apparently Mia was still at lunch. But that didn't mean that her mysterious letters were…

I bit my lip, glancing over both shoulders. I should have walked away. I should have gone back to wardrobe where Dusty was probably waiting for me. I should have known that as I tip-toed up the two metal steps leading the trailer's door and gingerly turned the knob that nothing good would come of breaking into a star's private trailer.

I should have.

But I didn't.

Instead I slowly opened the door and ducked my head inside.

"Hello? Mia?"

The interior of the trailer was a decadent contrast to the stark outside. Red velvet material covered a plush, four foot sofa along one wall. The blinds were not only shut, but layered with thick, brocade curtains in deep reds and golds. The floor was covered in a thick, plum colored rug that swallowed up the sound of my heels as I stepped into the room. This was a far cry from the trailer my mother had rented to drive us to the Grand Canyon when I was eight.

To my left was a small hallway, at the end of which I could see a bedroom, done in the same dark, opulent colors. To the right was a mini kitchen, complete with stainless steel appliances and granite countertops. In front of the sofa sat a coffee table, the top littered with scripts, notes, half empty coffee cups, and a stack of mail.

I raised one eyebrow. Fan mail?

I took a step closer, gingerly flipping one envelope over to see the address. It was hand written in loopy letters with little hearts dotting the "I"s. Bingo.

I did another over the shoulder, praying Mia took a long lunch, as I quickly sifted through the pile of letters. Three from teenagers asking Mia to their prom, one from a little girl in the hospital, two marriage proposals, and one housewife in Milwaukee wanting to know where Mia hired her gardener. Great fuel for my celebrity addiction, but none of them threatening enough to warrant a police presence.

I was about to concede that my snooping was just… well, snooping, when I spotted one more envelope, partially shoved under last week's copy of *Variety*. I picked it up.

The outside was a plain number ten, like the kind my phone bills came in. It was addressed to Mia Carletto, care of Sunset Studios, though I noticed it was missing a postmark. My heart sped up. Hand delivered? There was no return address, and the top had already been neatly slit open.

With my pulse picking up to marathon speeds, I gingerly slipped my fingers inside and pulled out the note.

Again, nothing special about the stationary. Plain white paper, typed note. Could have come from any computer. It started, "Dear Mia," but those were about the only repeatable words on the page. This guy seriously needed his mouth washed out with Ivory. He seemed to have a thing for the "f" word, coupled with the "b" word, with a few references to female genitalia thrown in for color.

But as vulgar as the letter was, it was the last paragraph that made a chill run up my spine.

I've been watching you. I've been waiting for you. I'm going to kill you.

Irrationally I looked to the closed blinds as if Mr. Potty Mouth might be watching me right now. Of course, I didn't see anyone, but that didn't slow the adrenalin shooting through my limbs. Suddenly Mia's trailer was the last place I wanted to be. I quickly shoved the letter back in the envelope and stuck it under the *Variety*. I did a hasty survey of the room to make sure it looked the same as when I'd entered, but really, all I wanted to do was get out of there. Now!

I grabbed the handle of the door and quickly twisted it open. If I hadn't been in such instinctive fight-or-flight mode I might have had the presence of mind to peek outside first. As it was I plowed headlong out the door.

And ran smack into something.

"Uhn."

It was something solid. Stiff.

I looked up.

Something pissed off.

I gulped down the fresh shot of adrenalin sitting in my throat like a lump and did a little one finger wave. "Uh… hi," I squeaked out, doing a great Minnie Mouse impression.

Two dark espresso eyes narrowed at me. A stubble covered jaw tightened into a hard line.

"What the hell are you doing here?" Ramirez ground out through clenched teeth.

I moved my mouth up and down but no sound came out. I cleared my throat and sucked in a big breath. Which did nothing to help me because it smelled like Ramirez and just sent my circuits reeling again in a whole new direction.

"I… I…"

His eyes narrowed into fine slits. "Yes?"

"I'm working?" I said. Only it came out more of a question.

"How the hell did you get on the set?" He glanced behind me as if looking for security rushing to catch up to the blonde who'd broken in.

"I was on the list." Okay, I'll admit I just liked saying that. I mean, how often does one get on that kind of list? "I'm working here. On the set. I'm the new wardrobe assistant."

Those eyes narrowed again. So far that I wasn't even sure he could see out of them. "New wardrobe assistant?"

I nodded, doing another dry gulp. I was ninety-nine percent sure that Ramirez was like an M&M. Hard coating on the outside, but kind of sweet and soft inside. But as I stood there, his dark, intent face hovering over mine, that white scar running menacingly across his eyebrow and his black tattoo peeking out of his sleeve (not to mention the fact that I knew he always carried a loaded gun somewhere on his person) I was a little intimated. Okay, fine. I was a *lot* intimidated. I pitied the criminal that had to come up against that face across an interrogation table. They'd crack like a cheap Naugahyde barstool.

Which, of course, is exactly what I did.

"See, here's the thing. I thought that maybe if I was on the set I could help you with this whole stalker dealie. I mean, people tell their stylist things they never tell anyone else. And I totally know *Magnolia Lane*. I mean, like mega-fan know it. And Dana decided we should go undercover, then we'd find the stalker, and you could go back to homicide and wouldn't have to spend your days babysitting a bunch of flawless actors. Speaking of which, I've heard that Mia is a bit of a pill, so you might not want to get too involved with her. I mean not that you're involved; I mean you wouldn't be and I'm totally *not* jealous at all because I know how *that* turned out last time, and I'm so not going there again, and I know that even if I was, you wouldn't. You know?"

Ramirez took a deep breath. And I could see him mentally debating the merits of throwing me over his shoulder and bodily carrying me off the studio lot.

Instead, he gritted his teeth, that vein in his neck pulsing double time. "I told you to stay out of this. To stay away from me. What part of that was so hard to understand?"

My turn to narrow my eyes. "Listen, pal, didn't you hear what I just said? I'm doing this for you."

Both eyebrows headed north this time. "For me? Don't you think you've done enough for me lately?"

"I said I was sorry about that."

"And yet here you are. Doing it again."

"I'm here to help."

"I don't need your help."

"You know, you don't seem all that happy to see me."

"Happy? *Happy*?!" Ramirez clenched his jaw together, and I could tell he was thinking a really bad word. "You don't ever listen, do you?"

"Look, you just do your job, and I'll do mine."

"Fine!"

"Fine!"

He leaned in so close that I could feel his coffee scented breath on my cheek. "Just stay the hell out of my way."

I ground my teeth together. But, to my credit, I didn't even shoot back a smart remark. Mostly because I couldn't think of one. The heat of his body so close to mine suddenly chased every logical thought right out of my head. Instead, all I could think of was the last time our bodies had been this close. And, if that vein bulging in his neck was any indication, how very long it could be until we were this close again. Without meaning to, I inhaled deeply. Fabric softener and woodsy aftershave. I felt my stomach flutter.

Damn traitorous body.

I watched Ramirez spin around and stalk into Mia's trailer, back straight, jaw clenched so tightly he'd need a crow bar to pry that sucker open.

I had a bad feeling that unless I repaired the damage I'd done with Ramirez quickly, there might not be anything left to repair.

* * *

I spent the rest of the afternoon washing, pressing, and patching clothes, in between running back to wardrobe for Dusty's last minute changes. The woman may be pierced in some weird places, but I was beginning to think she was a saint. Despite the outrageous requests from the actors (like Margo's insistence that she wear a three-inch, rhinestone-studded broach over her scrubs in the hospital scene), Dusty managed to not only make sure everyone was fully clothed for each scene, but keep some semblance of peace on the set as well. Even when it came to Mia. Who, I realized as the day wore on, just didn't want to do anything. Ever. For anyone. I found myself wishing it were Ashley in the coma instead of her husband. By the time Steinman, the director, yelled the longed for, "It's a wrap," it was growing dark outside, and I was beyond beat.

I picked up my bag and dragged my tired self back through the Sunset city and out the back gates, barely managing to drop Dana off at home and climb the steps to my apartment before collapsing fully clothed onto my futon.

And dreaming of getting up at 6:00 AM to do it all over again.

Isn't Hollywood glamorous?

* * *

Somehow I pulled my tired body out of bed at the crack of dawn and by 7:37 (only seven minutes late today – I was improving!) I made my way through security and onto the lot. Solo today. We were scheduled to shoot a bedroom scene between Ashley and Chad so, obviously, no extras were needed. Though, Dana assured me she was booked for the following two days and would be "back on the case." (Ever get the feeling your life has become a *Charlie's Angels* episode?)

After blindly stumbling through New York, Boston, and San Francisco (all the while wishing I'd gone for the venti latte instead of the tall) I came to a screeching halt outside stage 6G.

A crowd was gathering around Mia's trailer. And not the good kind of crowd where someone has just been nominated for an Emmy and we're all celebrating with early morning champagne instead of lattés. This was a hushed, speaking in whispers, pointing and doing that can't-look-away-from-the-car-wreck kind of crowd. I jockeyed myself into position to get a look at what they were all staring at. Only, being 5'1 ½", my chances of seeing anything were slim to nil.

I spotted Kylie standing a couple of feet away.

"Kylie!" I called her name as I approached.

She jumped as if I'd startled her. "Oh, hi. Wardrobe, right?"

I nodded. "What's going on?" I asked, gesturing to the crowd which I could swear was growing by the second.

Kylie grimaced, rolling her lips inward and stuffing her hands into her pockets. "You haven't heard? It was all over the morning news."

I shook my head. The only report I'd tuned in to had been traffic between Evanescence songs on Star 98.7.

Kylie frowned again, scrunching up her ski-jump nose. "It's Veronika," she said. "Mia's stand in."

"What about her? Is she okay?" I asked, craning to see again.

Kylie bit her lip, her voice cracking. "No she's not. Maddie, she's dead."

CHAPTER FIVE

I blinked at her, my vision going fuzzy. It was one thing to witness dead bodies on *Law & Order*, but the idea of someone I'd just seen alive and well yesterday suddenly needing a toe tag made my itty bitty latte in my stomach like the loop-d-loop coaster at Six Flags.

"Dead?" I repeated. "What do you mean dead?"

Kylie's throat bobbed up and down. "They found her this morning. In Mia's trailer."

"Mia's trailer?" My limbs turned to instant Jell-o. I leaned a hand on the side of the building for support, vividly remembering that creeped out feeling I'd had in her trailer just the day before.

Even though Veronika had looked the picture of health yesterday, I had to ask. "Did she have a heart attack or something?"

But I already knew the answer even as Kylie shook her head, whips of blonde hair whipping her cheeks. Pretty, young actresses didn't just have heart attacks. Especially not in the trailers of women being stalked by obsessive fans.

"No. They're saying she was..." Kylie lowered her voice to a whisper. "...killed. Can you believe it? Steinman said we should all go home. He's closing the set today, you know, because of all this..." She trailed off, staring at the hovering gawkers.

I took a deep breath, trying to get that churning latte under control. This was way too much to absorb before 9 AM. I craned to see through the crowd again. Grips mingled with extras, who mingled with hair and make-up, all straining for a glimpse of what would undoubtedly be *Access Hollywood*'s top story tonight. And mixed in with the curiosity seekers, I spotted someone I knew.

Someone who wasn't supposed to be there.

He hovered near the back in a rumpled white button-down, sneakers, and a pair of wrinkled khaki pants. He had to be the only person in the known universe that could wrinkle Dockers that badly. He looked like he'd slept in his car, or worse yet, not slept at all. His neatly clipped, sandy blond hair stuck out ever so slightly in the back and his jaw bore the tiniest dusting of blond hairs, giving him an overall lived-in look. He was one of the few people not craning his neck to get a better look at the gruesome sight I now knew hovered just beyond my eye line. Instead, he was talking into his hand where I'd bet anything he held a tiny voice recorder.

"Felix," I mumbled, stepping up beside him.

To his credit, when I hissed in his ear he didn't jump nearly as high as Kylie had.

"What are you doing here?" I asked.

"You're kidding, right?" he answered with the hint of a British accent in his deep voice. "This is the story of the century."

Felix Dunn worked as a reporter for The *L.A. Informer*, which, as I may have mentioned, is one of Southern California's sleaziest tabloids. In addition to regular photos of myself engaged in various… misunderstandings… they delighted in printing photos of celebrity cellulite, bat boy's secret lover, and Bigfoot's love child with the crocodile woman. Generally their stories were ten percent truth and ninety percent sensationalism. I had worked with Felix on one of his rare, real stories last year, purely out of need on my part, but I hadn't seen him since. Which was a good thing as far as I was concerned. Felix had an annoying habit of snapping unflattering photos of me, then pasting my head on Pamela Anderson's body.

"Isn't this a bit out of your league?" I asked. "I mean, there doesn't seem to be any indication that Sasquatch was involved."

"Ha, ha. Bloody funny. You ever think of dropping the whole shoe career for the comedy stage?"

I stuck my tongue out at him. What can I say? Felix brought out the second grader in me.

"For your information," he continued, "the *Informer* will pay thousands for a story like this. Not to mention photos."

I paused. Thousands? For a half second my bank account warred with my sense of morality. "Thousands? Seriously?" I asked.

Felix shrugged. "What can I say? Tabloids sell."

He lifted his hand up, ostensibly to scratch his head, but I noticed his palm was facing toward the trailer. Not only a voice recorder, but he also must have a camera tucked in there.

I couldn't help myself. Curiosity got the better of me.

"What do you see?" I asked, standing on tip-toe again.

Felix shrugged. "Not much. They've got the trailer sealed off. They haven't brought her body out yet. A bunch of guys with black bags have gone in. And there are cops all over."

At the mention of the word, "cops," my mind suddenly went to one cop in particular. Ramirez. I wondered if he was here, and if so, how badly his superiors would rip him a new one this time. He'd been assigned to this "babysitting" job, as he put it, to watch the set. And now look. A dead body. Ironically, he was back in the middle of a homicide investigation, but I wasn't altogether sure his superiors would see this as a good thing. Homicide detectives usual came on the case *after* the body was dead, not before.

As if he could read my mind, Felix said, "I saw your boyfriend go in a few minutes go. He didn't look too happy."

"Yeah, well most people aren't happy when someone's murdered. Unlike tabloid reporters."

"What? I'm sorry the poor girl died," he responded. He grinned, showing off a row of slightly crooked teeth and dimples in both cheeks. It was, as I was learning, his charming look, a la Hugh Grant. Luckily I knew him well enough not to be deceived by a little thing like charm.

"Uh-huh. That's why you're grinning like the Cheshire cat, Tabloid Boy."

"What can I say? I guess I'm just a happy-go-lucky kind of fellow." And with that he did a mock stretch and yawn, pointing his palm toward the trailer for a few more clicks.

"So, what happened here?" I asked.

Felix shot me a sidelong glance.

"Come on, I know you've got all the dirt."

He grinned again. "And suddenly Tabloid Boy has his uses."

I rolled my eyes. "You going to share or not?"

Lucky for me Tabloid Boy couldn't sit on a juicy story. "All right, since you asked so nicely. It appears the wardrobe girl-"

"Dusty," I supplied.

Felix raised one eyebrow, making a mental note. "You know the bird?"

"Met her yesterday. Go on."

"Okay, well it seems Dusty found her this morning around 6:15. She was in Mia's trailer, dead. Strangled with – you're going to love this part – a pair of pantyhose."

I always knew those things were evil. I grimaced as Felix continued.

"So far, the speculation is that she died sometime between midnight and 3 AM. They're questioning everyone with access to the lot. But what Veronika was doing in Mia's trailer, no one's sure of yet."

"And Mia?" I asked. "Where's she?"

Felix shrugged. "Probably surrounded by bodyguards at this point. I'll tell you one thing she's not doing."

"What's that?"

"Talking to the press. Don't suppose you could convince her, eh?"

I shot him a look.

He shrugged. "Oh well, it was worth a try, right, love?" Felix stretched and shot a few more frames of the crime scene.

The idea of someone on the set leaving threatening letters in Mia's trailer was disconcerting. The idea that one of the people milling around the scene at this very moment might be a murderer was downright chilling. I shivered despite the sunshine pelting down on us and wrapped my arms around myself.

I hung around for a few minutes more, but there honestly wasn't much to see. Instead, I walked back through the lot to my Jeep and dialed Dana's number on my cell.

"Yello!" she answered in a way-too-perky voice.

I jumped, pulling the receiver back from my ear. "Wow, what are you on this morning?"

"Sorry," she shouted. "I'm doing the treadmill thing. It's noisy."

Dana lived in a duplex in Studio City with a seemingly never-ending stream of other actors. Her various roommates had included No Neck Guy (with whom she'd had a brief thing until she'd caught him ogling another woman's "pecs" at the gym), Stick Figure Girl (who'd checked herself into an eating disorder clinic last summer) and, my all time favorite, Asian Guy Who Always Smelled Like Peanuts. Yick. Currently Dana was living with Daisy Duke, thus named for her endless supply of short shorts. Daisy had just landed a recurring role in a string of Budweiser commercials, so instead of taking on a third roommate this month, she and Dana had turned the extra bedroom into a home gym. Which didn't make a whole lot of sense to me considering that Dana worked at an actual gym, but to each her own. Me, I'd have turned it into one big shoe closet.

"So, what's up?" Dana asked, breathing heavily.

"Seen the news this morning?"

"You know I never watch that stuff. Too depressing." She paused. "Why? What happened?"

I gave her the quickie version of the morning's discovery, amidst her cries of, "no way!" and, "ohmigod!" When I was done, she was panting like a Doberman, and I wasn't entirely sure it was the treadmill.

"Ohmigod, a real live Hollywood murder! I can't believe it! The one day I'm not on the set. So unfair."

"Um, I guess." Only I had to admit this whole Hollywood glamour thing had worn off the second the words "dead body" had entered the picture. It was one thing to gawk at stars going down the red carpet, but when said stars were strangled with their own support hose, it was a whole different ballgame. "Listen, the set's closed today. You want to meet me for coffee?"

"Sure. I've got three more miles to do, then I'll be right over," Dana panted.

"Three more miles? Don't you have like a gazillion aerobics classes to teach today?" I asked.

"Yeah," she panted back, "but not until noon. I need to keep busy until then. Therapist Max says I have to find positive new outlets for my sexual frustrations. It was either running or macramé. And I've already got all the plant hangers I need."

* * *

Twenty minutes later Dana and I were sipping lattes at a corner table at the Starbucks on Ventura and Alcove. I was going over what little I knew about Veronika's tragic demise one more time, while Dana tried to keep her eyes on me and not the college kid in tight jeans serving biscotti behind the counter.

"Felix said they found her strangled with her own pantyhose. How cruel is that?"

"Totally sucks." Dana sipped at her latte (non-fat, decaf, soymilk).

I nodded, taking a big gulp of my mocha (full-fat, double shot, with extra cocoa powder. What can I say? Dead bodies made me seek comfort food.)

"So, let me get this straight," Dana said, "Veronika looked just like Mia?"

"They could be twins."

"She usually wore the same clothes as Mia?"

"That's the whole point of the stand-in."

"And she's found in Mia's trailer."

I nodded again. "Yep."

"So, maybe Mia was the target."

I took another warm sip of my drink, inhaling the coffee aroma. "That's what I was thinking. I mean, it would be a bit of a coincidence, the letters and now this, right?"

"So, the stalker was going after Mia and got Veronika by mistake?"

"It makes sense. It was late at night, dark. Chances are the guy probably came at her from behind. I mean, I can't imagine Mia or Veronika inviting him in for a chat."

Dana nodded, her gaze straying only minimally to Biscotti Boy, leaning over the counter to squeegee off the bakery case. "So we're back to the letters. Whoever has been writing them is our killer."

"Right." I sipped at my coffee again, wondering if Ramirez had made any headway on that front. Not that he'd tell me. Not that he was even speaking to me at this point. A thought depressing enough to tempt me into a second mocha. With whipped cream. And a chocolate chip muffin.

"Did the guy sign them or anything?" Dana asked.

I shook my head. "No name on the one I saw. Just, 'your adoring fan.'"

"Creepy."

"No kidding."

"Well, if there's nothing terribly distinguishing about the letters themselves, we'll just have to focus on the person delivering them."

I raised an eyebrow at her. "Meaning?"

"Meaning find out who on the set has the biggest grudge against Mia."

I did a mental shiver at the thought. "Speak for yourself, but I'm not particularly crazy about the idea of interrogating this guy face to face."

In fact, I wasn't even particularly crazy about the idea of going back to the set. Now that Ramirez's assignment had been bumped up to homicide, every cop in town would be on the Sunset lot. Honestly, what could Dana and I do that they couldn't?

"Hey," Dana said, cocking her head to the side as she watched Biscotti Boy bend over to pick up a stray napkin off the floor. "You think he'd go for an older woman?"

I shot her a look. "Seriously? I think he started shaving yesterday."

"Look at those glutes, Maddie. Don't they make you just want to sink your teeth into-"

"Down, girl. Remember your chip."

Dana bit her lip and did a little moan thing. "I think I need to go for another run."

* * *

After dropping Dana off at the Sunset Gym for her noon Spinning to the Oldies class, I pointed my Jeep in the direction of my studio. Like a good girl, I was going home and staying the heck out of Ramirez's way. (I made a mental note to remind him of this the next time he accused me of butting in.)

I took the 405 south until it merged into the 10 west to Santa Monica. I pulled my little red Jeep into my space just as Mrs. Alvarez from downstairs was letting her cat out. I gave her a friendly wave.

"'Morning, Mrs. Alvarez."

She nodded in my direction. "Someone left a package for you," she said, gesturing to the top of the stairs. I glanced up. Sure enough there was a brown box sitting on my doorstep. My heart lifted. The suede Michael Kors boots I'd ordered from Zappos dot com? Maybe this wasn't such a bad day after all.

"Thanks, Mrs. Alvarez," I called, taking the steps two at a time.

She nodded again before shutting the door and returning to *The View*.

I picked up the package, not even waiting until I got in my apartment before tearing off the tape and peeking inside.

"Ewwwwwwe!"

I did a big girly squeal and dropped the box at my feet, doing a jogging-in-place waving-my-hands-in-the-air dance to shake off the cooties. It was so *not* my suede boots. Instead, lying inside the box was a squirrel. Or, more accurately, most of a squirrel. The poor little thing looked like he'd suffered a run-in with a Ford Bronco on the 101.

I shut my eyes against the mangled image, now burned into my brain, and kicked the box down the steps with the toe of my Gucci pumps, willing myself not to vomit in Mrs. Alvarez's azalea bush.

I did a sweep of the street, searching for teenagers giggling behind trash cans at their prank. Nothing. The only sign of life was Mrs. Alvarez's cat licking its privates on the hood of my neighbor's Chevy. Doing one more icky squirm, I unlocked the door and quickly slipped inside my apartment.

Instinctively, I dialed Ramirez's number. Then, remembering how our last conversation had gone, hung up after the first ring. The way we'd left things had been a little tense. Okay, fine. "Tense" was sugar coating it. But suffice to say I wasn't altogether sure Ramirez would be happy to hear from me. Especially now.

If his superiors were angry before, I could just imagine how they felt after this morning. Forget Hollyweird duty. Ramirez would be lucky to get a job ticketing illegally parked cars on the Promenade.

And it was all because of me. Okay, so I hadn't actually killed Veronika, but thanks to his girl-whom-I-refuse-to-actually-call-my-girlfriend, Ramirez was in the really wrong place at the really wrong time. I wasn't sure if forgiveness would even be on the table after this.

And calling him about a dead squirrel wasn't likely to improve his mood.

Instead, I made a mental note to buy him one of those singing Hallmark cards (Did they make one that said, "I'm sorry I ruined your career, and a starlet showed up dead on your beat?"), grabbed a pint of Ben & Jerry's from the freezer and polished off the entire thing standing in my kitchen.

I nearly jumped out of my skin when the phone rang.

"Hello?" I asked. Half expecting it to be PETA, interrogating me about my curbside road kill.

"Oh my God, Maddie, don't tell me it's happening again?" Mom screeched.

"What's happening, Mom?"

"Maddie, I just heard about the young woman on that show you're working on. Is it true? Is she really dead?"

I debated the merits of lying, but remembering the way Felix was snapping pictures, it was unlikely I could keep this one from her. "Yeah, it's true."

"First the shoot-out-"

"*Misunderstanding*."

"-and now this?"

"It's that Mercury in retrograde. It can be a bitch," I heard Mrs. Rosenblatt shouting in the background.

"Maddie, please tell me you're carrying your pepper spray," Mom said.

I sighed. "Mom, I'm fine. I don't need pepper spray."

"I could always look for one of Ollie's guns," I heard Mrs. R offer.

"No!" I closed my eyes and did a silent mini-meditation. "Okay, fine. I promise I'll carry pepper spray to work tomorrow. Happy?"

"I'll be happy when your life stops making headlines."

Join the club.

"Just be careful, Maddie," Mom said. "And I'll see you on Sunday."

"Sunday?" I asked before I could stop myself.

There was a pause. Then Mom groaned. "Oh, Maddie, don't tell me you forgot about Sunday."

"Of course not," I lied, wracking my brain. In my defense, a dead actress and a dead rodent all in the same day did funny things to one's memory.

Mom sighed again. "Connor's birthday party."

Oy vey. I had forgotten. Connor was my cousin, Molly's, youngest spawn, just turning one and already known in our family as The Terror. The last time I'd visited, he'd spilled grape juice on my favorite white espadrilles. The time before that it was a half eaten lollipop in my Kate Spade. And the time before that, he bit me. Seriously. Right on the ankle like a little dog. Not something I was looking forward to again.

Especially in light of the fact that when I'd first gotten the invitation, I'd stupidly asked Ramirez to go with me. Now that I was on his shit list, I was going to have to endure Molly's brood, The Terror, Mom hinting at my own biological clock ticking like a time bomb, and my Irish Catholic grandmother's stories about how she had already birthed seven kids without anesthesia by the time she was my age. All alone.

Sigh.

"I'm not sure I can make it, Mom; I think I have something else to do that day." Like wash my hair. Or clean my belly button lint.

"Maddie!" my mother admonished.

"Okay, fine. I'll try to be there for The Terror's birthday."

"*Maddie*!"

Oops. "I mean, Connor's birthday."

I could feel Mom's frown through the phone. "You have a gift, right?"

"I have to bring a gift?"

The frown deepened and was accompanied by a low sigh. "I'll pick you up tomorrow after work to go shopping."

Great. Dead bodies, road kill and Toys R Us. Could this day get any better?

I decided I'd better hang up before I tempted Fate with that particular question.

"Sorry, Mom, I'm going through the canyon." I made fake whooshing sounds. Yeah, I know, I'm a terrible person for lying to my mother. "I think I'm losing you."

"I'll pick you up at five!" she yelled as I hit the "off" button.

I spent the rest of the afternoon alternately watching the reporters on E! flock like vultures to the story of Veronika's murder and trying to concentrate on the Pretty Pretty Princess designs for Tot Trots. Between shots of Mia's trailer and *Magnolia Lane* press photos, I added a mini heel and tiny pink bows to the patent leather Mary Janes. But my heart wasn't really in it. And by the time I watched them wheel Veronika's body out in a human hefty bag, I'd abandoned the kiddie shoes and was glued to the TV.

Granted, I hadn't even really known Veronika. In fact, I think I'd only spoken a total of three words to her yesterday when Dusty had asked me to fetch her for a fitting. But she'd been about my age, single. I wondered if she lived alone. If she'd had any plans for the weekend that would now go unfulfilled. When faced with strangulation by pantyhose, The Terror suddenly didn't seem so bad. Poor thing. Talk about the wrong place at the wrong time. I wondered how Mia felt about all this. Did she feel at all responsible that her stalker had offed the wrong person?

Knowing Mia, probably not. Probably she was just pissed that her pantyhose were ruined.

I ordered Chinese in, eating it in front of the television while watching *Entertainment Tonight*. So far there wasn't any new information beyond what Felix had told me that morning, though I did notice a couple of photos of Mia's trailer air that were suspiciously from Felix's vantage point.

On the nine o'clock news, the chief of police finally held a press conference, though it was filled with mostly "we have no information on that"s and "we can't comment at this time"s. I scanned the background for any glimpse of Ramirez.

The truth was, I had kind of hoped that Ramirez would call me. Besides the fact that my co-worker was found murdered this morning, he had to know I was dying to hear about Veronika. Okay, poor word choice. But it felt weird that he hadn't at least called to make sure I was okay.

And there was the fact that the last time we had spoken we'd been fighting. I hated fighting. I hated leaving things like this because a teeny tiny part of me, the part that freaked at the mention of the Cabana Club, worried that maybe he wouldn't call. Ever. Maybe this was it. He wasn't going to forgive me.

Maybe this time I'd actually gone too far.

CHAPTER SIX

The next morning my alarm clock began playing "Good Day Sunshine" at exactly 6 AM. I rolled over and smacked the snooze bar. Ten minutes later, "Pretty Woman" blasted through my apartment. I whacked the snooze again.

I have no idea how many snoozes later it was that I heard the William Tell Overture cut through my sleep. Instinctively, I banged my snooze bar, but that didn't do much good. I popped one eye open, grasping around for my purse and dug my cell phone out.

"What?" I croaked. Between dreams of dead squirrels and dead actresses, I was in no mood for a telemarketer this early.

"Where are you?" Dana chirped from the other end.

I blinked, rubbing sleep out of my eyes. "In bed. Like a normal person. Where are you?"

"You're still in bed? We're supposed to be on the set in, like, half an hour!"

I groaned. "For real? You want to go back?"

"Um, hello? Yes, of course. How are we supposed to catch the killer if we don't go back?"

I glanced at the clock. 7:15 AM. "Dana, the entire LAPD is looking for Veronika's killer. You really think they need Lucy and Ethel on the case, too?"

"Who?"

"Never mind," I mumbled, pulling the blankets over my head.

"Listen, my agent said that they're shooting the scene where Chad and Ashley finally find out who the father of Ashley's baby is. Don't tell me you're going to miss this?"

I pulled the blankets back. "Seriously?"

"Seriously. I even had to sign a disclosure thing promising not to spill the secret to anyone."

"I'll pick you up in ten minutes."

* * *

I did a quick turn under the blow dryer and dressed in skinny jeans, red kitten-heeled patent leather slingbacks, and an oversized black t-shirt with the neck cut out of it. I topped it off with a big red belt and a swipe of Raspberry Perfection on my lips, and I was out the door. Though, I did pause long enough to grab my can of pepper spray, because I had, after all, promised Mom. Okay, I grabbed it *mostly* because I had promised Mom. Partly, I was still a little creeped out by the punk that had left road kill on my doorstep. If I caught the little sucker near my door with a squirrel again, I was gonna spray him.

Half an hour later I had Dana in my Jeep, and we were pulling up to the studio *almost* on time. That is, we would have been almost on time if there hadn't been a line to get through the studio security that spanned around the entire block. Dana and I took a spot at the back, and I craned my neck to see what the hold up was. Blake, a.k.a comatose husband, was standing two people in front of me. I reached around and tapped him on the shoulder.

He jumped as if I'd hit him with a taser gun. Blake was five-foot ten, starting to thin a little on top and spread a little in the middle. There'd been rumors last season that he'd had a breakdown (and who could blame him, having to work with Mia every day) and had checked himself into a mental hospital over the mid-season break. And if today was any indication, his nerves were nearing their breaking point again.

"Sorry, I didn't mean to startle you."

Blake licked his lips nervously. "No, no. T-that's okay."

"I was just wondering if you know what's going on?"

"New security measures. They've got two guards on each gate today, and they're going to be locking down all the back gates after dark. They're even putting extra security on the main gate 24/7. They're being very careful after yesterday's… unpleasantness."

Unpleasantness. Now there was an understatement alert.

I craned again to see around him, but all I could make out was a long line of people checking their watches and tapping their feet.

Finally (half an hour later!), we got close enough to see exactly what the hold up was. A metal detector. A large, plastic archway with a little red indicator light blinking menacingly above it. Not only that, but they also had one of those scanner machines used in the airport to X-ray your luggage. Apparently everyone's purses and wardrobe bags had to be scanned before being let onto the lot.

Dana and I gave our names to the old guy in coke bottle glasses and a name tag that read, "Billy", who checked them against his list. Then, Dana set her Fendi (fake from eBay) down on the conveyer belt. I set my little Kate Spade (real because I choose to live on Top Ramen. It's all about priorities, people.) down next to hers, and we watched our bags disappear into the X-ray machine. Billy's magnified eyes roved the monitor, carefully scanning the entire contents of my purse for any knives, guns or suspicious looking electronic devices.

Beside him stood a bored looking woman in security blues who was the spitting image of Queen Latifah.

"Next," she called, waving Blake through the plastic archway.

Blake stepped through.

The machine beeped.

Blake did a little terrier yelp and clasped his hands together until his knuckles turned white.

"Your watch," Latifah said, pointing at the gold Rolex on his left wrist. He took it off, setting it in a little metal dish, then stepped back through the machine again.

Beep.

Latifah rolled her eyes, popping a wad of bubble gum between her teeth as Blake proceeded to take off his class ring, a big gold colored thing from USC, and pulled a key ring out of his pocket. And again he walked back through the plastic doorway, gingerly this time, almost wincing as he placed one loafer clad foot over the threshold.

Beep.

"Oh, for Pete's sake," Dana mumbled under her breath.

Latifah shook her head, popping her gum like little firecrackers. "Come on, I gotta wand you now."

She waved Blake through, then ran a plastic wand over his extremities. I could see sweat starting to break out on his forehead.

After he'd been thoroughly molested by her stick, the security guard let him pick up his watch, class ring, and battered shoulder bag, and Blake fairly ran in the direction of 6G.

"Finally," Dana said, stepping through the machine. Luckily, the plastic thingie liked her. No beeping.

Unluckily, (yup, you guessed it) it didn't feel the same way about me.

Beep.

"Shit," I murmured, stepping back through.

"Your belt?" Dana suggested.

Right. I unclasped my belt, setting it in one of the plastic tubs. "Sorry," I mouthed over my shoulder to the line of anxious people stacking up behind me.

Okay, let's try this again. I stepped through.

Beep.

I rolled my eyes heavenward and did a silent "why me?"

"Your shoes," the security guard said, cocking her head at me and popping her gum. "They got them little metal buckles on them. Try taking off your shoes."

I stared at her. Seriously?

But she didn't strike me as the joking sort. So, trying not to make any little icky sounds at the feel of the gritty pavement beneath my bare feet, I slipped my ruby slingbacks into another plastic tray, wishing them a safe trip through the scanner. Walking on tip-toes to minimized contact with the ground, I stepped over the plastic threshold. Again.

Beep.

Again.

I threw my hands up in the air. "I give up! Wand me."

Queen Latifah rolled her eyes and motioned me over. Then proceeded to run her plastic wand up and down my legs, getting way more intimate than Ramirez had in weeks.

"Arms out to the side," she said, in a monotone, then punctuated it with another pop of her Doublemint.

I complied, feeling like those guys on *C.O.P.S.* right before they get the handcuffs and the watch-your-head speech.

"Turn around."

I did, trying my best to hold on to some shred of dignity as the line at the metal detector grew to include two minor sitcom actors and a pair of grips who were smirking in my direction.

And just when I thought I was topping out on the embarrassment scale, I hit whole a new high.

Queen Latifah waved the wand over my breasts, and the damn thing beeped like a car alarm going off.

The grips snickered out loud.

Latifah raised an eyebrow at me. She moved the wand away, then back to my barely B's.

Beep, beep, beep!

My face went Lava Girl and I felt myself go into stammer and stumble mode. "Underwire!" I shouted out, as much to the snickering grips as the Security Guard (who looked slightly less bored with her job now). "It's the underwire, okay? I have to wear a lot of wire to make it look like I have any cleavage at all. I'm a B; we B's have to go to extraordinary measures to fill out a shirt. And I know someone as well endowed as you might not understand…"

She raised the other eyebrow at me.

"…but it's very, very important for us little girls to push that support up. I swear it's not a gun. I'm just wearing underwire!"

By now even the sitcom stars were barely concealing their laughter.

Luckily, Latifah took pity on me. "You're cleared," she said. Then covered a snort with another bubble gum pop.

Sure that my cheeks now matched my slingbacks, I ducked my head down, grabbed Dana by the arm and hauled ass out of there. Thankful that only about five hundred people had witnessed my boobs of steel moment.

* * *

"Ashley, the results don't matter. You know I'll love her even if she's Blake's baby."

"Oh, Chad, I don't deserve you."

"What you don't deserve is that husband of yours ruining our lives. Please, just divorce him."

"But, Chad, he's still in a coma! I can't be that cruel."

"Miss Culver?"

"Yes, Nurse Nan."

"I have the paternity results."

I shoved a fingernail into my mouth to keep from gasping out loud. I was watching from the wings as Ashley, Chad and Nurse Nan stood in the three-walled hospital waiting room (which the set dresser told me had also doubled as Blake's office last year before the coma) hanging on every word of dialogue as we shot the scene of the season. Bright lights shone down from the exposed rafters, and a guy with a huge fuzzy microphone on the end of a boom stood just outside of the shot. Behind Ashley, Dana sat at the reception desk, dressed in scrubs, silently pretending to answer the phones and trying (mostly successfully) not to ogle Ricky's tush, as camera one zoomed in to catch Chad's reaction.

"Chad, hold my hand."

"Of course, Ashley."

"Okay, Nurse Nan, we're ready. Who's the father?"

"Cut!" Steinman yelled.

A collective groan went up from the crew assembled in the wings.

"Ricky, you're too far away from Mia, we can't get both of you in the shot like that," Steinman said, stomping onto the set. Carl Steinman was 6'4" with the body of an ex-football player, and the booming voice to match. I put him somewhere in his fifties, just starting to go salt-and-pepper at the temples, and in need of thick wire-rimmed glasses, probably from too many late nights squinting at the dailies on his monitor. "Move closer together," he directed, moving Ricky toward Mia.

"She keeps pushing me out," Ricky protested.

"I do not!" Mia yelled. "You're in my light. Hey, you!" Mia pointed to one of the grips. "What the hell is wrong with you? Don't you know how to properly backlight someone?"

"The light is fine, Mia," Steinman said.

"Oh, sure. No one wants to see *my* face in this scene anyway," Mia retorted, laying on the sarcasm. "And you," she spun around, pointing at Dana.

Uh-oh.

Dana popped her head up, looking like a deer caught in the headlights.

"Yes?"

"I can hear you shuffling papers back there. I can't concentrate on my lines!"

Dana nodded, doing a zipping-it-shut-and-throwing-away-the-key thing.

"Oh, please," Margo cut in, fiddling with the lapels of her nurse scrubs. "It's not her fault you haven't studied your script."

"Why, you old cow," Mia lunged toward Margo, but Steinman was faster, positioning himself between them. I suddenly saw where his linebacker physique came in handy.

"Ladies," he coaxed. "Shall we try to get this shot before end of day?"

Mia stepped back, still glaring at Margo. Margo gave her a self-satisfied smirk.

"Okay, let's take it back a line," Steinman shouted, taking his place behind the monitor again.

I shoved that fingernail back into my mouth, trying not to fidget as I waited for the revelation of who-shot-J.R. proportions.

A PA with an electronic clapboard stood in front of the camera. "Speed. And… rolling!"

"Okay, Nurse Nan, we're ready. Who's the father?" Mia repeated.

"I'm sorry to tell you that the results aren't what we were hoping for."

"What?!"

"What do you mean, not what we'd hoped for?" Ricky asked, taking a step closer.

"Dammit, Carl, he's in my light again!"

"Cut! " Steinman yelled, rubbing one hand over his eyes. "Would someone get another spotlight in here, please? Everyone else, take five."

Walkie-talkies buzzed to life and two PA's took off, scurrying. The make-up woman descended upon Margo, dusting and powdering her forehead, and Mia stalked off to her trailer.

"Isn't this exciting?" Dana asked, skipping over to me.

"I think I'm going to pop a blood vessel if someone doesn't tell me who the father is soon."

"No kidding. Ohmigod, I hope it's Chad's. That man is h-a-w-t, hawt!" she spelled. She glanced behind me. "Hey, where's your purple haired friend today?"

"Dusty took a personal day." At least that's what they'd told me when I'd finally made my way onto the set that morning. Apparently, she was still shaken up after being the one to find Veronika's body. I didn't blame her. After just finding a squirrel's body, I'd been ready to spend the day in bed.

As it turned out, it was a good thing I hadn't, because with Dusty gone there was no one else. Nurse Nan might very well have still been wearing the gaudy day-glow orange, wool scarf and Crocs she'd been in when I'd arrived on set.

"Dana," the AD called her, "could you stand in for lighting?"

Dana did a little happy squeal before skipping over to a mark in front of the camera where the new spotlight had arrived.

I left her having a starlet moment and went in search of that Starbucks carafe.

Apparently I wasn't the only one in need of an afternoon pick-me-up. As I approached the craft service table, I spied Ricky pouring himself a steaming cup of coffee.

"Want some?" he asked, the carafe hovering over a fresh paper cup.

I nodded. "Please."

I tried not to stare at the play of muscles beneath his too-tight T-shirt as he poured me a cup. "Tried" being the key word here. Holy cow, the guy was built. And, I had to admit, up close he was even hotter than on TV. I touched a hand to the corner of my mouth to make sure I wasn't drooling as I accepted the cup Ricky handed to me.

"Wild day yesterday, huh?" he said.

"Very. I'm so sorry about Veronika. Did you know her well?"

Ricky shrugged. Then got kind of a sad look in his baby-blues. "We went out a couple of times when she first started working on the show."

I felt my internal radar pick up. "Really? What happened?"

Ricky shrugged again. "Nothin' much. We saw a movie out in West Hills, near where she lived. But, you know, we just didn't really hit it off."

Despite my earlier decision to leave it alone, I couldn't help asking, "How about Mia? Do you know if she's seeing anyone?"

Ricky shrugged. "I dunno." Then he paused, his eyebrows puckering together. "Why?"

"It's possible the killer mistook Veronika for Mia," I said slowly, watching his reaction. "She was in Mia's trailer after all."

Ricky's eyes went big, his mouth dropping open. "Wow. Heavy." He paused, churning this bit of info over in his head. "Well, I don't know if Mia's with anyone now, but a while back she was dating Blake."

I took a sip of my coffee to cover my surprise. Nervous Blake was the last person I'd expect a control freak like Mia to be attracted to. "Really? Any idea why she stopped seeing him?"

Ricky shook his head. "Nope. But I know that it was right before Blake checked himself into the hospital. And when he came back, Mia had convinced the producers to put him in a coma."

"The coma was Mia's idea?"

"That's what Blake told me. He was kind of ticked off because it's cut his screen time in half."

Iiiiinteresting. I sipped my coffee again, wondering if being in a coma were enough motive to want Mia out of the picture. I'll admit, I had a hard time picturing the shaky Blake actually strangling a woman without having a panic attack, but stranger things have happened.

A PA with a headset glued to his ear ducked his head around the corner. "Maddie?"

"Yeah?"

"You're wanted back in wardrobe."

Great, what now? I had a terrible vision of Margo bargaining to put the Crocs back on again. "Be right there."

I gulped down the rest of my coffee, praying that it was just a loose seam. Of course the fact that I haven't been to mass since my Irish Catholic grandmother dragged me to the midnight all-you-can-pray Christmas Eve service, was probably why God ignored this request. Instead, I could almost hear him giggling at his own private joke as I walked through the door of the wardrobe room to find two uniformed officers going through the racks as a guy in a rumpled suit with a gun bulge at his hip looked on.

And, in the corner, arms crossed over his chest, Bad Cop face firmly in place, Ramirez.

I made a mental note to go to mass more often.

Taking a deep breath, I did a little one finger wave in his direction.

No reaction. Oh boy.

"Miss Springer, would you please have a seat." The guy with the gun bulge indicated a folding chair beside him. He had graying hair and a face that looked like it had been left out on Venice boardwalk during a heat wave – tan, wrinkled, and in serious need of some moisturizer.

I sat down, giving a tentative glance to Ramirez. Still no reaction.

"I'm Detective Rodgers," Prune Face said. "I'd like to ask you some questions about the events of the last few days."

I nodded, gulping down a dry lump.

"Where were you between midnight and 3 AM the night of the thirteenth?"

The night Veronika had been killed. That lump grew, and I nervously cleared my throat.

"We have to ask all the cast and crew," Rodgers reassured me, a fatherly smile parting his wrinkles. Though, I watched enough *Law & Order* to wonder whether it was sincere.

"So, you think the killer *was* someone on the set?" I asked.

Ramirez narrowed his eyes at me, his jaw doing that tight, granite thing again.

"Please, just answer the question, Miss Springer," Rodgers said.

I gulped. "Right."

"Where were you on the night of the thirteenth?"

"Sleeping."

"Alone?"

I glanced at Ramirez. "Very alone."

He pretended not to notice.

"Can anyone verify this?"

Wait, what did he mean verify? "Wait, am I a suspect here?"

"Please, just answer the question."

I turned to Ramirez. "You can't possibly think I'm a suspect here."

"Maddie," he warned, his voice tightly restrained.

"Like I said, we're asking everyone," Rodger repeated.

"Then why are they going through the clothes?" I asked, gesturing to the uniforms.

"The nylons came from the wardrobe room," Ramirez said.

Rodgers shot him a look that clearly said ix-nay on the info-ay to the uspect-say.

"Well anyone could have walked in and taken them. The room's not locked during the day."

"What about at night?" Rodgers asked, flipping open a notebook and jotting something down.

"Yes, it's locked. But I don't even have a key!" I sputtered. "I'm just the assistant.

"Who does?"

I paused. "Dusty."

The detective exchanged a glance with Ramirez.

"But she wouldn't do this!" I protested.

"How well do you know Dusty?"

"Semi-well," I hedged.

Another glance exchange.

"But, I'm telling you she wouldn't do this. She's my college roommate's best friend's cousin! Plus, her best friend's ex-boyfriend's mother plays canasta with the producer's aunt!"

Rodgers gave me a blank look. Then, "Isn't it true that she and Mia had an altercation yesterday? Over the color of her shirt?"

I leaned forward. "So, you think Mia *was* the target?"

"Just answer the question!" Rodgers had dropped the fatherly thing, doing a full on exasperated-cop thing now. A routine that, thanks to Ramirez, I was all too familiar with.

"Mia has altercations with lots of people. Just now she had one with Margo, Ricky, *and* Steinman."

"I'm only interested in the one she had with Dusty, the day Veronika was killed. Did Mia threaten Dusty's job?"

I bit my lip. "Um, I'm not really… I mean…"

"Well?"

I looked to Ramirez for help. Nothing. It was starting to piss me off that he was just standing there, letting this guy grill his almost girlfriend.

Clearly, I was on my own here.

I crossed my arms and puffed out my chest as far as it would go. (Which, sadly, wasn't very far.) "I don't think I want to answer any more questions without an attorney present."

Ramirez lifted one eyebrow. Then muttered a, "Jesus," under his breath.

Rodgers gave me a hard stare and flipped his notebook shut with an audible thud. "Fine. We'll be in touch."

"So I can go?"

He nodded. Then to Ramirez, "Escort her back to the set."

"I don't need an escort."

Ramirez stood up and grabbed my arm. Hard. "Oh, yes you do," he said under his breath.

Ramirez steered me out the door and down the hallway. "This is police brutality," I hissed as his grip on my arm tightened. He opened a door and pulled me into an empty storage room. Then he spun me around with enough force that I feared whiplash.

"Ow!"

"What the hell was that in there?" he asked, his dark eyes blazing.

I froze. I'd never seen him like this before. Sure, I'd seen him exasperated, frustrated, even a little peeved with me at times. But this was different. This was downright angry. There was no hint of humor glinting behind the fire in his eyes. This time he was serious.

I bit my lip to stave off the unpleasant emotion bubbling up inside me. If I had to put a name to it, I'd say it was somewhere between anxiety and all out dread.

"You just don't get it, do you, Maddie?" he continued. "This is a *homicide* investigation. And that was a *homicide* detective. This guy isn't playing around."

"But you're a homicide detective, too," I squeaked out.

Again his eyes blazed, only this time I could see the exhaustion of the past week creeping into them. "No, I *used* to be a homicide detective. Now, I'm a glorified security guard."

"Thanks to me, right?" I finished for him. The dread was bubbling up so far it was stinging the back of my eyes now.

"I didn't say that."

"You didn't have to."

"Jesus, Maddie." Ramirez ran a hand through his hair. "Why didn't you just tell Rodgers what you knew, then you could get the hell out of here?"

"They think Dusty did it!"

"Yeah, and now he thinks *you're* covering for her. Does the word 'accomplice' mean anything to you?"

Does the word "girlfriend" mean anything to you? I longed to retort back. But I was suddenly too afraid of the answer. Instead, I let out a feeble, "Dusty's innocent."

"Maybe."

I shook my head. "No, you don't know Dusty."

"Do you?"

I bit my lip. "Maybe not. But why would she do this?"

"What about the argument she had with Mia?"

I shook my head again. "Dusty wouldn't kill over that. Besides, Dusty must have known Mia was right. With her coloring, she really is a Spring."

Ramirez narrowed his eyes at me. "That's it? You believe her because some woman is a season?" He shook his head. "Jesus, Maddie, I don't get you."

"No, you don't," I said, realizing just how true that was. Damn. The stinging was getting worse. Another minute of this and my mascara would be toast. "Look, Dusty's my friend, and I know she's innocent. And if you or your law-and-order posse have any more questions for me, you can ask them through my lawyer."

I turned and tried to stalk out of the room, making a really dramatic exit. But the stinging behind my eyes had morphed into tears that were suddenly blurring my vision. I kind of stumbled instead, half running half tripping down the hall and out the back exit onto the lot. I blindly ran through the Sunset city, not caring where I was going, just wanting to get away. Away from the accusations, away from the chaos of the set, and, most of all, away from the man who instead of comforting me was interrogating me!

Sure, Ramirez and I had had our ups and downs in the past. But this felt different. This felt like only downs. Where were our ups? Were we ever going to have one again? Not likely, the way things were going. Maybe Ramirez had been right all along – maybe we just weren't relationship material. I'd known from the beginning that Ramirez was a cop first. But somehow in the back of my mind I'd always hoped that he'd wake up one day and realize how much he wanted to put *me* first.

Clearly today wasn't that day.

I finally ran out of breath and sat down at a bus stop somewhere in New York. "Somewhere" being the key word here. As I wiped at my damp cheeks, I realized I had no idea where I was.

The fake city was eerily creepy in the fading dusk, the setting sun creating shadows across the New York skyline. I did a few unladylike hiccups, getting myself under control as I got up and walked down the street, half expecting a mugger to jump out of the dirty alleyway. Even though I knew the dirt had been spray painted on by set dressers, and the only rats on the lot were the agents.

But between the talk of murderous letter writers, and even more murderous murderers, the empty buildings seemed to take on an ominous feeling.

And then I heard it. The sound that made my heart start pumping double time.

Footsteps.

I paused, freezing in the middle of a street lined with brownstones (or at least brownstone facades). The footsteps continued for a beat, then stopped, too.

Okay, so maybe it was just a set dresser getting New York ready for that cop show tomorrow. Maybe it was a cleaning crew. Maybe it was an actor trying to soak up some of the East Coast atmosphere.

Maybe it was a homicidal maniac who strangled women in their trailers with their own pantyhose.

I started walking again, briskly, in the direction of my car. Only with the adrenalin-fueled fear pumping through my veins, I wasn't sure which direction my car was.

I quickened my pace, mini-jogging now as I rounded the corner and found myself suddenly in a tavern-lined street in Boston. The footsteps followed me, speeding up as mine did. I glanced behind my shoulder and let out a squeak. A figure loomed in the shadows just a few yards behind me. Clearly my imagination did not produce that. Frantically I tried the door to O'Shay's pub. Of course it didn't open, because, duh, it was freaking painted on. Nothing here was real!

Nothing, that is, except the murderer chasing me.

I was running now, trying not to trip over my feet as I heard the footsteps growing closer. I didn't dare look back for fear he'd be right on top of me. I rounded another corner, onto a San Francisco street lined with Victorians, and started jogging uphill.

I could hear him closing in. His breath coming fast as if he wasn't any more fond of San Francisco terrain than I was. I reached into my purse, grasping for anything that might be used as a weapon. Lipstick, tampon, change… pepper spray! I said a silent thank you to my overly protective (though in hindsight genius!) mother as my fingers curled around the canister. I felt around for the little button to push, still tripping uphill. I found it.

Just as I felt a hand clamp down on my shoulder.

CHAPTER SEVEN

More out of instinct than anything else, I let out a blood curdling scream as I whipped around and shot the contents of the spray canister blindly at my attacker.

"Sonofa-!" My attacker staggered backward, clawing at his eyes. "What the bloody hell did you do that for, Maddie!?"

I blinked, the adrenalin slowly receding from my limbs as I took in the rumpled khaki pants, sneakers, and slept-in white, button down. Felix.

"Oh crap!" I dropped the canister on the ground. "Oh, holy crap. I'm so sorry, Felix. Oh crap, are you okay?"

"No, I'm not bloody okay!" He was still rubbing at his eyes, his entire face turning redder than a Malibu sunburn victim. "What the hell was that?"

"Pepper spray."

He dropped his hands, his eyes tearing as he stared at me. "Pepper spray? You bloody shot me with pepper spray?"

I felt myself blush. "Sorry. But in my defense, you did kind of sneak up on me."

"I did no such thing. I was trying to catch up to you. You're bloody fast in flats. Dammit, this stuff stings."

"Water. We need to rinse it with water." I led Felix, who was pretty much blind now thanks to my blonde moment, through the streets until we found a drinking fountain in the Golden Gate Park that actually worked (as opposed to the three we passed that were just for decoration). I helped Felix splash water on his eyes, between his "bloody this" and "bloody that" curses.

Finally he stopped tearing and swearing, his eyes only marginally puffy. Okay, so he looked like a bee sting victim in some slapstick comedy movie, but since he didn't have a mirror, he didn't need to know that.

"Bloody hell, you're a menace, girl."

"Hey, I resent that. Besides, what do you mean chasing girls like that? What was I supposed to think? There's a killer on the loose, you know?"

"And you're going to defend yourself against him with cayenne pepper?"

I put my hands on my hips. "Worked, didn't it?"

He gave me a death look.

"So, what did you want anyway?"

"I wanted to see how your co-worker, Dusty, was faring."

I narrowed my eyes. "You mean you wanted to see if you could get an interview with her."

He grinned. "You know me so well."

I shook my head. "Unh-uh. No way, pal. Dusty's not talking to anyone, least of all a sleazy tabloid."

"Aw, come on. Throw me a little something? I've got to have some sort of follow up to print in tomorrow's edition."

"How did you even get on the lot?" I asked.

Felix smiled. "I've got the golden ticket." He pulled a laminated card out from his shirt pocket. "Press pass. It just so happens that the *Informer*'s editor-in-chief plays golf with the head of Sunset Studios. Thanks to the fact the chief throws every game, I've got carte blanche on the lot."

I scoffed. "Am I supposed to be impressed by that?"

"No, but here's something that might get your attention. The coroner's report."

"On Veronika?"

He nodded.

Damn. He was right. I was all ears now.

"Okay, I'll bite. What was in the coroner's report?"

Felix clucked his tongue and shook his head. "Nah, uh-uh. Not until you give me something first."

"Forget it. I'm not giving you any dirt."

Felix shrugged. "Okay, then I'll just keep Veronika's condition to myself."

I pursed my lips together. Dammit. He knew my weakness. What condition?! I was dying here. "How did you get a copy of the coroner's report? That gold ticket get you into the morgue, too?"

Felix shook his head. "No. My excellent computing skills got me into the morgue. Or, more accurately, their database."

"You hacked into the LAPD database?!" I'll admit, my tone was horrified, but inside I was actually a little impressed. The last time we'd worked together, Felix had proven himself competent at a range of lock picking, a skill he still hadn't totally explained. Now he was a computer hacker, too. Part of me was thinking I should be worried about this guy, but mostly I was wishing I had skills like those, too.

Of course, here was Felix offering to let me reap the rewards of said skills.

I did an angel-shoulder, devil-shoulder thing for about two seconds, before I finally gave in.

"Okay, fine. I'll give you a gossip tidbit you can run tomorrow. But cough up the report first. What condition?"

Felix gave a satisfied crooked smile. "She was pregnant."

"No way!"

"Way. About three months."

"Any idea who the father is?" Talk about life imitating art.

Felix shook his head. "Not yet. I'm sure the police are currently swabbing any male she's come in contact with lately. I'll let you know when anything pops across my screen."

I chewed at my Raspberry Perfection lip gloss as I digested this bit of information. Maybe we'd been too quick to judge. Maybe Mia hadn't been the target after all, but Veronika. She wouldn't be the first mother-to-be that had broken baby news to a less than enthusiastic father.

"Hey, you all right?" Felix asked.

"What?"

He reached out a hand and wiped a finger down my cheek. "Looks like you've been crying." He cocked his head to the side. "You all right?"

I sniffed hard, trying not to dwell on the irony that the most tender touch I'd had in days just came from a tabloid reporter. "I'm fine. Men just suck."

Felix raised one eyebrow. "Tiff with the boyfriend?"

"I don't want to talk about it."

Felix's face broke into his charming grin (which actually was a bit comical with his eyes still swollen). "Definite tiff with the boyfriend. And, I'd venture to say, a big one."

"I said I don't want to talk about it!"

His grin widened. "Okay, fine. How about we talk about the juicy bit o' gossip you're going to lay on me?"

"Okay." I cleared my throat. "Deveroux Strong is gay."

Felix scoffed. "Oh, hell, I know that. Everyone knows that. That's not news."

I shrugged. "Sorry, it's all I've got."

Felix glared at me. "That's it, then? I give you Veronika's pregnant, and all you can give me is stale gaydar?"

"Better luck next time." I waved and walked off in the direction (I hoped! Wow was this place a maze.) of studio 6G.

To the tune of Felix muttering "bloody hells" behind me. He really should learn to watch his language.

* * *

By the time I got back to the set, Steinman was just calling it a wrap. I grabbed my things and slogged out to my Jeep, pulling up in front of my apartment to the sounds of Mrs. Alvarez watching *Wheel of Fortune* and my stomach rumbling. I parked in the drive and carried my purse up the wooden stairs, mentally debating between the merits of pizza delivery versus Chinese take-out again.

I was having visions of chicken chow mien when my cell clucked from my purse. I fumbled with my keys at the front door as I balanced the phone between my ear and shoulder.

"Hello?"

"Hey, it's me!" Mom shouted.

I resisted the urge to jerk away from the receiver. "You don't have to yell, Mom."

"I'm on a cell!" she screamed.

I rolled my eyes.

"Listen, I'm sorry I'm late. There was traffic on the 101. But we'll be there in a couple of minutes."

I froze. "Um, you'll be *here*?"

Mom did her patented where-did-I-go-wrong? sigh. "You forgot?"

"No, of course not." Oh, hell. What now?

"Connor's gift. For his birthday party?"

"Right!" Mental forehead smack. "Oh, wow, um, you know what? It's been a really long day, and I totally trust you, so you know, maybe you could just pick something up for me?"

"Don't worry. I'm already on my way."

"Mom, really, I'm beat, and I-"

"Just a minute, we'll be right there."

"Seriously, I'm so not in a toddler toy place right now, and – wait, who's *we*?"

Too late. I looked up to see Mom's gold Dodge minivan pull up in front of my apartment. Mom waved her cell at me from the driver's seat. I could see Mrs. Rosenblatt's muumuu-clad outline in the back. And then the passenger side door burst open, and my cousin, Molly, waddled out. Waddled because, yet again, she was pregnant.

Molly had popped out four munchkins in the last four years and was the apple of my Irish Catholic grandmother's eye. There's nothing an Irish Catholic family loves more than a girl who gets married young and makes babies like a bunny. Don't get me wrong, I loved Molly. She just made my ovaries hurt sometimes.

"Mads!" she said, attacking me with air kisses.

"Hi, Molly," I mumbled, navigating a hug around her swollen belly.

"I'm so glad you're coming to the party. Connor is so looking forward to seeing his Auntie Maddie again."

Yeah, I'll just bet. He was probably planning his attack on my Cavalli pumps as we spoke.

"So, ready for Toys R Us?" Molly asked, her eyes twinkling.

I think my ovaries groaned.

* * *

Half an hour later I was in the preschool aisle of Toy Hell, surrounded by noisy, three foot high people with runny noses and sticky hands, pretending to shoot me with little red plastic laser beams.

"I don't see it," Molly said, scanning the shelves. "Where's Chicken Dance Elmo?"

A kid with freckles and pigtails made little *pow, pow* sounds at me and stuck out her tongue.

I resisted the urge to respond in kind. (Just barely.)

"How about this one?" Mom pulled a furry red monster off the shelf. She squeezed its tummy, and it told her she was special.

"No, no, that's Self Esteem Elmo. I need the Chicken Dance one. Connor wants the Chicken Dance one." Molly shoved packages aside on the shelf, digging in the back.

Considering Connor's entire vocabulary consisted of drool and spit bubbles, I seriously doubted he could tell one monster from another.

"This guy's kinda cute," Mrs. R said, grabbing a blue furry Grover doll. "Kind of reminds me of my last husband, Luther."

I raised an eyebrow.

"Luther was all gangly arms and legs," Mrs. R explained. "Real tall, never quite looked like he knew what to do with his body. That is until we got in the bedroom, if ya' know what I mean." Mrs. Rosenblatt waggled her drawn-in eyebrows up and down.

Muppets and sex, two topics that should never collide. Trying not to envision Mrs. R in bed with a six foot tall, furry blue monster, I pulled a puzzle off the shelf. "Here, this looks cute. I'll just get this."

Molly whipped around. "What's the age range?"

"Uh?" I scanned the box.

"In the corner," Molly pointed. Then shook her head. "It says ages 18 months to three years. It'll be too hard. Plus, the pieces are too little; Connor could choke on one. You have to read the age ranges, Maddie."

"Oh. Okay." I put the puzzle back. Then grabbed a plastic truck. "How about this?"

Molly shook her head. "No, we're only allowing gender neutral toys in the house. Experts say that social imprinting begins at a very early age, and male and female non-specific toys present them with the best chances for gender role socialization in a non-threatening and nurturing environment before they conceptualize gender constancy and their culturally determined roles."

O-kay. I put the truck back.

"I think this guy's kind of cute. You sure Connor wouldn't like him?" Mom squeezed Self Esteem Elmo again.

"*Be proud of your uniqueness*," it told her.

"You know, it's been ages since I saw Luther," Mrs. R said, putting Grover back on the shelf. "Last time was right after we signed the divorce papers. We bumped into each other at the Hometown Buffet. Then ended up back at my place for dessert." She did another eyebrow waggle. "If ya' know what I mean. I tell ya, for a skinny guy, that man could really eat."

I sincerely hoped she was talking about the pound cake.

"Where is it? The online ad said that Chicken Dance Elmo was ten percent off this week. If they advertise it, they should have it. I need that doll!"

Mom squeezed Self Esteem Elmo again. "*Elmo loves you just the way you are.*"

"How about this guy?" Mrs. R held up another red monster, this one in a pair of shiny silver pants. She pushed the "try me" button on his hand, and he began to gyrate to a hip-hop version of "Old Mac Donald's Farm".

"No, that's Bust-a-Move Elmo. He's last year's model. We need the new one. Connor wants Chicken Dance Elmo!" Molly pushed past the freckle-faced girl with the gun, frantically rummaging through the stuffed toys.

"You know, Luther wasn't much of a dancer. Unless, of course, you count the horizontal mambo. Man, that guy could mambo all night. He had this huge-"

"How about this?" I asked, quickly grabbing a teddy bear from the shelf, lest the freckle-faced kid get an anatomy lesson right here in the Elmo aisle.

Molly turned around. Then blinked her blue eyes at me. "Seriously? Ohmigod, Maddie what are you trying to do to the kid?"

Uh, give him a teddy bear?

Molly grabbed the bear from my hand. "The eyes are made of buttons. Connor could easily pop them off and choke on one. *Parenting Today Magazine* says all safe animals should have embroidered features. And the bow around his neck is secured with an elastic cord, which could get wrapped around Connor's throat. And look at the tag! The stuffing isn't hypo-allergenic, poor Connor could have a reaction to it, and the fur isn't even pre-treated with fire-retarding or Teflon. And to top it all off, it's made in China, probably by children in a sweat shop not much older than Connor. What kind of message would we be sending him by allowing him to play with this? It should be illegal to even sell safety hazards like this." Molly's nostrils flared, and her eyes had a scary Jack Nicholson look to them.

I slowly put the cuddly death trap back on the shelf, seriously contemplating a gift certificate.

"I still like this guy." Mom squeezed her Elmo.

"*You deserve respect and love*," he squeaked back.

"We're not getting that one!" Molly turned her attention back to the shelves, knocking boxes off onto the floor now in her search. "All the other kids at Mommy and Me have Chicken Dance Elmo. Connor needs Chicken Dance Elmo. What will the other mothers think if I can't find Chicken Dance Elmo!"

"Wait!" Mrs. R clapped a thick palm to Molly's forehead, her underarm jiggling with aftershocks. "Albert's speaking to me. She rolled her eyes back in her head. "Ohmmmmmmmm."

"Albert?" Molly asked.

"Mrs. Rosenblatt's spirit guide," Mom explained.

The freckled-faced kid took a few steps back and started calling for her mommy.

I didn't blame her.

Mrs. R rolled her eyes so far back all I could see was white. "Albert says… he says he thinks he saw Chicken Dance Elmo fifteen percent off at Toy Town with the purchase of a Power Ranger action figure of equal or lesser value."

"Really, fifteen percent?" Molly asked.

Mrs. R opened her eyes. "Give or take. Albert's usually correct within ten percent."

"To Toy Town!" Molly gave the battle cry.

Mom let out a squeak of excitement and hugged her doll.

"Elmo thinks you are a valid human being."
I think my ovaries just shriveled up and died.

* * *

By the time Mom finally dropped me back off at home and I was climbing the steps to my studio, we'd been to every toy store in the greater Los Angeles area, looking for a monster in a chicken suit. At the last one, a tiny little place in the Valley with bars on the windows, Molly finally found one doll left. For three hundred dollars. I almost choked when Molly gladly forked it over. Didn't she know how many pairs of pumps three hundred dollars could buy?

Since there was no way my budget (let alone my conscience – see shoe reference above) could allow me to spend that kind of money on a stuffed monster, I finally bought Connor a pair of baby Nike's. After, that is, making sure they didn't have any hazardous laces, elastic bands, buttons, zippers, or were made in a third world country.

I stretched my neck from side to side, working out the kinks, as I trudged up the stairs. The slight hum of traffic two blocks away on Venice the only backdrop to the blissful silence. I made a mental note to wait a few years (decades) before having any little monsters of my own, nursing a whopper of a toy store induced headache as I pulled my keys out.

I did an audible yawn and was about to slip my key in the lock when the toe of my ballet flats came up against something. I looked down at the top step.

Then froze.

Another package. A plain brown box, the top taped neatly down, just like the last. Instinctively I reached into my purse for my canister of pepper spray. Not there. Damn! I'd left it in San Francisco. Instead I looked over both shoulders and down the street as if the punk who'd left it here might still be watching, waiting for me to find the remains of another unfortunate victim of speeding on the PCH.

I weighed my options. I could just leave it there. Pretend I hadn't seen it. I could chuck it in the Dumpster behind the building.

But as morbid as it seemed, I was curious.

Gingerly, I reached down and pulled the tape off.

Grooooooooss!

My stomach churned as I stared down at his present. He'd escalated to dead birds tonight. A pigeon with a bent wing and tire treads through his mid section. Only this time, there was a note sitting on top of the mangled carcass. With visions of bird flu dancing in my head, I reached inside my purse and pulled out an old Taco Bell napkin, draping it over my hand as I held my nose and picked up the paper.

Then I really felt my stomach lurch, white dots dancing before my eyes as I scanned the page.

I should have killed you when I had the chance.

CHAPTER EIGHT

My gaze whipped wildly from side to side, as if I expected the boogey man to jump out of my neighbor's agapanthus bushes. I kicked the box of road kill aside, fingers fumbling with my keys as I tried to fit them into the lock. I was shaking so badly it took me two tries before I realized I was trying to unlock my front door with my Jeep keys. Finally I got the right one in, but by this time I was in serious panic mode.

I was a fashion designer. I drew little bows and sparklies on toddler shoes. Who would want me dead? How did they know where I lived? Had he been following me? What did he mean, "when he had the chance"? Was he watching me right now, waiting for another one? I pictured that poor little birdie with tire treads across his mid section and felt faint.

I quickly shut and locked the door behind me, making sure my metal security chain was fastened. Only in the face of a crazed killer with big-ass tires, the chain looked awfully small and pathetic. I grabbed a chair and stuffed it under the doorknob for good measure. Then, I grabbed my hairdryer and, wielding it like a club, searched the rest of my apartment for any signs of bad guys. Luckily, the only thing I found lurking in the shadows were some dust bunnies that spoke of my less than stellar skills as a housekeeper.

Once I was sure I was alone, I reached into my purse and pulled out my cell. My hands were still shaking as I dialed Ramirez's number. Three rings into it I was starting to work into a panic again that maybe he wasn't there, maybe the bad guy would come back, maim me, kill me and stuff me in a cardboard box, all because Ramirez was still too pissed off at me to pick up my call.

"Ramirez, here."

I did an audible sigh of relief. "Oh thank God. I got a bird. A pigeon. I think. Or maybe a sparrow. I'm not sure. But it had tire tracks! Just like the squirrel."

I think I heard him sigh on the other end. "Okay, what's going on this time, Maddie?"

The way he said "this time" was like a mother showing up for the bazillionth time at the principal's office. Was I that predictable?

I took a deep breath and tried to calm down, lest I become a caricature of myself.

"I got a death threat at my apartment."

This got his attention. "From who? Is he there now? Are you okay?"

"Yes. No. I mean, I'm fine." Sort of.

"What happened?"

As I told him about the road kill presents I'd been getting, and the last one with its menacing message, I could feel Ramirez tensing on the other end. "Look, I'm going to send a patrol car over to watch your place tonight."

Which should have made me feel better. Only, I realized as he said it that I'd been kind of hoping he would come over. The fact that he was sending a patrol car instead spoke volumes to the fact we were so not to the "ups" yet.

"A patrol car?"

He must have heard the disappointment in my voice. "Look, Maddie, I've got the captain and the DA breathing down my neck 24/7. I can't deal with this right now, too."

I felt a lump form in my throat. He thought I was something that had to be *dealt* with. Ouch.

"Right. Fine. I understand."

"The patrol car will keep an eye on you."

"I said it was fine."

Ramirez did a deep sigh into the phone. "You're not doing that girly thing where you say it's fine but really you're pissed off, are you?"

"No!" Yes!

He paused again. "Okay, I'll be right over."

"You know what, don't bother. I'm fine by myself."

Another deep sigh. "Jesus, Maddie, don't do this to me right now."

"To you? I'm sorry; I thought I was the one who just got a death threat via bird guts!"

"So let me come over."

"I said I'm fine! What, you think I can't take care of myself? You think I *need* you? I don't need you. I'm fine!" Never mind that I was wielding a hair dryer as a weapon. There was no way I was going to let Ramirez think I wanted him here when he so obviously *didn't* want to be here.

I slammed the phone down in its cradle. Then picked it up and slammed it down a couple of more times for good measure.

I stared at the kitchen chair barring my door. The truth was, I was so not fine. I was still shaking (though part of that could be anger at this point) and the thought of spending the night alone barred up in my apartment, wondering if some maniac was lurking just outside the window with more animal carcasses, left my insides whimpering like a five year old.

I picked up my cell and called Dana at the Actor's Duplex. Unfortunately, I was informed by Daisy Duke that she'd just watched three episodes of *Magnolia Lane* and, thanks to Chad's shirtless scenes, headed off to the nearest SA meeting. I left a message for Dana to come over once her inner beast had been tamed.

I hung up, sudden silence permeating my tiny studio. I flipped on the TV to distract myself, watching images of the Sunset Studios fill the *Entertainment Tonight* screen. The hot topic of the day was that the police now suspected someone on the studio lot was the killer. Mary Hart even speculated that it could be another member of the cast. I watched as images of Blake, Ricky and Margo flitted across the screen. Last but not least was Deveroux Strong. They'd captured an image of Deveroux coming out of a trendy boutique in Hollywood wearing tight leather pants and a form fitting turtleneck. He was carrying a large pink shopping bag and standing just a little too close to his "personal bodyguard." Felix was right. It was no national secret that this guy was gay.

The next image to grace the screen was Mia's face in a montage of shots: outside her Bel Air home, in Versace at the

Emmys, on vacation in the Bahamas. I wondered again if she'd really been the target. Veronika's secret pregnancy put a whole new twist on things. Maybe the killer had taken advantage of the press surrounding Mia's letters as an easy scapegoat. Despite what the police thought, it would have been an easy thing for anyone to walk into wardrobe and help themselves to a pair of pantyhose. Hell, Margo was in and out of there with costume jewelry at least fifteen times a day.

The real question was, who was the father of Veronika's baby? I thought back to the conversation I'd had with Ricky earlier. He'd admitted to going out with her; maybe he was the father? Maybe the pretty-but-duller-than-a-pair-of-Keds act he had going on was just that, an act. I made a mental note to ask Ricky tomorrow just how serious things had been between him and Veronika.

I was still going down my list of available baby-daddies on the *Magnolia Lane* set when a knock sounded at my door.

I let out a little squeak and picked up my discarded hair dryer in a white knuckle grip. "Who is it?" I called, half expecting the person on the other side to answer, "The Big Bad Wolf; open up so I can eat you."

"It's me, Maddie," Dana called. "I got your message to come over."

I quickly scooted the guard chair out of the way and undid the chain, letting Dana in. "Ohmigod, I'm so happy to see you. You will not believe the night I've had."

"I might," she said. Then gestured behind her. "What's with the cop car?"

I peeked around her to see a patrol car parked across the street. Never in my life have I been so glad a man didn't listen to me.

"Long story. Come on in, and I'll tell you."

While we watched the E! special Hollywood report on Veronika's death, I filled Dana in on my conversation with Ricky, my run-in with Felix, my road kill stalker, and last but not least, my conversation with Ramirez.

"I think he hates me."

Dana shook her head. "Your boyfriend does not hate you."

"I'm not even sure he's my boyfriend. I'm not even sure he can say the word 'boyfriend.'"

"He's just under a lot of stress."

Right. Because of me.

I gulped down a big lump of guilt.

"So, who do you think is threatening you?" Dana asked. "Do you think it has anything to do with Veronika's death?"

I shrugged. "I dunno. I can't see how."

"Well, have you pissed anybody off lately?"

I picked up the remote and started flipping through channels. "Besides Ramirez?"

She gave me a look.

"No, I haven't. I mean, unless you count how grouchy Tot Trots was when I turned in the Dora the Explorer light-up sandals two weeks late."

Dana got up and crossed the room to the kitchen, rummaging in my cupboards. "Well, one thing's for sure."

"What's that?"

"Ricky is on the top of our list of suspects." She paused. "Too bad. He's so totally hot. You know, I think he looked at me today. I mean, he was talking to Nurse Nan, but I think he kinda looked past her at me for a second."

"That's right; what happened on the set while I was gone? Who's the father of Ashley's baby?" I asked, leaning forward.

"Argh!" Dana threw her hands up. "You would not believe it. We never got the scene finished. Mia refused to come out of her trailer until Margo apologized. And Margo refused to apologize until Mia apologized for calling her an old cow. And then Steinman got so mad he said they both owed him an apology. Then you showed up, and we all went home. Maybe tomorrow." She paused, holding up a box of Cap'n Crunch. "Maddie, do you have any idea how bad this stuff is for you? It's like eating pure sugar. Please tell me you don't eat this stuff for breakfast."

I ignored her, surfing through the cable channels. I passed through Animal Planet (where a guy was poking a "beauty of a snake" with a stick), Lifetime (where Valerie Bertinelli's husband was leading a double life with a secret second wife), and VH1 (airing a mud wrestling match between two overweight has-been celebs). I paused when I hit Spike. Usually I only stopped on this channel to watch those hot guys on the CSI reruns. But this time, my clicker went still for a whole new reason.

"Lonely tonight? Need a little company? My girls are always ready to play."

"Oh brother."

"What?" Dana popped her head out of the kitchen.

I gestured to the TV where "Sexy Jasmine," wearing a black lace teddy, was strutting seductively across the screen.

"Hey isn't that-"

"Yep."

"I thought I saw her on a billboard down on Pico. Wow, she's on TV now, too?"

"Come visit my website. We're open twenty-four hours a day, and we're always having fun." Then her web address flashed across the screen as she pouted and said, *"You know you want to watch."*

"Do guys really go for this stuff?" I asked.

Dana shrugged. "There's this guy at SA, Gary; he's totally addicted to internet porn. He loves those live web cams. Says the girls do anything he asks them to."

"Creepy."

"Want to know what's even creepier?"

"What?"

"How much sugar is in these crackers? Maddie, you really should take better care of yourself."

* * *

I was standing on the edge of a cliff, a sheer drop off the side, with water rushing beneath me. And the water was rising. I had to get across. I was starting to freak. Then I spotted him. On the other side of the cliff. It was Ramirez. He was silhouetted against the sky like some cowboy hero. I waved, trying to get his attention. But he didn't move. Just stood there. I called out his name, screaming at the top of my lungs as the water rose higher and higher. My feet were soaked now, the water covering my ankles. But still, Ramirez didn't move to help me.

Then, out of nowhere this giant squirrel rose up from the water. He had huge teeth and sharp claws and a big tire tread across his middle. In the distance I could hear the roar of an engine.

"You're next," the squirrel told me. Then pointed over my shoulders. I turned around just in time to see a huge, monster truck. Heading straight for me.

I screamed, calling out Ramirez's name again, and started running. But somehow my legs just wouldn't move. It was like they were stuck in molasses. It was getting closer and closer, the roar of the engine echoing through my head.

* * *

I sat up in bed, sweat pouring down my back. My eyes flew around my apartment as if expecting a giant rodent to appear out of nowhere.

No squirrels. No monster trucks.

Just the sound of my phone ringing.

"Make it stop," Dana mumbled from the futon beside me, a little puddle of drool forming at the side of her mouth.

I fumbled for the receiver, finally finding it beneath a crumpled Macy's bag, and croaked out a, "Hello?"

"Maddie? Um, hi, it's Dusty."

"Dusty?"

"Yeah, sorry to call so early."

I rolled over and looked at the clock. 6:15. No wonder my voice sounded like I'd swallowed Kermit the Frog. "No, it's fine. What's going on?"

"I, uh," she paused, stammering. "I-I'm not going to be able to make it in again today."

"Why?" I sat up in bed. "What's going on? Dusty are you okay?"

"Uh-huh. Yeah. Fine. Look, I just wanted to let you know. So, if Steinman's looking for me, just tell him, uh, just tell him I'm taking another personal day."

"Okay. But, Dusty-"

But I realized she'd already hung up.

"Who was that?" Dana asked, rolling over.

"Dusty. She's not coming in again today." I stared at the receiver. Dusty had sounded odd. Nervous. I wondered what was going on. Had finding Veronika really hit her that hard?

"Holy crap, is that the time?" Dana rolled over, pointing to my alarm clock.

"Yeah. Why?"

"I've got a seven o'clock call time today."

I did a stretch and yawn, still trying to shake the strange dream and the odd note in Dusty's voice from my head. "You hit the shower; I'll make the coffee."

After dressing in a pair of jeans, cork-heeled wedges, and a pink, sleeveless blouse, I threw my hair into a quick French twist, and Dana and I were on the 101, heading toward Hollywood.

The traffic gods were with us, and it only took a record twenty minutes before we were pulling into the garage behind the Sunset Studios. As with yesterday, there was a string of PA's, extras and assistants lined up at the security checkpoint.

Dana and I took our place behind an extra lugging a suitcase and wardrobe bag. Two beats later an out-of-breath Kylie came jogging up behind us.

"Oh, wowzers, can you believe this line?" she panted.

What was hard to believe was that anyone over the age of twelve used the word "wowzers." Though, looking at Kylie, it was kind of hard to believe she was over the age of twelve. She was like Britney Spears (pre K-Fed), Jessica Simpson (post Newlyweds) and Nicole Richie (pre-eating disorder) all rolled into one. Perky little ski jump nose, fresh pink cheeks, round, sort of vacant blue eyes, and blonde hair cut in a flirty layered look. This morning her locks were pulled back in a messy chic ponytail and she wore Uggs with pink sweats that read "Juicy" on the butt.

"It's, like, so unfair we have to go through this," she said, pulling a compact out and dabbing concealer over an invisible blemish. "I mean, Veronika was killed with pantyhose, not a gun. What's with the freaking metal detector, ya know?"

I had to admit, she had a point.

One that seemed more and more valid as we inched forward in line until I spied my nemesis. The plastic security doorway.

"God, I hate this thing," I muttered under my breath.

"It's no big deal," Dana said, slipping her Fendi off her shoulder and onto the belt. "Oh, crap, I forgot my cell in your Jeep. I'll be right back. Grab my bag on the other end for me, k, Mads?"

"Fine, leave me alone with this thing."

Dana waved me off, jogging back to the parking lot.

Considering there were about fifteen guys lined up behind Kylie, I figured all I could do was plow ahead.

I gave Bug Eyed Billy my name, then set my Spade down on the belt beside Dana's fake Fendi. Then I carefully took off my shoes, my watch, my hoop earrings, my toe ring, and my necklace. And today, despite the noticeably flattened appearance of my chest, I was sans underwire. I <u>would</u> make it through this time.

Queen Latifah was on duty again. She waved me through the plastic doorway with her wand. "Next!"

I took a deep breath, bit my lip, and stepped one foot over the frame. Nothing.

Hallelujah! I felt like hugging Latifah, I was so happy. Forget graduating college – this was a major life accomplishment!

"Uh, ma'am," Bug Eyed Billy spoke up from behind his monitor. I turned. He was holding Dana's fake Fendi. "Is this your bag?"

Uh-oh.

"Uh, well, it's my friend's bag," I said, glancing toward the parking lot.

"I'm going to have to inspect the contents for non-approved electronic devices."

"Uh, okay." I stepped over to the monitor and watched as Bug Eye Billy proceeded to paw through Dana's Fendi, pulling one item after another out onto the now stagnant conveyer belt. Lipstick, credit cards, checkbook, pen. I winced as he pulled out two condoms and saw a couple of PA's in line lean forward.

But then Bug Eyed Bully really hit the jackpot.

He pulled out a slim, pink, battery powered device with a soft rounded tip.

I felt myself grow hot as my jaw dropped open. Dana's pocket rocket!

"Ohmigod," Kylie giggled behind me.

Bug Eyed Billy inspected it as if he'd never seen one before, holding it up to his thick glasses. Of course, the PA's were a little quicker to catch on, openly laughing, and I think I heard someone snicker, "hot stuff," from the back of the line. Good God, they thought it was mine!

If I hadn't just gotten my nails done, I would have seriously considered clawing at the asphalt to dig a hole I could crawl into.

"That's not mine!" I protested hotly.

Bug Eyed Billy raised an eyebrow at me. "What is it?" he asked.

I heard a snort of laughter from one of the PA's. "Yeah, honey, tell him what it is."

I clenched my fists into balls. I was so going to get Dana for this.

I leaned in close, trying to be discreet. I know. Lost cause at this point. "It's a personal massager," I whispered.

Billy tilted his head to the side, still inspecting Dana's little friend. "Like for your neck?"

More snorting from the peanut gallery.

"Um, yeah. Like for your neck… or something."

Billy contemplated it for a moment, no doubt trying to figure out just how that might work, but finally he shrugged and, to my immense relief, dropped it back into the fake Fendi. "All right." He nodded. "You're cleared."

I grabbed the bag, shoved my shoes back on my feet and quickly scrambled up the rest of my belongings just as Dana made an appearance at the back of the line. She cheerily waved her cell phone and motioned that she'd meet me inside.

Some days, I think having friends is overrated.

* * *

"Speed. And, rolling!"

"Okay, Nurse Nan, we're ready. Who's the father?"

"I'm sorry to tell you that the results aren't what we were hoping for."

"What?!"

"What do you mean, not what we'd hoped for?"

"I mean it seems that neither Chad nor your husband are the father of your baby, Ashley."

I gasped, covering my mouth with my hand as I watched from the edge of the sound stage. Neither one? Wow, that was a bombshell. I thought back to last season's episodes. Who else could it be? I mean, there'd been that one guy who used to be on *Sex and the City*, but they wrote him out when he poisoned the next door neighbor to cover up his gambling addiction that led to him mortgaging his sister's house and forcing her to work as a high class call girl.

"There's someone else, Ashley?"

"No, Chad, I swear it. There's just been you. And my husband."

"Then explain these results."

"I... I... I'm so sorry. Please forgive me, Chad!"

"I'm not sure I can, Ashley."

"And, cut! Brilliant, take five everybody." Steinman beamed from ear to ear behind his monitor. Grips slapped each other on the butt, and even Margo and Ricky did a high five. The only one who didn't seemed pleased was Mia, still shooting daggers across the soundstage at Margo.

Dana skipped out from her perch behind the reception desk and mini-jogged over to me. "Oh, wow, did you catch that?"

I nodded. "No freaking way the baby is someone else's!"

"My money's on the electrician across the street."

"But he's been dating Tina Rey ever since she saved him from that drunk driver in season two."

"Yeah, but Tina Rey's been seeing that undercover detective on the sly."

"Ooooh. Right. I forgot about that." God, I loved this show!

"Hey," Dana said, elbowing me in the ribs. "Ricky's alone. Now's our chance to grill him."

"Grill him? What is he, a rib eye?" But before I could protest, Dana grabbed my arm and was dragging me across the stage to where Ricky was trying to extract himself from his clip-on mic. She stopped just short of him and did a less-than-subtle throat clearing thing, accompanied by another shot to my ribs.

"Ow! Okay, geeze," I mumbled. "Uh, Ricky?"

Ricky looked up. "Oh, hey. Maddie, right?"

"Right."

"Ah, heh, hem!" Dana cleared her throat again.

"And this is my friend, Dana."

Dana stuck out her hand, doing her best flirty-blonde. "It's a pleasure to meet you."

"Hey." Ricky shook it, and I swear I saw Dana melt on contact, doing a sixth-grade giggle thing.

"Uh, anyway, I was wondering if I could ask you something?"

"Sure." Ricky pulled his microphone through his sleeve. "Shoot."

"You mentioned yesterday that you and Veronika had dated. When was that?"

Ricky pursed his lips together. "Um, I'd say about three months ago. Why?"

Alarm bells louder than one of Mrs. Rosenblatt's muumuus clanged in my head. Three months was exactly how far along Veronika had been. I tried to keep my voice calm and even as I asked, "Why was it you two broke up again?"

Ricky bit the inside of his cheek, his eyes doing a slow survey of the soundstage behind me. "We, uh, we just didn't hit it off."

"Oh, I totally know how that goes. Compatibility is so important," Dana gushed. She laid a hand on Ricky's arm and batted her eyelashes.

"And Veronika felt the same way?" I asked.

Ricky shrugged again. "I guess. I dunno."

"You never talked to her about it?"

"Uh, well, um, not really." Ricky fidgeted with the microphone in his hand, looking about as uncomfortable as when I wore those cheap leatherette pumps from Bargain Barn last summer during that heat wave. Obviously I wasn't getting the whole story.

"Ricky?" I prodded.

He glanced nervously from side to side. Then sighed. "Okay, fine." He paused, leaning in closer. "But this stays just between us, okay?"

"Absolutely," Dana promised. Punctuated by a big toothy smile.

I held up two fingers. "Scouts honor."

"Look, we went out a few times, and then this one time I took her to the movies and dropped her back off at home. Her neighbor was outside watering her lawn. She saw me and recognized me from the show. I mean, she was nice enough, so I signed a couple of autographs for her."

"Go on," I prodded, wondering where this was all going.

"Well, then this lady asks me what I'm doing here, and I told her I was taking Veronika home. Then she kind of got quiet. So, I figured something was up."

"Such as?"

"Well, she tells me that she'd seen some *other* guy go home with Veronika the night before. And he didn't leave until morning. Well, I mean, come on. I'm just not into that. I mean, I'm a one woman kind of guy."

I think I heard Dana sigh beside me.

"So, I broke it off."

"Any idea who this other guy was?"

Ricky shook his head. "Nope. I didn't ask. Honestly, kinda didn't want to know, you know?"

I nodded, disappointed.

"Anyway, please don't tell anyone, k? I mean, my publicist has worked really hard to make me look like this bad-boy womanizer. If word got out that I'm into monogamy, my image would be toast."

"I think that's so sweet," Dana said, her eyes glazing over as she stared up at him.

"Remember the chip," I mumbled to her.

"Chip schmip," she whispered back.

"Hey, you don't happen to have Veronika's address, do you?" I asked Ricky.

"Sure." He pulled a pen from his pocket and wrote it on the palm of my hand.

"Thanks."

"Hey, no sweat," he said. Then flashed us both one of his trademarked hunky gardener smiles.

This time I'm sure I heard Dana sigh. Though I had to admit, as he walked away the rear view was hot enough to make me sigh a little, too.

"I think I'm in love," Dana said, tilting her head to the side for a better angle.

"So, do we believe him?" I asked.

Dana rounded on me. "Of course we believe him! Did you see those tight glutes?"

I rolled my eyes. "All right, what do you say we go pay Veronika's neighbor a visit?"

* * *

Thanks to the shifty-eyed AD, Dana had to wait until lunch to get away. But as soon as Steinman yelled, "Cut", we bolted for the garage and pointed my Jeep in the direction of the address Ricky had given us: 1342 Coronado Court.

I made a right on Melrose, then a left onto Highland before getting caught at a red light between Santa Monica and Lexington.

As we idled, Dana leaned down to flip on the radio.

Which, as it turned out, was a good thing. Because had she been sitting up in her seat, her head might not have survived the impact as a car slammed into the driver's side of the Jeep.

"Uhn!" I felt my neck jerk to the right like a rag doll. Instinctively, I tightened my grip on the steering wheel. I looked up to find a white Range Rover munched up against the side of my car. I blinked hard, trying to get my bearings as adrenalin surged through me.

"Ohmigod, someone just hit us!" Dana yelled, stating the obvious.

What wasn't obvious was why the Rover was backing up.

Then surging in for another attack.

CHAPTER NINE

I braced myself against the steering wheel as the SUV slammed into the side of the car again.

"Holy shit! Is this guy nuts, or what?" Dana screeched, grabbing onto the dash in a white-knuckled grip.

The light in front of us turned green just as I saw the Range Rover back up for another run.

"Go, go, go!" Dana yelled.

I admit, up until that point I'd been paralyzed with shock. But as I saw the Rover's tires spin, revving toward us again, adrenaline kicked in full force, and I slammed my wedge down on the gas pedal, hard enough to send my Jeep fishtailing through the intersection.

I watched with horror in the rearview mirror as the Rover cut into traffic behind us and sped up to kiss our bumper.

"Ohmigod, who is this creep?" Dana asked, swiveling around in her seat. "What does he want?"

I bit my lip, my eyes ping ponging between the cars in front of me and the SUV closing in behind us. We were coming up on Sunset, and the traffic was three lanes thick. "Hold on," I warned, making a sharp right turn onto a side street, just barely missing the curb. The Rover didn't have quite our turning radius, jumping up on the sidewalk and knocking into a bus stop as it followed.

"Dammit, he's still coming after us," Dana said, her eyes glued to the back window.

A point he illustrated by surging forward and ramming into my back bumper.

Dana and I both whipped forward.

"Uhn." My head snapped back against the headrest so hard it rattled my teeth. I pushed the gas pedal down as far as it would go, quickly making another right and swinging into an alley behind an all-night diner.

The Rover followed and, since it had about fifteen horses on my little Jeep, easily caught up to us. Only this time instead of ramming us from behind, it pulled up alongside us, so close that Dana could reach out and touch the white metal beside her window. She let out a whimper and ducked as the driver swerved left, bumping us against the side of the building. I could hear the sickly sound of metal scraping as we careened out of control down the alleyway.

"Ohmigod, ohmigod," Dana chanted in the seat next to me.

Ditto. Only my adrenalin was pumping too hard to form actual words. Instead, I closed my eyes, prayed, and slammed on the brakes, pulling hard to the right.

The Rover sailed past us as my little red Jeep whipped around in a circle, tires squealing against the pavement. When the world stopped spinning, we were facing the opposite direction. I switched to the gas again and surged out of the alleyway as fast as I could, making a hard right into the parking lot of a Hollywood Video before pulling the car to a stop.

I cut the engine, the only sound Dana and I panting like Rottweilers as we both tried to bring our heart rates to something slightly lower than a Pomona drag race.

Dana was the first to recover, digging her fingernails out of the dash and slowly flexing her limbs. "Ohmigod, Maddie. He could have killed us!"

A vision of my squirrel friend with the tread marks flashed through my head. "I think that was the general plan." I pried my hands off the steering wheel, doing a slow mental check of my person. My neck was starting to tense up, but other than that everything else seemed to work. Toes wiggled, arms moved. I looked down. Miraculously, I hadn't even wet myself.

"Are you okay?" Dana asked, rubbing her temple.

"I think so. You?"

She nodded, even though I could see a bump starting to form on the side of her head.

I tried my door handle. Wouldn't budge. Not surprising since what I could see of the driver's side looked like it had been shoved in a trash compacter. My poor baby!

Luckily, Dana got hers open and, after navigating over the gearshift, we both climbed out on legs that felt like overstretched rubber bands. I gingerly walked around the car to assess the damage.

"Wow," Dana said.

All I could do was stare. The driver's side door was smashed beyond recognition, the front lights busted out, the back bumper hanging on by a thread. The entire rear quarter of the Jeep was twisted at a 45 degree angle, and my back tires were flat.

"It's, like, totally totaled," Dana said.

I felt tears well behind my eyes. She was right. The Jeep was toast.

That's it. I was so gonna get this guy.

"Do you think we should call the police?" Dana asked.

I thought about it. For about half a second. Calling the police meant calling Ramirez. And calling Ramirez meant another chapter in the "what's Maddie gotten herself into now?" book. I was already verging on tears; the last thing I needed was another confrontation with Ramirez to top off my day.

Instead, I pulled out my cell and dialed the one person any independent, competent adult calls when a true crisis hits.

Mommy.

Thankfully, Mom picked up on the first ring. "Hello?"

"It's me. Listen, I've been in a little bit of an accident-"

"Oh my God, you've been shot!"

"No, no, I haven't been shot."

"The pepper spray, you sprayed yourself?"

"No, Mom, I-"

"Don't tell me you've been mugged?"

"No!" I yelled. "It's my car." I looked down at the carnage that was my Jeep and felt that lump in my throat return. "It's been in a little accident."

"An accident? Oh, honey, are you okay? Do you have whiplash? Did you get their insurance information?" Mom fired off in rapid succession.

"Yes. Maybe. And no. He sped off."

"A hit and run? My baby's been in a hit and run!?"

I felt my neck growing more tense and wondered if maybe this wasn't the wisest person to call after all. "Mom, I'm okay. Really. I just... Dana and I need a ride."

"Baby, don't move. I'll be right there."

After I gave Mom the address, I hung up and dialed information for the nearest towing company who said they'd be there in half an hour. I sat down on the curb to wait next to Dana, who was digging in her purse for an aspirin, and stared at my crushed baby.

"Look on the bright side," Dana said. "At least he didn't have a gun."

You know your day sucks when the high point is you haven't had a gun pointed at you.

Ten minutes later Mom's minivan screeched to a halt beside the remains of my Jeep. She barely had the engine turned off before she vaulted out of the car, followed closely by Mrs. Rosenblatt. And Pablo The Parrot.

"*Squawk. Love my lady lumps.*"

Mrs. R held Pablo's cage by the top and waddled towards us.

"What is that thing?" Dana asked, peering between the bars.

"This here is Pablo. Marco said he'd give me twenty dollars to take him for the afternoon."

"Maddie!" Mom yelled, wrapping me in a rib-crusher hug. "Are you okay?"

I winced as my neck seized up again. "I'm fine." I think.

"What happened?"

I gave Dana a sidelong glance. But before I could send her the psychic message to wait until I'd formed an edited-for-Mom version, she flipped her hair over one shoulder and launched into dramatic monologue mode.

"Ohmigod, it was, like, totally out of a movie or something. This SUV, like, totally slammed into us, and we were like, 'Holy crap, he just slammed into us!' and then he, like, did it again. So then Maddie did, like, this total street racer move down this alley, and then this SUV, he jumped a curb and comes up beside us and totally starts trying to smash us against the wall! So then we, like, slammed on the brakes and did this killer spin, then flew into the parking lot. I totally think he was, like, trying to kill us or something!"

Mom blinked. Then grabbed me in another fierce hug.

Mrs. Rosenblatt shook her head. "I tell you, that Mercury in retrograde makes people nuts. Did you try shootin' him with your pepper spray?"

"Oh, well, I, uh, I kinda lost my spray."

"Lost it?"

"Um, yeah. Sorry."

Mrs. R dug around in her purse, pulling out a canister. "This here is from my personal stash. I always carry one. I used this sucker on a creep in this bar once. Knocked him flat. 'Course, I took him home after that, and he turned out to be my second husband, Carl."

I rolled my eyes. But, considering I was still dealing with adrenaline aftershocks, I slipped the spray into my purse.

"Really, it was her car that took the brunt," Dana said, gesturing to what was once my Jeep.

Mom took one look at the smashed Jeep and hugged me again. Honestly, though, this time I didn't mind. Staring at my car, I kind of needed a hug.

After the tow truck arrived and hauled my mangled Jeep to the nearest service station, Mom, Mrs. R, Dana, Pablo and I all piled into her mini van, and she drove us back to the studios. All to the tune of Pablo singing his little heart out. "*Don't you love my lady lumps! Squawk.*"

Mrs. Rosenblatt should have held out for fifty.

* * *

By the time we got back to the lot, Dana was way late, and Steinman was yelling out for that "new wardrobe girl" to get that hideous pair of chandelier earrings off Margo. After that it was changing Ricky's sweater so it didn't clash with the shoes Mia wanted to wear, and after that it was pinning Kylie's hem higher so she didn't look, and I quote, "all old 'n' stuff". After that I was in serious need of an aspirin. With a tequila chaser. My neck was so stiff I couldn't turn to the right, and my head was starting to ache. I was just contemplating an early leave when Steinman caught me at the Starbucks carafe.

"Wardrobe, right?" he barked.

I tentatively looked up from my cup. "Yes?"

"I need Blake out here in his hospital gown now. We're shooting Mia and him in fifteen."

"Okay, but then I need to go-" I started to say, but Steinman had already walked away.

So much for leaving early.

On the other hand, I hadn't yet had a chance to talk to Blake alone. And while Veronika's baby-daddy was at the top of our list, I couldn't ignore the fact that being forced into a coma could give a guy one heck of a motive for murder.

I downed my coffee and, after stopping off at wardrobe to grab his gown, made my way out back to the trailers. I passed by Mia's, now void of the ugly crime scene tape, and the one marked, "Talent", until I got to Blake's. The outside was the same white, corrugated metal as the others, though I noticed it looked a couple of feet shorter than Mia's.

I climbed the steps and gave a sharp rap on the closed door. "Wardrobe!" I called out.

I heard a muffled, "Come in," from inside and turned the metal latch.

While the exterior of the trailer was a match to Mia's, the inside couldn't have been more different. Instead of the custom drapes, plush furnishings and granite covered kitchen, Blake's trailer looked like your standard issue motor coach for the retired and idle. A small bench style dinette sat in the middle, the top covered in papers, while a tiny kitchen holding a microwave and mini fridge done in 70's olive green sat to the right. The carpet was a matted brown that was so thin I'd bet my Spigas it was laid right on top of the plywood. The curtains were a dull, pleated polyester and the entire place smelled slightly of burritos and stale Chinese.

"Dusty, is that you?" Blake called from down the hallway.

I peeked my head to the left and noticed a bedroom, as in Mia's trailer, this one considerably smaller and done in wallpaper made to look like wood paneling. "Actually, it's

Maddie. Steinman wants you in your hospital gown for the next scene."

Blake groaned, then appeared from the bedroom, his slacks and white shirt looking rumpled, as if I'd caught him napping. "I don't know why he even bothers. It's not like I'm any more than a glorified prop at this point."

"Sucks being in a coma, huh?" I asked, handing him the gown.

Blake shrugged his shoulders and shot me a sad look. "Well, at least I don't have to stress over my lines."

"How long has Preston been comatose?" I asked.

He did a deep sigh. "Months."

"Any idea when he's waking up?" Okay, I'll admit, this was just the TV junkie in me asking now.

He shook his head. "No. No end in sight. Be right back, I'll just…" He trailed off, gesturing to the gown, then shuffled back down the little hall to the bedroom.

Keeping one eye on the door, I walked over to the dinette, gingerly sifting through the papers. Mostly racing forms, crossword puzzles, a few fan letters thrown in, though certainly not the pile Mia had. "So, I heard that the coma was originally Mia's idea?"

"That's right," Blake replied from behind the door. "She thought it would add some drama to her and Nurse Nan's relationship."

"Was that the only reason?" I quickly scanned through the fan mail. Nothing threatening, though I noticed that Blake's fan base tended to be a bit older than Mia's. There was one woman asking him to appear at her bingo club, another wanting to take him for an early bird special at Applebee's.

Blake popped his head out of the room and I quickly took two steps back from the table. Luckily, Blake didn't seem to notice. "Why? What have you heard?" he asked.

"Nothing…" I hedged, watching his reaction. "Just that you and Mia had dated, then she suggested that your character be put in a coma."

Blake emerged from the bedroom, his hospital gown flapping pathetically around his bare ankles above black dress socks and loafers. "It's true, things didn't exactly end well between us."

I raised one eyebrow. "Oh?"

"No. She said she wanted to see other people, I didn't. I…" He paused, biting his lip. "Well, I'm sure you've heard by now. I had a breakdown. It wasn't just Mia, it was the whole pressure of the show. The press conferences, the interviews, the appearances."

I could well imagine how Blake wasn't suited to being in the public eye. I could see him starting to sweat just talking about it.

"Anyway, it was after I came back that they put me in the coma. I guess Mia just felt it too awkward to work with me."

I phrased my next question carefully. "And you weren't upset by this?"

Blake shrugged. "A little. But not terribly surprised. Before the coma, Kylie and Deveroux's characters were the hot items in the ratings. Tina Rey and the electrician were getting all the press. Mia was in danger of slipping into a supporting role. The coma's slowly pulling up her numbers. Well, that and the press she's been getting lately over these letters hasn't exactly hurt her."

"And you?"

Blake did the sad smile thing again. "At least no one's hounding me for interviews. I better get to the set."

I watched as Blake shuffled out the door and into the soundstage. Honestly, he didn't strike me as the killer sort. More of the lie-down-and-take-it-like-a-doormat sort. Then again, he was, after all, a trained actor. I wondered just how much lying down and taking it a man could do before he snapped?

* * *

It only took Mia fifteen takes to get her monologue in Blake's hospital room right. By the time Steinman yelled an exhausted, "That's a wrap," my neck was stiffer than a new pair of leather boots, and I was ready to drop.

I gathered up my purse, thankful that tomorrow was Sunday – the one day the crew took off during shooting season, and met

Dana near the rear gate. The bump on her head had grown and was starting to turn purple.

"Do you think maybe you should get that looked at?" I asked.

Dana shook her head. "I'm fine. Just a little bump. All I need's an aspirin."

I dug through my purse and came up with one, which I handed over.

"So, are we ready to go try Veronika's neighbor again?" Dana asked as she swallowed the pill.

I groaned. "I don't exactly have a car."

"No prob." Dana held up a pair of keys dangling from a rabbit's foot key chain. "Ricky let me borrow his."

I raised one eyebrow. "Ricky?"

Dana blushed. "Isn't he just the sweetest?"

Uh-oh. I felt my internal radar pricking up. "Dana, please tell me you're not-"

"No!" she cut me off. "I'm celibate, remember? Besides, he's, like, totally famous. I'm sure I'm not even remotely his type."

I had a bad feeling Dana was every guy's type.

Dana twirled her borrowed keys in one hand. "So, we going to go talk to the neighbor or what?"

While my head was screaming for a long, hot bubble bath and a big, frosty cocktail (not necessarily in that order) I had to admit the idea of going home to my apartment alone wasn't all that appealing. The last thing I wanted to find was more road kill. Or, worse yet, Mr. Road Killer himself, waiting in his menacing SUV. So, despite the whiplash and brewing headache, fifteen minutes later we were in Ricky's silver Porsche on the 101 heading up through the hills and west toward the Valley.

We exited at Topanga Canyon, making a left on Victory as we wound our way into West Hills, a suburban area on the westernmost edge of the Valley. Strip malls lined the major streets, while residentials clamored up the hillside, each just a little higher than the other to capitalize on the view.

Dana slowed as we approached Coronado, a tree lined street set into the natural hillside flanked with a hodgepodge of oversized homes, fairly bursting from their modest-sized lots.

Most were set behind manicured lawns with mature, blooming foliage, and driveways sporting BMWs and racy looking Italian sports cars.

Dana parked in front of 1342, a faux Mediterranean villa set behind a row of neatly clipped palm trees.

"This is where Veronika lived?" Dana asked, gaping at the near mansion. "'K, I know how much a stand-in makes. Twenty bucks says she had a sugar daddy."

Considering her prenatal state, that wasn't a bet I was willing to take.

"Come on, let's go talk to the neighbor."

We locked the car and walked up the flagstone pathway to the house Ricky had indicated, just to the right of Veronika's. This one was done in an English Tudor style, with exposed wood beams running diagonally across the stucco face. Dana knocked on the solid front door, which was opened two beats later by an older woman in a pastel blouse with little Scottie dogs running through it. She held a TV remote in one hand, and I could hear static in the background.

"You here to fix the cable?" she asked, narrowing her eyes at us. "'Cause it's been busted all morning."

"Uh, no. Sorry, we're not from the cable company."

"Then I don't want whatever you're selling." She started to close the door, but Dana was quicker.

"Actually we worked with your neighbor, Veronika. On *Magnolia Lane*."

"Oh?" The woman paused. "Oh, you're TV folk?" She brightened up, standing a little taller. Then squinted her eyes at Dana. "I don't remember you. Were you on last season?"

"No, I'm an extra."

"Oh." Her interest waned again.

"Anyway," I jumped in before we lost her, "we were wondering if we could ask you a couple of questions about Veronika?"

The woman snorted. "Hmph. That tart. She thought she was really something. You know, when I heard she was gonna be on the TV, I went and baked her a pineapple upside down cake, just like the one I seen them make on the Food Network. Anyway, she ate the whole thing, then when I asked if maybe she could get me that Mia's autograph, she just laughed at me. Said Mia wouldn't give the likes of me the time of day. Can you believe the nerve of that girl? Prima donna."

I hated to say it, but Veronika was probably right.

"Do you know if Veronika was dating anyone?" I asked.

Her wrinkled cheeks parted in a smile. "Well, I don't know about *dating*, but I do happen to know that she went out with that hunky gardener fellow from the show. Now, *he* gave me an autograph."

"Yes, he told us that you might be able to help us."

"He mentioned me?" She smiled so widely I feared her face might crack.

Dana nodded. "Uh-huh. He said you knew everything that went on on this street. That we could just ask you."

The woman laid a hand on her chest and blushed. "What a nice young man."

"Isn't he?" Dana gushed.

I rolled my eyes.

"He said that you told him you'd seen Veronika come home with a man? The night before he met you?" I prompted.

"Oh, yes." She nodded vigorously. "Now, I'm not one to spread rumors; I keep to my own business, you see. But I'll tell you I seen a man go in late at night, just about when Jay Leno come on, and he didn't come out until the ladies from *The View* had their first guest the next morning." She nodded sagely. "Doesn't take a genius to figure what they were doing."

Now we were getting somewhere. "Did you recognize him?" I asked. "Maybe from the show?"

She pursed her lips together. "No, I don't think so. But it was dark. And the next morning I just got the faintest glimpse of him. But," she said leaning in, "I will tell you he wasn't the only one."

My ears pricked up. "Really?"

"Oh, yes. Men are always going in and out of that place." She gestured next door. "Girls too. It's like a cheap motel, that house. Complete den of iniquity. I tried to get the neighborhood association to fine the owner, but she just claimed she had a lot of friends. I've got a mind to call that gal on Channel Four that does those neighborhood grievance reports."

"So, Veronika doesn't own the house?"

"I knew it," Dana mumbled.

"Goodness, no. She just rents a room. She moved in a few months ago. That place had been going south long before then."

"Do you know the landlord's name?"

"Ask her yourself," she said. "She just got home a few minutes before you pulled up."

"Thanks."

"Anytime, and, uh, tell that nice young gardener fellow I said, 'hi.'"

I eyed Veronika's house as the woman closed her door and went back to her cable guy vigil. A lot of friends, huh?

"Maybe we should go pay our condolences to the landlord," I suggested.

Dana followed as I picked my way over the moist lawn and up the gravel lined pathway to the front door. The home itself was a pale adobe colored stucco, with white columns flanking the front door and large, flowering birds of paradise in glazed planters on the porch. The front windows were all closed and shaded behind heavy curtains. Unless you knew someone was inside, there'd be no way to tell.

I rang the bell beside the dark, imposing front door and waited while footsteps approached from inside. Two seconds later I heard the sound of a lock being thrown, and the thick door swung open.

"Yes? What do you want?"

I stared. Blinking as I took in the woman's liposuctioned thighs encased in tiny spandex shorts, her obviously man-made chest barely contained by a little red crop top, and those familiar collagen enhanced lips, the likes of which I'd last seen six feet high on a billboard above the Taco Bell on Pico.

Jasmine.

CHAPTER TEN

Jasmine put a manicured hand on her hip and raised one eyebrow (which, of course, due to regular Botox injections, did little to change the expression on her placid face.). "Well?" she asked.

I swallowed. "Hi, Jasmine."

She cocked her head to the side, one finger twirling a lock of dyed, red hair. "Do I know you?"

"Maddie," I supplied.

Still nothing but a blank stare on Porn Star Barbie's face.

"Maddie Springer. Richard's ex-girlfriend."

More blinking. "Oh, right. You're the chick that stabbed that girl's implant." She crossed her arms protectively over her double D's. "What do you want?"

"We, uh, we're friends of Veronika's," I said, stretching the truth just a little. "Your neighbor said that you lived here together?"

"She was my tenant. I own this place."

Dana did a low whistle. "Business must be very good."

Jasmine smiled (which, with her highly lifted face, was something akin to the Joker in Batman). "Very. I've got a billboard up on Pico."

"I noticed," I mumbled. "So, Veronika rented a room from you?"

"More like worked for me. I run a twenty-four hour web cam. Veronika was one of my girls."

Mental forehead smack. "Veronika was a cyber sex girl?"

Jasmine frowned. (Or tried to. See Botox reference above.) "It's not just cyber sex. Yes, we do some private chats, but mostly we just let the cameras run and go about our daily lives."

"And men pay three ninety-nine a minute for that?" Dana asked, peering into the house over Jasmine's bony shoulder.

"Well, we are naked most of the time."

Ah ha.

"You're awfully nosey," Jasmine said, planting her hands on her hips again. "What's all this about?"

"We're helping the police investigate Veronika's death," I lied. Hey, the police were investigating; we were investigating; it was almost like we were working together.

"Veronika was killed on the set, not here. Besides, I saw on *Extra* that Mia was the real target anyway."

"Maybe," I hedged. "But we're looking into all possible leads." Wow, that sounded official. Finally, all those hours of watching *Law & Order* were paying off.

"Well I didn't do it," Jasmine said, crossing her arms protectively over her boobs again. "I've got nothing to hide. Everything we do here is perfectly legal. See for yourself." She stepped back to allow us entry.

I admit, curiosity got the better of me. I'd never been inside a real live den of iniquity before.

As we stepped into the marble tiled foyer, I realized that the inside of the house was even more decadent than the outside. To the right lay a sunken living room, lined in plush red velvet sofas. A black lacquered coffee table sat in the center of the room, in the corner a matching bar, fully stocked with colorful bottles. The walls were painted in deep reds and burgundies and the windows were all covered in heavy curtains, though bright, strategically placed spotlights on metal stands blazed throughout the room.

And in each corner, mounted into the ceiling, were white web cams, little red lights blinking on each of them.

"Are those on?" I asked.

"Always," Jasmine responded.

I resisted the urge to cover my face.

Two girls walked past us, into the living room (both clad only in their itty bitties), sat down on one of the sofas and started to play a game of Go Fish.

"Seriously, guys pay for this?" Dana asked.

Jasmine smirked. "And girls. I cleared three mil last year."

I was so in the wrong business. "Three mil?" I gasped out. I looked over at the Fish players, wondering if they needed a third.

"What can I say? Sex sells."

"So, Veronika worked here for you. Doing what? Playing…" I gestured to the two girls. One was taking her top off now. Apparently it was strip Go Fish. "…cards?"

Jasmine nodded. "Among other things. I gave her room and board free, and her hours were flexible so she could go on auditions. Most of my girls are aspiring actresses. Of course, when she landed the gig as Mia's stand-in, it cut into her hours here some, but she worked nights. I gotta get my beauty sleep, you know."

"Do you know if Veronika was seeing anyone special?" I asked. "Maybe a boyfriend?"

Jasmine puckered her collagen enhanced lips. "Veronika kind of kept to herself. Not real friendly. Unless, of course, the cameras were on her. I remember she did bring this one guy home once. After that she started getting the same guy logging in to watch her every day. I figured maybe it was a boyfriend."

"When was this?" I asked, mentally crossing my fingers.

"I dunno. About five months ago. Maybe four. But, like I said, he's logged in every day since then."

"What about since Veronika's been gone?" Dana asked.

Jasmine cocked her head to the side. "Once or twice, I think. Mostly just quick stints. Nothing longer than a couple of minutes."

"Any way you could find out this guy's name?"

Jasmine shook her head, her red hair whipping across her cheeks. "Nope. All our transactions are done through a secure online payment system, PayMate. The clients enter their credit card information; the company tracks their online time, then sends me a check. It's all anonymous. The clients can't find us, and we don't know who they are."

"Well, surely someone at PayMate must have his personal info then?"

"Someone," Jasmine replied. "But it ain't me. Now, if you'll excuse me, I have to go to work. You can let yourselves out?"

With that, Jasmine walked into the living room to join the rousing Go Fish game. She stripped off her spandex shorts to reveal a pair of Brazilian cut panties so skimpy they left little to the imagination as to what else might be Brazilian on Jasmine's body.

Dana and I quickly ducked out the front door and down the pathway to her borrowed Porsche.

"So," she said, once we'd settled in, "how do we get to PayMate's records?"

Chances were, if they catered to the adult industry, they weren't likely to give out their clients' names and addresses to a couple of blondes just because we asked nicely. What we needed was someone who knew computers and how to get around them.

Unfortunately, I only knew one computer hacker.

Felix.

I debated the merits of calling him. It felt a little like poking at a slug – like some of that slime might rub off if I stood too close. On the other hand, the fact that Jasmine had bought our "we're working with the police" spiel, meant the actual police had yet to attack her with the same line of questioning. They were so busy focusing on Dusty's altercation with Mia, that they'd likely have Dusty handcuffed, fingerprinted, and on her way to San Quentin before anyone ever got around to checking PayMate's records.

So, figuring I was doing a favor for a friend of a friend of my college roommate, I dialed Felix's cell.

He picked up on the first ring. No doubt hoping I was a hot lead on Jessica Simpson's latest nude sunbathing location.

"Felix Dunn," he answered.

"Hey. It's Maddie."

He paused on the other end. "Yes?" he asked cautiously. Apparently he knew how I felt about the slime factor.

"Listen, I need a favor."

He laughed. "Don't you always. And what do I get in return for this favor? You know, my editor wouldn't even print that story about Deveroux being gay? I got bumped to below the fold."

"Oh, don't pout. One story about Liberace's ghost and you'll be back on top."

"You know, for a girl who needs a favor, you're not being very nice to me."

He was right, I wasn't. What can I say? Old habits die hard. "Sorry. How about this, pretty, pretty please will you do me a favor?"

"Am I going to get a real story out of it?"

I looked up at Jasmine's Mediterranean. "Uh-huh."

"Does it involve sex or starlets?"

"In spades."

"I'm in. What's the favor?"

I quickly explained Veronika's involvement in Jasmine's website, the credit card company, and the regular customer. As I talked I could hear him mentally putting together a sensationalized headline: Cyber-sex Starlet Slain by Sweetheart – Bigfoot involved? (Okay, I added that last part, but ten to one he'd be in the story somewhere. I mean, this was the *Informer* we were talking about.) By the time I finished he was practically salivating into the phone. He said to meet him at his place in twenty minutes, and he'd pull up the PayMate site.

* * *

The address Felix gave me was in the Hollywood hills. Up Laurel Canyon, down Mulholland and winding around until we broke through the trees and were treated to a spectacular view of the city that made my breath catch in my throat faster than a lungful of freeway smog. Below us the entire valley spread out like a fine mosaic of twinkling lights and through the trees I could make out the Hollywood sign, starkly white against the dark hills. It was the kind of view that would make a location scout stand up and cheer.

And the house standing in front of it wasn't any less impressive. It was a large glass structure, constructed of sleek modern angles. I could tell it was the work of some famous architect, the angles leaning to the side as if they might topple over with a strong Santa Ana. The front of the house was paneled in pale, blond woods, while what I could see of the back was one solid wall of glass. In the driveway, as if to mock the grandeur of the structure, sat a blue Dodge Neon with a dented front fender.

Last year while working with Felix on the story in Vegas, I'd learned that, while he was swimming in family money from his father's side (though he wouldn't divulge just how much), he was a cheapskate of the highest degree, courtesy of his mother's Scottish upbringing. I'd teased him at the time about being a cheap rich guy. Though, I hadn't realized until now just how rich he must be.

"Wow." Dana stared up at the imposing structure. "You sure your tabloid guy lives here?"

"He's not *my* tabloid guy," I protested a little more loudly than I'd meant to. "And, I guess we're about to see."

Dana locked the Porsche, doing the little beep beep thing with her rabbit's foot remote, and we walked down the neatly laid stone pathway and up a flight of slate stairs to the front door.

"How come you haven't introduced me to this guy before?" Dana asked, taking in the multi-million dollar view. "What, is he like hideous or something?"

"Not if you like slugs," I mumbled as I heard the door open.

Felix was dressed in the same rumpled button down shirt he'd been in the last four times I'd seen him, though tonight he was going casual, pairing it with jeans, ripped at the knees. His feet were bare and while his hair was still sticking up in that messy-chic way (though knowing Felix it was a messy-didn't-bother-to-comb-my-hair-after-rolling-out-of-bed way), I was glad to see he'd at least shaved since the last time I'd seen him, giving his face a deceptively boyish look.

"Maddie," he said.

"Felix."

I felt Dana nudge me in the ribs. "Ohmigod, he's Hugh Grant-alicious!" she whispered in my ear.

Uh-huh. With the moral fiber of pond scum.

"Some place you've got here," I said as I pushed past him. The floors were a polished hardwood, the furnishings simple, yet stylish. Obviously the work of an interior decorator who knew when to stop knick-knacking. Low sofas, pale woods, smooth, clean lines. Overall a calming atmosphere made to showcase the natural beauty of the surrounding hills.

Felix looked around himself, as if he hadn't really noticed. "It's a roof."

"How many square feet have you got?"

He grinned. "Enough."

"Hi, I'm Dana." I watched as Dana thrust her hand out at Felix, doing a big-eyed eyelash-batting thing.

Oh brother.

I almost felt sorry for Felix. (Almost. He had, after all, spliced my head on Pamela Anderson's body.)

"Pleasure to meet you," Felix said, pumping Dana's hand. "Felix Dunn."

"Oh, I know! Maddie's told me so much about you." Dana fluttered her eyelashes and leaned in closer.

"Has she now?" Felix asked, cocking an eyebrow my way.

I pretended not to notice.

"Oh, yes. I think it's so cool that you're a reporter. You must see some amaaaaaaazing things," she said, drawing out the word with a Betty Boop giggle as she laid a seductive hand on his arm.

Oy vey. It was only a matter of time before the flattery started laying down thicker than sunblock on a Venice lifeguard.

"Yes, just last week he saw Bigfoot run off with the Crocodile woman," I added.

Felix grinned, extricating his hand (with no small effort) from Dana's grip. "Our Maddie's ever the comedian, isn't she?"

The sad thing was, I think the *Informer* had actually printed that story last week.

"No, I'm on to bigger and better things," he continued. "Like starlets who work for cyber sex sites, right?"

Right. I forced myself to rein in my sarcasm. "Where's your computer?"

"This way, m'ladies." Felix did a mock bow, gesturing to the back of the house.

Dana giggled and touched his arm again.

Good grief. One week off sex, and already her standards were dropping faster than Paris Hilton's panties.

My wedges echoed on the hardwood as we followed Felix through the foyer and down a small flight of stairs to a large office overlooking the back of the house. The wall of glass capitalized on the unobstructed view of the valley. Beyond the glass sat lush, obviously professional landscaping and a bubbling hot tub perched atop a large wooden deck.

"Wow, what a great view," Dana said, pressing her nose to the glass. "And check out the size of that hot tub. I bet you could fit fifteen people in there, easy."

"Honestly, I've never tried. But it fits one quite nicely."

"Or two…" Dana purred.

That's it. I was driving her straight to an SA meeting after this.

Felix crossed the room to a large, Craftsman style desk. Beside it, an array of printers, fax machines, scanners, and lots of other scary looking electronics lined the low bookcases. A slim, state-of-the-art computer hummed to life on the desktop, a flat screen monitor bigger than my television just above.

Felix sat behind it and jiggled his mouse until the screen came to life.

"What's the name of this bird's site, then?" he asked, his fingers hovering over the keyboard.

I gave it to him, and as he typed it in, almost instantly Jasmine's pouty lips filled the monitor, the caption, "You know you want to watch", beneath her. He clicked the "enter here" button, surfing through the free trial pages. I tried not to look as images of the red velvet living room flashed across the screen. A pair of brunettes who looked like twins were playing a game of strip Candyland. Apparently badly, as neither was still wearing much.

He clicked through to a different page and came up with a shot of the kitchen, where two women were doing something completely unsanitary on the counters. Ewwww!

"This the site?" Felix asked.

"Yeah, that's it. Jasmine said all their credit card info goes through a company called PayMate. Do you think you can hack into it?"

"Hack is such a crude word," Felix chided me. "I prefer to think of it as visiting."

I rolled my eyes. "Fine. Can we pay them a visit?"

"I'm going to set up an account with Jasmine's girls," he replied, clicking through the motions as he talked, "to find out what ISP the information is going through. Then, hopefully I can find some sort of back gate to their system that will unlock the security code."

"Won't that be hard to do?" I asked. "I mean, it is a credit card company. If just anyone could hack into their system, they'd be ruined."

Felix grinned at me, showing off a pair of dimples. "Luckily, I'm not just anybody."

"Wow, you must be, like, really smart to know this much about computers," Dana crooned, tearing herself away from the window. "Where did you learn this stuff?"

Felix shrugged noncommittally. "Around." I watched as he created a screen name. Ppingtom07. Cute.

Finally a screen verifying his account came up; then it asked him if he'd like to make a secure payment now. He clicked "yes", and as the screen transferred us to PayMate dot com's home page, Felix opened a new window. This one had a black screen with a little flashing cursor prompt.

"Bingo," he said.

"What, are we in?"

He chuckled. "Hardly. As you said, it's no simple task to break into a secure network like this one. But, I've got their location now. It's a start."

He did a few more clicks, and a sequence of numbers started appearing on the black screen.

"Are those supposed to mean something?" I asked.

Felix didn't look up, intently watching the numbers grow. "Not yet. Give it time, love."

Fifteen minutes later my eyes were starting to bug out from watching numbers fly. I rubbed at my neck, trying in vain to work out some of the stiffness. I rummaged in my purse for an aspirin, then remembered I'd given the last one to Dana.

"Hey, do you have an aspirin or something?"

Felix motioned down the hall. "Bathroom's the first left. Check the medicine cabinet." He looked up from the screen. "You all right?"

"Just dandy," I told him as I went in search of relief.

I followed the hallway and made the first left into a bathroom the size of my entire studio. A sunken Jacuzzi tub took up one side while a marble-topped vanity spanned the other. To the right of it hung a beveled medicine cabinet. I swung the door open and, to my relief, spied the aspirin right away. I downed two with water from the faucet, resisting the urge to snoop through Felix's cupboards.

Okay, *almost* resisting.

With a quick over-the-shoulder, I opened the two beside the sink, disappointed to find only a stash of clean linens. I tried the next two, coming up with a water pick, a hair dryer (that, judging by the perpetually tousled state of Felix's hair, had likely never been used) and a Costco three pack of Listerine. Well, at least he valued dental hygiene. I opened the next cupboard and instantly blushed as I saw that mouthwash wasn't the only thing Felix bought in bulk. A double pack of the biggest Trojan boxes I had ever seen. A bright red sticker on the front touted, "value pack – 30% more free!" I couldn't help picking one up and checking the size. (Hey, I was already snooping, I might as well go all out, right?) My blush turned into an all out full body flush when I found it. Magnum, extra large. Either someone had an inflated image of himself or there was more to Tabloid Boy than met the eye.

I quickly put the box back and scuttled back down the hall to the computer room, ducking my head to conceal my ruby studded cheeks.

I found Dana hovering over the monitor, her head bent toward Felix's as they whispered about something.

"Ahem," I said, clearing my throat loudly.

Both Felix and Dana jumped at the sound of my voice. Dana got a sheepish look on her face and began guiltily twirling a lock of hair between her fingers. No doubt thinking what Therapist Max would have to say about flirting with tabloid reporters.

Felix cleared his throat. "Say, this looks like it could take me awhile. Why don't I call you when I have something on this guy?"

"Works for me." I grabbed my purse and, steering the reluctant Dana by the elbow, made for the front door.

"It was so nice to meet you," Dana called over her shoulder.

"Likewise," Felix replied, a few steps behind us.

"Like I said, give me a call if you ever want company in that hot tub." She added a couple of eyelash bats for good measure as I shoved her out the door ahead of me.

Felix chuckled. "I think your friend likes me," he said as we watched Dana beep open the driver's side door.

I turned on him. "She's in SA, you know. She's celibate, and the last thing she needs is to get involved with another Mr. Wrong." Even as I took an indignant pose, I couldn't help my gaze straying down his Khakis into "Magnum" region.

One side of his mouth quirked up. "Are you warning me away from her?"

I snapped my eyes up to meet his and crossed my arms over my chest. "Yes." *Don't look down, don't look down*!

The other side lifted into a full fledged smile. "Don't bother. She's honestly not my type."

I snorted, keeping my eyes (with difficulty – I mean, who really buys extra large Magnums?) on his. "Oh really? Tall, stacked, blonde aerobics instructor isn't your type? What is then?"

He paused, his smile faltering as he stared at me, his eyes blinking back what I could swear was a sincere emotion bubbling just below the surface.

For half a second I was almost afraid of his answer.

But then the Tabloid Boy I'd come to know and dread resurfaced. "You know me, I live for the story. The only thing that gets me hot and bothered is a report of the Loch Ness Monster surfacing to chat with Bigfoot."

"Very funny. Who's the comedian now?"

He grinned, showing off twin dimples. "Listen, Dana told me about your fan in the Rover today. I know you've got wicked accuracy with the pepper spray, but I think you should consider something a little more serious."

"What do you mean, 'serious?'"

"I mean a real weapon."

"The pepper spray is fine. It stopped you, didn't it?"

He shot me a look.

"All the pepper spray did was piss me off. Were I really bent on harming you, I still could have." Felix went to a low cabinet along the wall and opened a drawer. He pulled something out and slipped it into my hand. "Here."

I looked down and blinked. "A gun?!"

"It's a .38 pistol. Easy to use, all you have to do is pull the safety back like this," he flipped a little metal switch, "then point and shoot. Simple."

I shoved it back at him. "No, I don't want a gun."

"Maddie, someone out there is trying to harm you. You walked away from them today, but that doesn't mean they won't be back tomorrow. Please, just take it."

If I didn't know better, I'd have sworn there was genuine concern in his voice.

Before I had a chance to respond, Felix shoved the .38 into my purse.

I suddenly felt like my Kate Spade was carrying a ticking time bomb.

"Are we leaving or what?" Dana called from the drive.

"Coming," I shot over my shoulder. Then turned to Felix. "You'll call me the second something comes up on our PayMate search, right?"

He nodded and held up two fingers. "Scouts honor."

Satisfied, I jogged over to the car and got in as Dana revved up the engine. I could see Felix still shadowed in the doorway watching us as we pulled away. The weight of my purse eerily unnerving.

* * *

Half an hour later Dana dropped me off in front of my studio, hightailing it to an SA meeting in Van Nuys. (First heartthrob Ricky, then, as she'd put it, Brit-o-yummy Felix, were more than her positive sexual sobriety self could take.)

The patrol car was still comfortingly parked across the street, and I gave the uniformed cop a little wave as I climbed my steps. No response. Figures. I didn't have real good luck with cops lately.

Probably due to the police presence, my doorstep was thankfully road kill free as I let myself into my apartment and saw my message machine blinking like mad. I hit the play button, letting the mechanical voice tell me I had two new messages as I stripped off my clothes in favor of an oversized Aerosmith T-shirt.

"First new message," it informed me. "Maddie, this is Mr. Shuman at Tot Trots." I groaned, staring at my abandoned design table. "I just wanted to remind you that we're expecting the Pretty Pretty Princess designs by Monday. Mrs. Larson's threatening to reassign the My Little Pony flip-flops this summer if you're late again."

I made a mental note not to neglect my real job and finish those sparklies and bows tomorrow. If I lost the My Little Pony account, there went rent. Not to mention those strappy Santana sandals I'd had my eye on.

The machine clicked over to the second message and Dusty's shaky voice filled my studio. "Hi, it's Dusty. Um, listen I… I kind of need to talk to you, Maddie. It's important. Please call me back as soon as you get this message. I… it's important."

"End of messages," the machine informed me.

Something about the urgency in Dusty's message had the hairs on the back of my neck standing up. I quickly grabbed the receiver and dialed her number. It rang three times. Then four. Five. Finally I gave up after the tenth ring and redialed. Still no answer.

I hung up, reluctantly telling myself that if it really was that important, she'd call back. I crawled into bed, but instead of falling into the deep sleep I'd been dreaming of all evening, I tossed and turned, uneasy feelings churning in my belly as I mentally replayed Dusty's message over and over.

I swear someday I'll learn to listen to those feelings.

CHAPTER ELEVEN

True to my promise, as soon as I woke up the next morning, I went straight to my drawing table and sketched out the patent leather buckle closures for the Pretty Pretty Princess shoes. I worked straight through the morning, careful not to get any of my strawberry frosted pop tart on the drawings, before rolling them up and popping them into a mailing tube, ready to send off first thing Monday.

Those My Little Pony flip-flops were so mine.

Feeling pretty pleased with myself, I hopped into the shower, letting the hot water work out any lingering stiffness in my neck. Next to push-up bras, hot running water has got to be one of the greatest inventions known to man. I stood an eternity under the spray until finally the water started to turn tepid, and my tiny bathroom was filled with so much steam even my eyelashes were beginning to frizz. I stepped out, wrapping myself in a big fluffy towel and plopped down on my futon to treat myself to a fresh coat of toenail polish. I was halfway through the second foot when my doorbell rang. I did a heel-walk, careful not to let my wet toes touch, as I called a, "Coming," and peeked through the security hole.

Then froze.

Dark hooded eyes, thick black hair, just a little too long, T-shirt fairly painted on that I-can-bench-press-a-Buick body, arms crossed over his chest, causing that sleek panther to trail dangerously down one bulging bicep.

Ramirez.

I hugged my fluffy towel closer to my body, the sight of him sending a sudden shiver down my spine.

I debated the merits of throwing on a pair of pants first, but his fist banging impatiently on the other side of the door made the decision for me. I undid the security chain and slowly opened the door just enough to stick my head out.

"Hi."

He gave my disembodied head a funny look. "Hi. Can I come in?"

"Um…" I looked down at my towel, which in the face of Ramirez's George Clooney stubble and worn in the right places jeans, suddenly seemed way too small.

"Please?" Eyes dark, voice low and intimate. That shiver transformed into instant heat, starting in the pit of my stomach and settling somewhere distinctly lower.

What the hell, he did say please, right?

I stepped back, opening the door. The second he stepped into the room, my studio felt about ten times smaller, bursting at the seams with sexy detective. I shifted nervously from foot to foot as his eyes gave me and my itty-bitty towel a slow up and down. I'm not totally sure, but I think I heard him groan somewhere in the back of his throat.

Or maybe that was just me.

"Uh, so, what are you doing here?" I asked, tugging at the hem of my towel. "I mean, not that I don't want you here. Or that you shouldn't be here. I mean you can be here any time you like. If you like. Which, you do, 'cause you're here, but I mean we kind of left things… I mean I wasn't sure where we… I mean with all the fighting and all…"

I trailed off as Ramirez licked his lower lip, an innocent movement that somehow erased every single thought from my head.

"The birthday party," he said, bringing his eyes (with difficulty) up to meet mine.

"Huh?"

His tongue shot out again, and I started having the kind of thoughts that could land a person in SA.

"Your nephew, Connor? You invited me to his birthday party, remember?"

"Oh. Right." Then I paused. "Wait - and you still want to go?" I was pretty sure that the whole "talk to me through my attorney" thing was free license for him to skip any and all family functions he'd previously agreed to accompany me to.

And Lord knows I would have taken the out if I could. I cocked my head to the side. "Really?"

He grinned, deep dimples punctuating his stubble covered cheeks. "I'm here, aren't I?"

Wow, he had a nice smile. I mean, like, completely-aware-I'm-not-wearing-any-panties nice. So nice I could feel any lingering anger I might have had at him melting faster than a push-pop on the Venice Boardwalk.

"Right," I said, clearing my throat in an attempt to rein in those pesky little hormones of mine. (Which totally failed by the way.) "So, does this mean that we're… I mean am I… we're sort of…"

His grin widened. "It means we're going to be late if you don't get dressed."

I glanced at my digital VCR clock. One fifteen. He was right. We were so late. "Oh crap! Molly's going to kill me."

I quickly heel-walked over to my closet and pawed through the pile of clothes sitting near the hangers. (I know, I know, <u>on</u> the hangers would be better. But I'm a woman on the go. I'm lucky if the clothes are clean.) Thankfully I found a little pink sundress (clean!) and white sweater (pretty clean) that perfectly matched the pink leather heels I'd put the finishing design touches on last month.

I leaned over to step into a pair of clean panties and heard that groan behind me again.

I snapped up straight and turned around to find Ramirez grinning from ear to ear, his eyes glued to the rising hem of my towel.

"Um, do you wanna wait outside?" I asked.

The grin widened, and he slowly shook his head from side to side. "Uhn-uh."

I rolled my eyes. "Come on, I'm late. I have to get dressed."

His eyes crinkled at the corners. "Honey, you don't have anything I haven't seen before."

Yeah, but that was before we'd turned into the Hatfields and the McCoys. After being at each other's throats the last week, I wasn't quite ready to do a strip tease in my living room for him.

I tugged at the hem of my towel again.

"At least turn around."

Ramirez raised an eyebrow at me, but complied, turning to face the door.

I quickly stepped into my panties and slid the dress over my head.

Even though I was ninety-nine percent sure he was peeking.

Ten minutes later me and my half-painted toenails (luckily the pumps were closed toed!) were in the front seat of Ramirez's black SUV pulling out of my driveway.

I glanced across the street. "What happened to the patrol car?" I asked, noticing the conspicuously absent spot between my neighbor's garbage cans and the mailbox.

"I sent them home." Ramirez sent me a sly sideways look. Then rested one hand on my thigh. "You're all mine today."

I did a dry gulp and crossed my legs.

Oh boy.

* * *

My cousin Molly lived in a fifties-style bungalow in the Larchmont district of L.A., just south of the 101. Larchmont was a popular shopping area filled with little mom and pop bookstores, trendy boutiques, and three coffee houses on every block. On the weekends it was home to locals browsing for bargains, and on the weekdays, actors memorizing their lines and moms pushing strollers two by two. Molly was one of those moms. Only there was no way her stroller would fit two by two anywhere. With four rugrats under the age of five, I think Molly was applying for sainthood in the near future.

Either that or head of the west coast division of Mommy and Me.

"Mads! I'm so glad you could make it," she said, throwing open her screen door and attacking me with air kisses. I awkwardly tried to navigate a hug around her swollen belly.

"Come on in, everyone's already here," she chided.

Hey, I was only fifteen minutes late. That was a record for me!

"Ma, ma!" The Terror yelled, toddling across the carpeted living room floor. He had on a teeny tiny pair of chinos and a dress shirt that was already stained with three different colors of baby drool. Instinctively my new heels and I took a step back.

"That's right, Connor. Auntie Maddie's here."

I gave the little person an awkward wave. It's not that I don't like kids. Kids are great. I might even have one someday. It's just that I was never quite sure how to talk to them. Somehow I couldn't do the high-pitched mommy-voice Molly did, but I felt slightly ridiculous talking to a drooling, baldheaded guy in a diaper as if we were meeting at Starbucks for lattes. So, I settled on the non-committal wave.

"Hey there, big fella," Ramirez said, leaning down and giving Connor a high five.

Connor blew him a spit bubble. "Ablablabla!" he screamed.

I resisted the urge to cover my ears.

"What do you want, Connor?" Molly asked. "You have to sign it. Sign it to Mommy."

Connor blew some raspberries and yelled, "Aboooboooboo."

"Sign it, Connor. Mommy can't understand you." She turned to me. "We're teaching Connor baby sign language. All the experts agree that it's the best way to foster early communication skills and ensure proper conceptualization of interpersonal dynamics at a young age."

Connor smiled at me and drooled onto his Chinos.

Oh yeah, a baby genius in the making.

"Now," Molly said, crouching down and slowly enunciating to the drooling wonder, "use your signs, and tell Mommy what Connor wants."

"Mabooooogoooo," he yelled, going red in the face.

"Use your signs," Molly prompted.

The Terror stomped one foot. Then let out a wail that could wake the dead. "Mamabooogooooooo!"

He raised one chubby fist in the air and, I could swear, lifted his middle finger.

How's that for sign language?

Molly sighed and shook her head. "We're still working on it," she reassured us. "Anyway, come on out back, everyone's here." She grabbed Connor under the armpits and slung him onto one ample hip as she led the way through the Fisher-Price-littered house into the spacious backyard, strung with streamers, balloons, and "Happy First Birthday" signs. Molly's brood of munchkins were on the lawn playing some kind of game that involved sticks, paper hats, and lots of loud war whoops. A pony stood in the corner, being petted by my cousin, Donna's, kids, and under an oak tree Molly's husband, Stan, was stringing up a big, blue piñata shaped like a dog. On the patio sat an inflatable Spiderman-themed jump house filled with shouting kids and my teenage nephew, Johnny, who recently started wearing his hair in a green Mohawk. My Irish Catholic grandmother sat straight backed in a deck chair, sipping at lemonade and plugging her ears. I spied Mom and Faux Dad standing next to the jump house, glasses of merlot in hand.

Alcohol. Just what was needed to make it through a family gathering unscathed.

"Let's find the booze," I mumbled to Ramirez as Molly's oldest came running towards us, swinging a wooden baseball bat and yelling for candy.

Ramirez jumped back just in time to avoid being piñata practice, mumbling something in Spanish. (I'm guessing it was something along the lines of, "Gotta remember to buy condoms.") "Good idea."

Near the back fence, Molly had set up two folding tables, both covered in bright red and blue tablecloths. Trays of cookies, cupcakes, candies and a jumbo-sized birthday cake shaped like a blue dog sat on the first table next to a big bowl of red punch. The second held clear plastic cups, a beer cooler, and boxes of wine.

Ramirez grabbed a beer and moved over to the corner of the yard as Molly's kid came in for another swing. I opted for wine box number one, an indistinguishable pink wine, and filled my glass to the brim.

"Hi."

I spun around.

Then let out a little eek as I encountered a man in thick white makeup with a bright red nose, standing close enough that I could smell the breakfast burritos on his breath. His hair puffed out in red curls all around his ears, and he had a big goofy smile painted over his lips. The effect was supposed to be cute, but with him standing so close, it was kind of creepy. I took a step back.

"How's it goin'?" the clown asked.

"Uh, fine."

"Got any more of that?" He pointed to my glass of pink stuff.

"Excuse me?"

The clown stepped around me and flipped the tab on box number two, filling his plastic cup with cheap merlot. He tilted his head back and downed it in one gulp. "Wow, that hits the spot."

I blinked. "Uh, hello?"

"What?"

"You're a clown!"

He stared at me. "Yeah. So?"

I gestured around at the backyard full of little people. "Don't you think you should be setting a good example?"

Drunkie the Clown refilled his glass, taking a long swig. "Cut me some slack, dollface, I'm only doing the clown gig 'cause they fired me from *Days of Our Lives*." He downed the second glass, then walked away, his oversized shoes squeaking with each step.

"Did he just call you dollface?" Ramirez asked, coming up behind me. His eyes narrowed as he popped the top on a second Heineken.

"Okay, everyone! Piñata time!" Molly yelled.

Kids poured from every corner of the yard toward the oak tree, nearly knocking the grown ups over in the process. Johnny barreled through, loot sack in hand, and pushed his mohawked self to the front of the line.

"Birthday boy first," Molly decided, extricating the wooden baseball bat from her oldest and handing it to Connor. She tied a bright red blindfold over his eyes.

"Can you see anything, Connor?" she asked.

"Maabaaagooo!"

"Oh, this can't end well," Ramirez murmured in my ear. He casually rested one hand at the small of my back, and I suddenly couldn't care less what Connor did with that bat. I tried to tell myself it was inappropriate to get turned on at a child's birthday party.

"Okay, here we go, honey. Swing for the piñata." Molly gave Connor a nudge in the general direction of the blue dog. The other kids danced on their tip-toes, poised to make a dive for flying candy. Connor toddled forward and swung, missing the piñata by a good two feet.

"Lower, Stan, they can't reach it."

Stan let the slack out on the piñata as Connor took another blind swing, this time barely missing Faux Dad.

"Lower, Stan!"

Stan lowered the piñata again. This time Connor swung so hard the momentum spun him around and he knocked into the clown (who seemed to have refilled his glass yet again).

"Lower! For heaven's sakes, no one's going to get the candy like that. Lower Stan!"

Stan lowered.

I backed up as Connor went in for another shot. He took a swing that came nowhere near the piñata. (Though it almost knocked Johnny in the shins.)

"Uh. Maybe we should take the blindfold off…" Mom said.

Too late.

Connor took one more Barry Bonds worthy swing and came in direct contact.

Unfortunately, not with the piñata.

I saw it happen in slow motion. Connor spun around, wielding the bat like a club. Faux Dad jumped back. Molly lunged for The Terror. Mom yelled, "Look out," and Ramirez turned around just in time to collide head first into Connor's wooden bat. The sound of skull on Louisville slugger action echoed through the yard, and everyone did the collective groan and scrunched ouch-face.

"Oh my God, are you okay?" I asked as Ramirez staggered backwards.

He gave me a dazed kind of look. "What happened?"

"Connor hit you with the bat."

Ramirez glanced over at Connor. He was giggling and blowing more spit bubbles.

"Let's not ever have kids," Ramirez mumbled.

At the moment, I had to agree.

Mom ran into the house and came back with a bag of frozen peas which she promptly stuck on Ramirez's forehead. I settled him in a deck chair next to my Irish Catholic grandmother, who was clucking disapproval about how kids in her day were lucky to get a pair of underwear for their birthday, let alone a piñata.

"I'm so sorry," I mumbled, sitting next to Ramirez.

He did a grunt behind the peas.

"I had no idea Molly would give an actual bat to The Terror."

Grandmother arched an eyebrow in my direction.

Oops. "I mean, Connor."

"Uh-huh," Ramirez grunted again.

"Is there anything I can do? Do you need anything?"

Ramirez shifted the peas and peeked out at me. "Another beer would be a start."

"Right." I popped up and crossed the yard, thinking that more booze wasn't altogether a bad idea. I grabbed another Heineken from the cooler for Ramirez, and I flipped the little plastic tab on the pink box for me.

"That one's running on empty, doll," Drunkie the Clown said, appearing at my side. "Try the other one," he slurred.

Great. The clown had beaten me to it. I managed to squeeze a couple of drops out of the pink and half a glass from the merlot. I know, sacrilege mixing wines, but was it really going to make much of a difference? It came from a box.

I took a big gulp… then choked on it as I felt something pinch me from behind. Ohmigod. Did that clown just *grab my ass*? I whipped around.

Drunkie was grinning and swaying on his feet. He waggled his painted eyebrows up and down at me suggestively.

I opened my mouth to give the fresh clown a piece of my mind.

But I never got the chance.

Before I could speak, I caught a glimpse of Ramirez out of the corner of my eye, rising from the deck chair, frozen peas in one hand, look of death on his face.

Uh-oh.

Ramirez lunged for the clown, who, by the way, was pretty quick for a guy who'd just drained a whole box of wine. He ducked, sliding his oversized red feet to the right. But Ramirez was a trained cop. Even with a slight concussion, a guy in a red nose and squeaky shoes was no match for him. He lunged again, this time hitting his target. I watched in horror as Ramirez's fist collided with Drunkie's painted, white jaw. The clown's head whipped around, and he tripped backward, stumbling over his too-big shoes. He knocked into Connor, who fell flat on his diapered bottom, then careened to the right, straight into – you guess it – me.

"Uhn." I reeled backward from the impact, flailing at the air for balance. But it was too late. I was a goner. I slammed, face first, into the dessert table, upending a plate of cookies, sloshing punch to the ground, and doing a ten point face plant right into the blue icing of Connor's birthday cake.

For a second I couldn't breath, my life flashing before my eyes as frosting went up my nose. I heard Molly scream, the clown groan, and Connor do another delighted giggle.

Was it wrong to hate a one year old?

"Maddie, are you okay?" Mom came rushing to my side, pulling me out of the ruined cake.

"I think so," I said. Only since I had a mouth of full of blue icing it came out as, "I ink o."

"My cake! My beautiful cake!" Molly screeched. "You ruined the cake."

"Sorry," I mumbled, wiping raspberry cream filling off my sundress.

"This can't be happening. I planned the perfect birthday party. This was supposed to be Connor's special day! We never even got a picture of the cake. What am I going to put in the scrapbook?" Molly was starting to hyperventilate.

I looked down at Connor. He giggled and drooled.

Then gave me the finger.

* * *

I did my best to wipe the majority of vanilla cake chunks from my sundress before getting into Ramirez's car, so by the time we finally pulled up in front of my studio (me looking like I'd lost a food fight with Betty Crocker and Ramirez growing a purple goose egg on the side of his head) I was relatively sure I hadn't left raspberry-cream butt prints on Ramirez's leather seats.

"Well, that was fun," I said as he pulled into my drive and cut the engine.

Ramirez gave me a look. "I think that kid flipped me off."

"Yeah, he's charming like that."

I got out of the car and started up my steps, leaving a Hansel-and-Gretel-like trail of cake crumbs in my wake. Ramirez was one step behind me and almost plowed into my back as I paused at the top step.

My door was opened a crack.

Ramirez spotted it too, silently slipping his gun from its holster and pushing in front of me.

"Go back downstairs," he whispered, his jaw tense, his body instinctively going into cop mode. I stood rooted to the spot as he slowly pushed the door open, his gun straight-armed in front of him.

Go back downstairs. Good advice. I'd do that.

Just as soon as I saw the asshole who'd broken into my place. I tippy-toed in behind Ramirez, trying to make myself small and unnoticeable.

I had to stifle a gasp when I saw my studio. It looked like the big one had hit. All my kitchen cupboards were opened, plates broken, food on the floor, box of Cap'n Crunch tipped upside-down. My futon cushions were strewn across the room, mixed in with drawing pens, clothes, shoes and my very non-threatening hair dryer.

I covered my mouth with my hand and bit back tears as I spied my favorite pair of silver slingbacks, both heels broken off. Who would do such a thing?

"Shit."

Ramirez had finished his quick walk through of the apartment, and his gun now hung loosely at his side as he stared in at my bathroom.

"What? Oh God, please don't tell me they trashed my make-up. Do you know how expensive that Lancôme moisturizer is?" I rushed to his side. Then looked up at the bathroom mirror and felt the blood drain from my face.

Written in blood red lipstick across the vanity were the words:

I'm going to kill you, bitch.

CHAPTER TWELVE

I crumpled to the ground, my butt hitting the cold tile with a thud. I put my head between my knees to keep the room from spinning. Or at least to keep myself from revisiting my lunch as dizzying fear washed over me in waves. I took deep breaths, having to concentrate on the steady in and out.

"You okay?" Ramirez asked.

"Yeah. Sure. Dandy," I said. Which might have been a whole lot more convincing if I hadn't been wrapped up in a fetal position.

"Honey, you're a terrible liar," he said, kneeling down beside me. He put one hand on the back of my neck and began gently kneading. I hated to admit how comforting the gesture was.

"I'll be fine." Just as soon as the urge to vomit passed.

Ramirez seemed to understand, wrapping one arm around my shoulders and hunkering down beside me. I'm not sure how long we sat like that, but finally the world stopped feeling like a tilt-a-whirl, and I peeked my head up.

"Thanks," I said.

He forced a grin. It wasn't very convincing. "Anytime. So," he gestured up to the mirror, "maybe you should tell me again about the other threats you received."

I took in a big gulp of air, letting it out on a breath that was shakier than I would have liked. "Okay. They started with the squirrel. Then the bird and the nasty note. Then he tried to run me off the road yesterday. Now this."

"What? Wait, back up – run you off the road?" Ramirez blinked at me.

Oops. I bit my lip. I forgot I hadn't told him about the whole road rage thing.

"Uh, well, he kind of ran into my Jeep. A little. But Dana and I were fine. Just a couple bumps on the head and some minor whiplash. No biggie," I said, trying to make light of the whole thing. Which, by the way, I think was very brave of me considering my apartment had just been vandalized, and I was fetal on my bathroom floor.

"And you're just telling me this now?!" Ramirez's jaw tightened, and I could tell it took all he had to keep that vein in his neck under control.

"In my defense, this did happen during the we're-not-speaking–to-each-other phase."

"Please tell me you at least filed a police report."

"Um, well… not really…"

Ramirez looked at the ceiling and muttered something in Spanish. I had a feeling the words "blonde" and "last nerve" were in there somewhere.

"You're mad again, aren't you?"

He gritted his teeth. "No," he lied.

"Then why is that vein bulging?"

Ramirez looked at me. His jaw flinched. His eye twitched. Then he consulted the ceiling again, blowing out a long breath. "I'm not mad at *you*, Maddie. I just…" He trailed off, shaking his head. His gaze resting on the death threat via Maybelline on my bathroom mirror. "I just sometimes wish like hell I had a normal girlfriend."

He stood up and brushed off the seat of his jeans. "Look, I'm going to go call this in. Don't touch anything!"

I watched him walk out into my living room and pull his cell from his pocket. But I honestly couldn't have moved if I wanted to. I was staring after him, utterly stunned.

Did he just say *girlfriend*?

* * *

Fifteen minutes later my apartment was swarming with crime scene guys in SID jackets, taking photographs of my bathroom mirror, checking the window locks, and dusting my design table for fingerprints. I winced as black print dust settled on my pair of white leather Gucci boots. That stuff washed off, right?

It was after I told one SID guy with a bulging gut and bulbous nose to please, please, please not spray any of that florescent body-fluid magnifying stuff near my two-hundred dollar Kors sandals that the police chased me downstairs and back out to Ramirez's SUV. I was instructed to wait there. Which I did. Though the longer I waited, the more anxious I felt.

As glad as I was that Ramirez had taken this threat seriously enough to call in the big guns, the sight of said big guns turning my apartment into something out of CBS's primetime lineup was less than comforting. It was one thing to watch police gather evidence on TV. It was another when it was *your* trash they were pawing through for clues and *your* drains they were checking for hair and fibers. The fact that the place I'd always associated with safety and home was now being treated as a crime scene was a little unnerving. Okay. It was a *lot* unnerving. So much that I was back to doing the head between the legs thing by the time Ramirez finally came down the stairs to check on me.

"You sure you're okay?"

"Uh-huh," I lied.

Ramirez lifted my chin with his finger, forcing me to look at him. He raised one eyebrow.

"I know, I know. I'm a terrible liar."

Ramirez grinned and pulled me toward him. He wrapped both arms around me and planted a kiss on the top of my head. "Come, on," he said, "let's go home."

I gestured up the stairs. "Home's currently being invaded by the LAPD."

"I meant *my* home."

I blinked. "Oh." More blinking. "Okay."

So, here's the thing. I'd only ever been to Ramirez's place once before and, even then, I hadn't actually made it inside. His pager had gone off while we were necking in the car, and he'd had to turn around and drop me off at my place on the way to a murder-suicide in the Hollywood Hills. Ramirez lived in a two bedroom bungalow in West L.A. It was an older neighborhood that might have been advertised as "family friendly" back in the fifties when the little stucco structures had been built, but fifty years later it was bordering the fringes of neighborhoods where you didn't walk alone unless you were carrying an industrial-sized can of mace. For a guy like Ramirez, this wasn't a problem. He fit the neighborhood perfectly, just a little on the fringes of dangerous himself. But, for a barely-tall-enough to make the height requirements at Six Flags blonde wearing a pink sundress and matching rhinestone studded pumps, it was the kind of neighborhood where I wouldn't want to loiter on the front porch.

But it wasn't his shady neighbors that had me biting the traces of frosting off my lip.

First he showed up to take me to a family function, then he used the "G" word, now he wanted to take me home? This was more attention than I'd gotten from Ramirez in weeks. Months. Maybe ever. The neurotic side of me started to wonder if it was because he liked me, or because I'd suddenly turned into a case.

Though, I didn't have time to wonder long.

"Ready?" he asked, his voice so close that his hot breath tickled my ear. My body responded immediately, sending a quiver through my belly that ended somewhere slightly lower.

I told Neurotic Chick to give it a rest. Haven't-gotten-any-in-longer-than-Dana Chick needed a night out.

"Ready."

* * *

Half an hour later I was standing in Ramirez's living room wondering if everyone in L.A. had a nicer place than mine.

Heavy, wood furnishing filled the room, along with overstuffed chairs and a dark, leather sofa. A copy of the *L.A. Times*, opened to the sports section, littered thc top of a dark, maple coffee table, along with a remote control that looked like it could land the space shuttle. A big screen TV took up one wall, while a fireplace with a thick wood mantel spanned the other. The walls were painted a warm coffee color and decorated with family photos, dozens of smiling, framed faces staring back at me. Overall, the room was cozy, yet completely guy. I'd never really pictured Ramirez as having a home, but now that I was standing in it, I realized it fit him perfectly.

"Nice place," I said, peeking down the small hallway to the right. I could see a couple of bedrooms and what I assumed was a bath at the end.

Ramirez took off his jacket, throwing it casually over the back of a Lay-Z-Boy pointed at the TV. "Well, it's old, needs a little work still. But it's a nice place to come home to."

"Well, it certainly beats my place at the moment."

At the mention of my apartment slash crime scene, he got a slightly pained look, his eyebrows pinching together in concern. "Look, Maddie, I need you to promise me something."

I licked my lower lip. "Okay…"

"Promise me that if you ever see this guy again, see his car, or see any more boxes on your doorstep, promise that you'll call me first."

I opened my mouth to respond, but Ramirez talked right over me.

"Not call Dana to pull another Lucy and Ethel act. Not call your mother to borrow a can of pepper spray…"

"She forced that stuff on me!" I protested, "I didn't even want it!"

Ramirez crossed the room in one quick stride, standing just inches from me. "Please, Maddie, just promise me you're going to keep me in the loop from now on. No more half-cocked, harebrained schemes, okay?"

I nodded. "I promise." Honestly, his concern was touching. Even if the whole "harebrained" thing was a little uncalled for.

"Thank you," he said, his voice softer. And lower. His eyes roved my face, the pleading look fading into something darker and a whole lot more inviting.

He leaned in, his breath hovering over my lips, his body pressing tightly against mine.

Yowza.

I felt my breath catch in my throat as evidence of Ramirez's Mr. Haven't-gotten-any-in-a-while pressed against me.

He reached one hand out and slid it around my middle, the scents of aftershave and leather warring together as he nibbled at my lower lip. He smelled good. Really good. Almost good enough to overpower the lingering smell of icing on my dress.

And then he *really* kissed me. Covering my mouth with his in a slow, sensual movement. Trailing his hand up my waist and inside my sundress.

I think I had an on-the-spot orgasm.

"But I'm covered in cake," I protested. (Feebly, I might add.)

He got that big bad wolf look in his eyes.

"I like cake."

He leaned in and nipped at my ear. I shivered as his lips glided over my skin, licking a stray smudge of frosting from my cheek.

I sighed. Yes, actually out loud. He was *that* good.

He slipped one strap off my shoulder… then the other. And suddenly he was nibbling a whole lot lower. I groaned and refrained from pointing out that there wasn't any cake there.

"So, does this mean all is forgiven?" I asked, going slightly light-headed as his hands slid up my thigh, taking my hemline with them.

He chuckled, his hot breath tickling the hollow of my throat. "Maybe."

His mouth dipped lower, leaving a shuddering trail down the V of my top. "Maybe? Anything I can do to convince you?"

He paused. Then did a big wicked grin that was all teeth.

"Oh, yeah."

In one fluid movement he wrapped his arm around my waist and lifted me off the ground, carrying me down the little hallway were I got the close, personal tour of his bedroom.

All night long.

* * *

I awoke to the sound of birds chirping outside the window, small children laughing, and bright, airy sunlight streaming through the curtains.

Okay, so in reality, it was the glare from the neighbor's TV streaming through the curtain. And the children were more swearing at each other than laughing. And the chirping bird thing was actually the sound of a garbage truck backing up down the block. But they all sounded pretty perfect to me. In fact, life was pretty perfect. I couldn't honestly imagine it getting any perfecter. I was in Ramirez's bed, sleeping on Ramirez's sheets, basking in the afterglow of Ramirez's seriously talented body. Life did not get any better than this.

And then, amazingly, it did.

"Morning, beautiful."

I opened my eyes and looked up to find Ramirez hovering over me, a cup of coffee in one hand. His hair was wet and curling around his temples a little, like he'd just showered. He smelled of Ivory and aftershave, and was dressed in a pair of worn jeans and a white T-shirt that clung to his chest tighter than Saran Wrap. I licked my lips, going warm beneath his sheets again.

"Coffee?" he asked, handing me the steaming cup.

Was this guy good or what?

I took a sip. French Roast. Just a little milk. Heaven.

"Get much sleep?" he asked, a glint of humor in his voice.

I couldn't help the middle-schooler giggle that escaped me. "Enough."

He reached one hand out and tucked a strand of what I feared was serious bed-head behind my ear. "You know, you snore a little."

I gasped. "I do not!"

Ramirez's mouth quirked up, hinting at that deceptively boyish dimple in his left cheek. "Relax. I thought it was kind of cute."

I took another sip of coffee to cover my blush.

"Listen, the crime scene guys called this morning. They analyzed the stuff from your apartment and kicked out a name."

I sat up, propping myself on my elbows. "Oh yeah?"

"Isabel."

I paused, trying for a moment to place that name. Isabel… Isabel… I knew it sounded familiar…

"The Cabana Club?" Ramirez prompted.

Mental forehead smack.

"You mean that crazy chick with the gun?"

Ramirez nodded. "That's the one."

I shook my head. "But, why? What does she want with me?"

Ramirez sighed. "What I've gathered from the guys in vice is that apparently after her boyfriend, Snake, saw the club shooting on the news and found out she was talking to the authorities, he dumped her. She blames you."

"Me?! But I didn't have anything to do with it!"

Ramirez gave me a look.

"Okay, maybe I had a teeny tiny bit to do with it. But I'm sure she's better off without him anyway. I mean, what kind of guy has a name like Snake?"

He cocked one corner of his mouth, his eyes crinkling at the corners. "Good point."

"Thank you."

"Anyway, Isabel isn't the most stable, rational person I've ever met-"

"Understatement alert."

His eyes crinkled again. "So, I think it might be safer if you stayed here for a while."

I froze, coffee cup halfway to my mouth. "*Stayed* here?"

Okay, so, yes, waking up in Ramirez's bed was heaven. And spending the night in it had been… well, heaven didn't even begin to describe it. Let's just say the words "multiple" and "orgasm" came into play. But that had been *one* night. Staying one night with someone and staying *a while* were two different things. A little snoring might be cute after one night. After a while it made you want to smother the other person with a pillow.

I blinked and realized Ramirez was still talking.

"…and we'll stop by your place later so you can pick up a few things."

"You don't have to do this. I mean, I don't want to intrude."

Ramirez's gaze lingered on the hem of the sheet, flirting with my barely B's. "No intrusion at all."

"But what about Tot Trots? I need my drawing table to design. I can't do that here."

"I thought you said you finished your last assignment?"

Oh yeah. Right.

"But, what about my mother," I said, grasping. "What will she say if I tell her I'm staying here? You know," I gestured to the wrinkled sheets, "with you."

Ramirez's lips parted in a slow grin. "Honey, your mom offers me condoms every time I see her. I don't think she's exactly under the impression you're a virgin."

"Oh. Okay."

I took another sip of coffee to cover my rising panic. Hearing the "G" word last night had been great. Wonderful. Terrific in fact. But going from the "G" word to cohabiting was a big leap. We're talking diving off the 110 overpass into rush hour traffic kind of leap.

Again I couldn't help but wonder if it was me or the case he was really interested in. What would happen when this was all over? When Isabel was behind bars, and the *Magnolia Lane* killer was doing time in San Quentin? Would he still be Mr. Attentive, or was it back to canceling dinner plans and running out on me at the mere chirp of a pager?

I wasn't sure. But, since Horny Chick had had her fun, Neurotic Chick was back, and she decided the only way to know for sure was to call his bluff.

"Okay," I heard myself say. "I'll move in."

His face broke into a wide grin, and he leaned in for a kiss.

"But," I stopped him, carefully watching his reaction over the rim of my coffee cup, "don't you think I should have my own key?"

Ramirez paused. "Key?"

"Uh-huh." I nodded, bobbing my bed-head up and down. "A key to your place. My own key. You know, since I'll be living here and all. That way I can come and go *any time I want.*"

"I, uh, don't have a spare copy," he hedged.

"No problem. I'll make myself one."

I saw him bite the inside of his cheek, his eyes narrowing at me.

I gave him my best wide-eyed innocent stare.

We sat like that for an agonizing two seconds. Until finally he stood and said, "Don't worry about it. Just leave the front door open."

Ahnt. Wrong answer, pal.

"But-" I was about to protest.

Only I didn't get the chance, as Ramirez's pager chirped to life on his belt. He looked down, a frown settling between his brows as he read the number.

"Work," he said, slipping his cell out of his back pocket.

I sucked on my lower lip, staring into my now tepid cup of coffee. And tried to stave off the panic that my little game of chicken was backfiring miserably.

There was no way I could move in with Ramirez. I was so not ready for him to see the unbuffed, unpolished, drooling on her pillow at 3AM Maddie that woke up with bed-head to rival Don King's. And I seriously was not ready to have him see the parade of beauty products it took to keep up appearances. What would he say the first time he saw me putting on my pore-cleansing acne mask? Or anti-wrinkle night cream? There were some things a man just should not know about a woman until after he's married. (i.e. legally required to love her despite her jumbo sized box of tampons sitting where his issues of *Sports Illustrated* used to be.)

I had just about worked myself into a state of hysteria the likes of which I hadn't experienced since the after Thanksgiving black Friday sale at Macy's last year, when Ramirez hung up the phone and turned to me.

The frown between his brows had worked itself into an all out scowl.

"I have to go," he mumbled, standing up and throwing on his leather jacket. "Now."

Uh-oh. I didn't like that tone.

"What's wrong?" I asked, unconsciously clutching my coffee cup tighter. "What's going on?"

Ramirez didn't answer, instead shoving a ring of keys into his pocket and slipping on his holster.

"What? What is it?"

He turned to face me, his Bad Cop look already firmly in place.

"Please?" I asked, really starting to worry now. "You know I'll find out eventually anyway."

I'd like to think it was the "please" that softened him, but more likely it was the fact that he knew I was right. "It was my captain." He paused, rubbing one hand over his eyes and suddenly looking very tired. "They've found another body."

CHAPTER THIRTEEN

I blinked, my mind going blank as I white knuckled the coffee cup to keep from spilling it all over Ramirez's white sheets.

"Whose body?" I asked.

But it was too late. Ramirez was already out the door. I sprang up from the bed, wrapping the sheet around my middle as I trailed after him into the living room.

"Wait! Whose body?"

Ramirez was at the front door, shoving his wallet in his back pocket. "Look, just stay out of this, okay, Maddie? You've already got some psycho pissed off at you. Just stay here, and I'll be back later."

"Jackson Wyoming Ramirez, don't you dare walk out that door!"

Ramirez paused, hand hovering over the doorknob, and raised one eyebrow at me.

"Um, please?"

He shook his head at me, and I could swear the corner of Bad Cop's lips quivered ever so slightly. "Look, I don't know whose body yet. They just said they found a woman in the Central Park section of the lot. She was strangled, just like Veronika."

I shivered, suddenly cold beneath my thin make-shift toga. "I'm going with you." I dropped the sheet and grabbed my discarded sundress, cake stains and all, from the living room floor.

"No!" In one quick movement, Ramirez was across the room, grabbing one end of the dress in a tug-o-war. "No way. You are staying here."

I tugged back. "Like hell I am."

"Maddie, I'm warning you…"

"Let go of my dress!"

"Not until you promise to stay put."

"You're going to stretch it."

"Then let go."

"No, you let go!"

"No, you-"

But he didn't get to finish that thought as the horrible sound of ripping fabric filled the air, and I went flying backwards, landing on my bare tush on his hardwood floor. I looked down. I had half a cake stained sundress in my hands.

"You ripped my dress!" I moaned. "This was a discontinued Betsy Johnson summer collection baby-doll dress! It's irreplaceable. And now I have nothing to wear!"

For a half a second Ramirez looked like he might have been sorry. But as he stared down at me, that wicked grin stole across his face again.

"Well, I guess you're staying here then."

That's it, he was dead meat.

I lunged for him, but thanks to his quick cop-reflexes, he was out the door before I could even peel myself off the floor.

"I am so *not* moving in with you!" I yelled to the closed door. But I'm pretty sure he didn't hear me over the sound of his SUV screeching out of the drive.

Great. Now what?

I pulled the sheet back around my middle and plopped down on the sofa. I stuck one fingernail in my mouth as my mind twisted over just whose body Ramirez was racing to view. Could it possibly be Mia? Had the killer really been after her this whole time? Or maybe it was another victim of the killer baby's daddy. Maybe Veronika hadn't been the only one he was fooling around with. Or maybe it was someone who had seen him offing Veronika. A witness? Maybe it was completely unrelated to anything. A copycat?

I grabbed Ramirez's space shuttle remote and tried to turn on the news. Only since my technical skills ended at being able to program my Mr. Coffee, all I could get was a giant screen full of snow and static. I gave up, instead grabbing Ramirez's cordless from the end table and dialing the one person I knew who just might know more than the cops.

"Felix Dunn," he answered. I could hear sirens and loud voices in the background.

"It's Maddie. You've heard about the body?"

"Yeah," he responded, "I'm at the studios now."

I held my breath. "Who is it?"

"No idea, love. Police aren't releasing her name yet. But I saw Mia giving a tearful comment to *Entertainment Tonight* just now, so I know it's not her."

I let out a small sigh of relief. I could just imagine what Ramirez's superiors would say if it had been his ward. (Not, mind you, that he wasn't still on my shit list after the demolition of my Betsy Johnson.)

"Any luck with the PayMate site last night?" I asked.

"Some." Someone shouted in the background, and I strained to hear what was going on. "I was able to get into their system, but the files are still all encrypted."

"Can you read them?"

I could hear him shaking his head. "Not yet. Honestly, I'm thinking the easiest way to find this guy is to catch him in the act when he logs in again. Now that I'm in their system, I can trace back to his address if he stays online long enough."

"Really? You can do that?"

"You underestimate me, love," he said with a hint of humor in his voice. "Problem is, we'd have to know when he's logging on."

I chewed my lower lip, an idea brewing. "Hang on, I'm going to put you on speaker phone, Felix."

After only three tries I found the right button to push on Ramirez's phone, and the living room filled with the sounds of a Hollywood crime scene.

"Still there?" I yelled.

"Bloody hell, no need to shout, girl."

"Sorry. Okay, hang on."

I dug my cell phone out of my purse and dialed information for Jasmine's number. Only a 900-number under Jasmine's Girls, but under her own name, Jasmine Williams, I hit pay dirt.

"Okay, I'm dialing Jasmine," I yelled at the speakerphone.

"I'm right here, no need to shout."

"Sorry."

I keyed in the number and waited while Jasmine's phone rang on the other end. She picked up after the third one.

"Yeah?" came her high-pitched Barbie voice.

"Jasmine, it's Maddie."

There was a pause. "Who?"

"Maddie Springer."

Nothing.

I sighed. If I ever got this chick to remember my name, I'd feel it was a life well lived. "The one who popped the boob and is now working with the police."

I heard Felix snicker from the speaker.

"Oh right. You. Wadda you want?" she asked. I could hear her popping a wad of gum between her bleached white veneers.

"I have a favor to ask. That guy who logged on to see Veronika, could you call me at this number if he logs in again?"

"And why should I do that?" she asked. (Pop, pop.)

"Because it may lead us to Veronika's killer."

Jasmine snorted. "So?"

Gee, such a loving soul. My eyes roved the apartment as I wracked my brain for anything I could barter with. Then they settled on the speakerphone.

"How about a free ad in the L.A. Informer?"

I heard Felix shouting, "No!" from the speaker.

"What was that?" Jasmine asked.

"Television. So, what do you think?"

"I don't know…"

"Uh… okay, how about two months of free ads. Full page," I added.

"Do you have any idea how bloody expensive that is?" Felix shouted from the speaker.

I covered the mouthpiece of the cell with my hand. "Relax," I whispered back at him. "I know you can afford it. Besides, think of the story you'll get."

Felix did a pained groan but didn't say anything.

"So," I said, into my cell, "do we have a deal, Jasmine?"

"You promise, full page?"

"Promise."

"Okay. Fine. I'll call you the next time he logs on. But, I'm warning you, I have no idea when it will be."

"Thanks Jasmine!" I said, flipping my Motorola shut.

"We got it," I shouted to Felix.

His groan filled the room. "You couldn't have offered her a free subscription instead?"

I ignored him. "I'll let you know the second Jasmine calls me. In the meantime, just be ready to track him."

"This better be one hell of a story," he mumbled. I heard more noises in the background and someone else shouting. "Listen, they're moving the body. I've gotta go if I'm going to get any decent pictures." Then he paused. "Oh, hell."

"What?" I pulled the sheet up over my shoulders to ward off the sudden chill in the air again. "What is it? What do you see?"

"You'd better get down here, Maddie."

"Why? Felix, who is it?"

But he'd already hung up.

Shit.

I looked down at my tattered sundress. What were the chances Ramirez had anything in his closet in a size 6?

I scooped my cell back up and dialed Dana's number.

Luckily, Dana was up early, and I quickly filled her in on the morning's developments. After the appropriate amount of "ohmigod"s and "he ripped your Betsy Johnson!"s, she promised to pick me up in twenty minutes with a new outfit in hand.

In hindsight, I guess I should have been more specific about what kind of outfit. It's not that Dana doesn't have good taste in clothes. It's just that she just tends to have a little bit *different* taste than I do. Me, I wear clothes that make me feel confident, pretty, even sometimes a little kick-butt. Dana tends to wear outfits that either a) are made entirely of workout friendly spandex or b) are cut low enough to cause car crashes on the 101.

I stared down at the dress in Dana's hand as she walked in Ramirez's front door.

"What is that?"

Dana looked from the scrap of fabric (which from here appeared to be both spandex *and* cut to the navel) to me. "What?"

I held it up to my body. It was a blue form fitting dress, hemline hovering somewhere just below my panty line, neckline plunging somewhere just north of that. "Seriously?" I asked, giving her the one-eyebrow thing.

"What?" Dana blinked innocently. "You asked for a dress."

I did a mental einie-meenie-minie-mo between a pair of Ramirez's oversized sweats and the reject from the J-Lo Awards dresses collection. In the end, I slipped the dress over my head, hoping my barely B's didn't fall out of the neckline clearly designed for someone about two letters larger. I slipped on my pink heels, cringing just a little at how badly they clashed with the electric blue spandex, and grabbed my purse before hightailing it out the door and off to the Sunset Studios.

* * *

If it was possible, security was even tighter today than it had been before. And, to make matters worse, in addition to the actors, grips, and crew members, the line spanning around the block also included various TV reporters, cameramen and paparazzi, all vying to get through the metal detectors and into the thick of Hollywood's hottest story.

Dana and I stood anxiously in line as I tried Felix's number again. Straight to voicemail. I chewed on a fingernail, wondering just what he'd meant by, "You'd better get down here."

"Hi, Dana!" A guy in a black cap and jeans, passed by us, giving Dana a little wave before finding a spot at the back of the line.

Dana waved back, sinking her teeth into her lower lip as she watched his denim-clad rear retreat.

I nudged her in the ribs. "Who was that?"

"One of the other extras. Carl. Awesome biceps, huh?"

I peeked over my shoulder. "Not bad. Which reminds me," I gave her a pointed look, "how's the SA thing going?"

"Right. Um, great. Wonderful in fact. Fantastic. Day five!" she said with false cheer bordering on Mary Poppins creepy.

"So, no relapse yesterday?"

Dana shook her head, her blonde hair whipping her cheeks. "Nope. I taught three spinning classes at the gym, went for a four mile hike, did some Pilates, then dropped Ricky's car back off at his place last night."

"Ricky's place?" I raised an eyebrow at her. "I'm not sure Therapist Max would approve?"

"Oh!" she exclaimed, ignoring me as she latched onto my forearm with a death grip. "Guess what Ricky told me last night?"

"Spill it," I encouraged as we inched forward in line.

"Well, after I dropped his car off at his place, he gave me a ride home – you know, he's such a gentleman that he didn't even make a move on me at all, and I was totally wearing this short little micro mini that, well, I have to say, looked pretty damn hot on me."

I made a circular get-to-the-point motion with my wrist.

"Yeah, okay. Anyway, we got to talking about Mia and Margo and their whole blow-up on set the other day. Well, it turns out that Margo was originally cast for the part of Ashley. Mia was supposed to play Nurse Nan, but she convinced the producers that Margo was too old to play opposite Ricky. She got the parts switched."

"Wow, Mia really knows how to make friends, huh?"

Dana nodded. "Apparently, there's been bad blood between them ever since."

I didn't blame Margo. If I'd lost out the part of Ashley Culver because some diva had called me old, I'd be pretty pissed too. I was beginning to wonder if maybe the LAPD were right after all. Maybe Mia was the target in all this.

Which made me wonder again just who was DOA in Central Park.

I shoved that fingernail back in my mouth, chewing anxiously, as Dana and I finally made it to the front of the line. After Billy checked our names against the list, I set my bag down on the conveyer belt, took off my shoes, ring, necklace, and, just for good measure, unhooked my bra, slipping it out through my right sleeve and dropping it into the front pocket of my purse. I was taking no chances this time.

Feeling confident (especially since I'd made Dana stash her vibrator in the car), I stepped through the metal detector. Nothing. Nada. Not a beep. I gave Queen Latifah a triumphant smile.

But, honestly, when was my luck ever that good?

"Miss?" Bug Eyed Billy called out, holding open my purse.

"It's just my bra," I explained. "I didn't want the underwire setting off the metal detectors." Again.

Billy peered at me through his coke bottle lenses, his jaw set in as hard a line as a jowly eighty-year-old's can get. Then he sent a warning look to Latifah. "It's a two-fifteen."

"A what?" I asked.

But apparently Queen Latifah knew exactly what a two-fifteen was, as she sprang into action, pulling her walkie-talkie from her belt and shouting into it. "Code two-fifteen, we've got a code two-fifteen at the west entrance. Requesting backup immediately."

"Whoa – backup?" My gaze whipped between Billy's hard stare and Latifah's frenzied shouting. "What's going on here?"

I blame it on the fact that I'm blonde, have been a little preoccupied with my crappier-than-a-tractor-full-o-fertilizer love life, and a set full of whacked out actors (not to mention dead bodies) that I didn't catch on sooner. That I didn't remember the last time I'd seen Felix and the fact that, in my morning-after glow, I'd completely forgotten all about…

Bug Eyed Billy used a sharpie to pull Felix's handgun out of my purse by the handle. The grips in line jumped back, one of them actually gasping. Queen Latifah's hand hovered over her own weapon and she escalated her shouts into her walkie-talkie until she sounded like she'd gone for the triple shot espresso that morning.

"Ohmigod, Maddie! You have a gun?!" Dana shrieked behind me.

"Look, I can explain," I said, holding my hands out in front of me. "It's not loaded." I think. "And it's not even mine."

Bug Eyed Billy narrowed his eyes at me. "Just like the *neck massager* wasn't yours?"

"Right!" Only I realized too late that that was Billy's attempt at sarcasm. "No! I mean, no, not like that. That was a misunderstanding. This is… it's not mine!" I protested, really starting to worry now.

And then worry turned to downright panic as three more security guards rounded the corner, hands hovering over their weapons.

"Miss, please put your hands in the air."

"I… I…" I sputtered.

"Just do it, Maddie. They look serious," Dana advised, taking a few steps backwards.

I lifted my arms above my head, hoping my neckline didn't shift low enough to give the grips a free show.

"Get down on your knees," one of the security guards barked.

"Is this really necessary-"

But Queen Latifah cut me off, tackling me from behind and slamming my body onto the ground beneath hers.

"Uhn." I felt the air rush out of me, my head going fuzzy as she pinned me with her bulk. This chick should seriously think about calling Jenny Craig.

"I got her! I got the two-fifteen!" Latifah called. I watched as three pairs of feet scuffled toward me, one of them pinning my hands behind my back a second before cool metal handcuffs slapped against my wrists.

"No, wait, it's not like that… please, you don't understand…"

But it was useless. Even as I protested my innocence, the three security guards lifted me up by my armpits and were dragging me, still in my bare feet, toward the back of the lot.

"Don't worry, I'm right behind you," Dana called.

I looked over my shoulder. The grips were giving Dana a wide berth while Bug Eyed Billy copiously went through her handbag.

* * *

Since my watch was in my purse, which had obviously been confiscated, I had no idea how long I sat at the folding table in the four-by-six room at the back of the Sunset Studios security office. But it was long enough that I was starting to fidget beneath the glare of the buzzing florescent lights. I nervously twirled one strand of blonde hair between my fingers, wondering what the charge for carrying a weapon onto studio property was. I wondered if it was even registered. Or legal? Maybe I was carrying a hot gun?

That's it. I was so switching back to pepper spray.

I was just wondering if Mrs. Rosenblatt had any more of her secret stash, when the door opened and in walked Detective Prune Face, followed closely by Ramirez.

Gone was any trace of the guy who'd brought me coffee in bed this morning. Instead, his eyes were dark and unreadable, his jaw set into those hard lines of granite, his posture stiff and unyielding as if it took every ounce of strength he had not to reach over the table and strangle the blonde in slutty spandex.

I gulped down a dry lump.

Oh boy.

Prune Face looked at me, recognition dawning. "Wardrobe girl again." He turned to Ramirez. "You wanna take this one?"

Ramirez's granite jaw flinched. He nodded almost imperceptibly.

Prune Face hovered at the door a moment, his gaze bouncing between us. Finally he shrugged and backed out of the room. "Good luck."

I wasn't sure if that was directed at Ramirez or me. But by the death look in Ramirez's eyes, it was clear I could use all the luck I could get.

I shifted nervously as Ramirez sat down in the folding chair opposite me and crossed his arms over his chest, silently staring me down.

"Okay, so here's the thing. The gun – totally not mine. And I didn't even remember I was carrying it. It just kind of slipped into my purse. Well, I guess technically, Felix slipped it in-"

"Felix?" he interrupted.

"The reporter, remember? From the *Informer*. He's… uh, a friend."

Ramirez narrowed his eyes at me. "Friend?"

I bit my lip. "Yeah. Sorta."

His eyes did that fine-slits thing again. "This the same friend that got you kidnapped last year?"

"Uh…"

He snorted. "That Felix is some guy."

"Hey, he was just trying to offer me some protection. He was concerned about me."

I'm not sure what made me defend Tabloid Boy, but clearly it was the wrong move. Ramirez leaned forward menacingly.

"I'm the *only* guy that gets to be concerned about you."

If he didn't look so scary right now, I might have been touched.

Instead, I gulped down another dry lump.

"What the hell are you even doing here?" Ramirez asked. He gave a long glance at my dress (lingering in what would have been the cleavage area, were I actually big enough to fill it out) and I could hear him mentally adding, *In that*. "I thought I told you to stay put."

I crossed my arms over my chest, obscuring his view. "And I'm just supposed to do as I'm told, huh?"

"Once in a while, it might be nice."

"You know, you have some nerve. Asking me to move in with you, then interrogating me."

Ramirez raised one eyebrow. "*Move in* with me?"

"This morning you said I should stay at your place."

Ramirez snorted again. "For a couple of days. Maddie, I didn't say you should *move in*."

I gulped back another lump, this one slightly larger. I know, I know. *I'd* been the one having the commitment freak-out just this morning at the thought of cohabitating. But he didn't have to sound so repulsed by the idea.

"I know!" I said a little too loudly. "I mean, it's not like I thought you meant *permanently*. Of course you weren't *actually* asking me to move in. I mean, hell, you're the guy that can't even bring himself to give me a key."

Ramirez scrubbed a hand over his face and muttered, "Jesus," under his breath. "Look, just stay away from this Felix guy, okay?"

My turn to narrow my eyes. "I don't think you're exactly in a position to tell me who I can and can't be friends with."

"The guy slipped a loaded gun in your purse! You realize you could have been arrested for carrying that thing onto studio property?"

"He was just trying to help!"

"What would help is if you stayed the hell out of this investigation. Look, just go back to my place and wait for me there."

"I can't," I yelled, tears piling up behind my eyes. "I locked the door!"

Ramirez muttered another, "Jesus." He rubbed a hand at his temple as if just talking to me gave him a headache. "Look, I'll have a uniformed officer drive you home. He'll wait with you there. Okay?"

No, not okay. I hated being treated like I needed a babysitter. But since I was currently without home, car, or decent wardrobe, (not to mention being stalked by a crazy woman) I didn't have much choice. "Fine," I muttered. "But tell me one thing first?"

He rubbed at his temple again. "What?" the word came out on an exasperated sigh.

"Whose body did you find in Central Park?"

Ramirez paused, putting his Bad Cop face firmly into place.

"I'm going to find out sooner or later anyway," I reasoned.

He gave me a look. Then blew out a deep breath. "Oh hell," he said, caving. "I'm sorry Maddie. It was Dusty."

CHAPTER FOURTEEN

For some inexplicable reason the room began to mambo in front of my vision, like I'd had one too many cosmos on the dance floor. "D-Dusty?" I sputtered, my voice sounding oddly disconnected even to my own ears.

It couldn't be her. Dusty was fine. She was just a little shaken up about Veronika, right? She was just taking a few personal days. She was fine. Wasn't she?

"Are you sure?" I asked, my voice high and threatening to crack.

Ramirez gave me a sympathetic look. "I'm afraid so. Purple hair, multiple piercings?"

He was right. It was pretty hard to mistake Dusty for someone else. "B-but how? Why?" I asked, my mind racing over the last message Dusty had left me. She'd sounded upset. Or had she been scared? Fearing for her life?

Ramirez shook his head. "The why, we don't know yet. But she was strangled, the same as Veronika. Only this time the guy used a bright orange scarf."

I paused. Why did that ring a bell?

"An orange scarf? Orange wool?"

Ramirez cocked his head at me. "I don't know about the wool part, but it was thick. Why? Do you know something?"

I licked my lips, willing the room to sit still. "Maybe. Margo has one. She tried to wear it on the set the other day but I made her take it off." I gulped down another crack in my voice. "Ohmigod, it's Margo! Margo did it, didn't she? Because she was jealous of Mia?"

"Hold on there, Nancy Drew." Ramirez held one hand up. "What did Margo do with the scarf after she took it off?"

I closed my eyes, thinking back. Things had been a bit chaotic that day (what else was new on *Magnolia Lane*?). "I think she put it in the wardrobe room."

"You think?" he prodded.

"Yes, I'm sure." I nodded my head, gaining conviction. "I told her the scarf and the Crocs had to go, so she put them both on the sofa in the wardrobe room because she didn't have time to go back to her trailer before the scene started. We were kind of running behind in wardrobe because Dusty..." I trailed off, remembering how Dusty had been absent from the set the last few days. I suddenly felt guilty. I should have tried harder to call her. Whatever had been bothering her, she'd never be able to tell me now. I wondered if maybe it was what had gotten her killed?

"So, anyone could have picked up the scarf?"

I gave myself a mental shake, pushing thoughts of Dusty to the back of my mind. "Maybe. But did you know that Margo has a serious grudge against Mia?"

"Oh?" He raised one eyebrow, leaning forward slightly.

I nodded and relayed the info Dana had shared with me that morning, watching his face for any sign of agreement. "If Margo did have it in for Mia," I finished, "maybe Dusty saw something she wasn't supposed to when Margo offed Veronika, only Margo thought that Veronika was Mia, but maybe Dusty knew it was Veronika, or at least she did after she found her in the trailer the next morning." Yes, I realize put like that, my theory was about as twisted as an L.A. Freeway. But that didn't mean it wasn't accurate. As I'd learned lately, people could be pretty twisted, too.

Ramirez sat back in his chair, his face a complete blank as he digested this.

Remind me never to play poker with this guy.

"So, what do you think?"

"I think it's time for you to go home."

I rolled my eyes. "I meant about Margo."

But Ramirez didn't answer, instead scraping his chair back as he made for the door. "Wait here. I'll get a uniform to drive you home."

"But-" I started to protest. But gave up. What was the use? Actually, I'd gotten off pretty lucky. He hadn't arrested me, and neither of us had stormed out. All in all it was one of our better conversations lately.

I picked at my flaking nail polish (mentally making an appointment at Fernando's) as I waited in the little room again. Finally, a guy with a greasy, black mustache in uniform blues walked in, my purse in one hand, my shoes in the other. I had never been so glad to see anyone in my life. I thanked him profusely as I donned my pink pumps and followed him outside to slip into the back seat of his patrol car.

Under the uniform's watchful eye, I dialed Dana's cell, letting her know what had happened. She told me Steinman had, obviously, closed the set again today and that she was going back to Ricky's place to help him run lines instead. I told her to remember her celibacy pledge and I'd call her later.

I sank back into the vinyl seats as we rode in silence toward Santa Monica. Even though I wasn't under arrest, I felt slightly criminal sitting behind the barred divider between Officer Mustache and me, knowing that my doors didn't open from the inside. I wondered how many big-time bad guys had occupied this same seat on their way to prison where they knew they'd spend the rest of their lives. Carjackers, rapists, murderers. Murderers like Margo? I wondered. She was one of the few people on the set that I hadn't talked to much. Though, until today she'd always struck me as harmless enough. In fact, she had a habit of fading into the background and, with the exception of that one blowup on set, you tended to forget she was even there. I wondered if that would have been different if Margo had gotten the role of Ashley. If Mia were out of the way, I wondered what would happen to Nurse Nan's character? She had been gaining momentum lately, especially with the baby's daddy storyline.

Which brought me back to Veronika. Was it just a coincidence that she'd been pregnant and dating a mystery man? And if Mia had been the target, what was Veronika even doing in Mia's trailer? I'd never been a big fan of puzzles, and this one was making my head hurt.

I was just about to reach into my purse and dig for an aspirin when the William Tell Overture burst out from its depths. Officer Mustache glanced at me through the bars in the divider.

"My cell," I explained, flipping it open. "Hello?"

"Hey, it's Jasmine."

My heart instantly sped up, and I gave a guilty glance at Officer Mustache as if he could telepathically feel a "harebrained scheme" being cooked up in the backseat.

"Hi," I said in a low voice. "What's up?"

"Why are you whispering?" she asked.

I cleared my throat. Then louder, "No reason. What's up?" I gave Officer Mustache a reassuring smile in the rearview mirror. It came off a little feeble, but I think I saw him return it under his bristled lip.

"You asked me to call when he logged on?" Jasmine said in a bored voice.

I held my breath. "Yes?"

"Well, he's on. Logged in a couple of minutes ago."

"A couple of minutes?! You were supposed to call me the second he showed up."

"Hey, I have stuff to do. I can't just jump when you tell me, blondie."

I thought a really bad word.

"Okay, fine. Look, just keep him on. I'll be right there."

Officer Mustache glanced at me in the rearview, seemingly picking up on the panic in my voice. I sent him a one finger wave. No return smile this time. Crap.

"Fine. I'll try. But hurry." Jasmine punctuated this by hanging up on me with a loud click.

I flipped my phone shut and tapped on the bars.

"Uh, excuse me?"

Officer Mustache glanced in the rearview again. "Yeah?"

"Um, could we possibly make a little stop?"

He frowned. "No can do. Detective Ramirez was very clear, I should take you straight to your place and wait for him there."

Damn. My babysitter was well informed.

I shifted in my seat, the vinyl giving an unladylike burp, as I tried a different tactic. "Um, what address did he give you?"

"10 Ocean View Road."

I crossed my fingers and hoped that Ramirez was up for forgiving me just one more time.

"That's the wrong address."

Officer Mustache gave me a confused look over his shoulder. "What do you mean 'wrong?'"

"I moved. Recently. Ramirez gave you my old address."

Mustache gave me a scrutinizing look. I held my breath, trying to look as innocent as possible.

"Maybe I should call Ramirez to verify it."

"No!" I shouted.

Mustache jumped in his seat.

"I mean, uh, no need to do that. No need to bother him over something so trivial. Right?"

He narrowed his eyes at me again in the mirror. I did a poor imitation of Dana's eyelash batting thing.

Officer Mustache gave me a long stare. Then slowly nodded his head. "Yeah, okay."

Mental sigh of relief.

"Anyhoo… let me give you my new one." I recited Jasmine's address and felt a little lift of triumph as he pulled off the 2 and made a U-turn, heading back to the 101.

I quickly dialed Felix's number, which, thankfully, he picked up this time.

"Felix Dunn."

"Where are you?"

"On my way home from the studio. Why?"

"We're a go," I said.

"Cyber guy?"

"Yep."

"All right, I'll get the trace on him, ASAP. Just keep him logged in."

"I'll try. Call me the second you have him. I'm not sure how long Jasmine can keep him on the line."

"Done."

Felix hung up, and I felt a little lift of excitement. With any luck, we'd have our baby's daddy identified in a matter of minutes.

As it turned out, Officer Mustache was a cautious driver, and by the time we pulled up in front of Jasmine's den of iniquity, I'd picked every bit of nail polish off my fingernails and was tapping my foot so hard I feared I might break a heel.

"You live here?" Mustache asked, doing a low whistle as he parked at the curb.

"Yup. Thanks for the ride!"

"Detective Ramirez told me to wait."

"Oh. Right. Okay, sure, whatever." Honestly, at the moment, I couldn't care less if Officer Mustache cooled his heels at the curb. All I cared about was whether or not Veronika's boyfriend was still logged into the system.

I practically raced up the pathway to Jasmine's front door, the mix of adrenalin and sudden exertion leaving me panting like a Saint Bernard by the time she answered my knock.

"Is (in) he (out) still (in) logged (out) on?"

Jasmine gave me disgusted look (apparently Barbies don't pant) and rolled her eyes. "Yeah, but I don't know how much longer I can keep him hooked."

I followed her into the house, past the living room and up a set of curved, wrought iron stairs. Jasmine then led me down a wide hallway full of closed doors, the walls punctuated with pictures of half naked women doing acrobatics on the hoods of sports cars.

"I've got Anna entertaining him in one of the private chat rooms, but he's already losing interest," she continued. "He's already typed, 'I gotta go,' like, three times."

I looked down at my cell, willing it to chirp to life with Felix's number. Nope. Silent. "Can't she keep him on just a little longer?"

"She's trying. But Anna's a brunette. This guy really prefers blondes."

"So, send in a blonde."

Jasmine shook her head. "With Veronika gone, the only blondes I have are the twins, Mandi and Candi. They're off today shooting a Doublemint commercial." Jasmine paused. Then gave me a slow up and down. Her eyes settling on my down-to-there neckline.

Uh-oh.

"Oh, no. No, no, no, no. Not me. I can't do this kind of thing!"

Jasmine raised one eyebrow at me. "Really? 'Cause you're certainly dressed the part."

"No, I'm not… I, mean, I don't… Look, I can't even talk dirty to my boyfriend without blushing."

Jasmine scoffed at me. "It's easy. Guys don't need anything flowery. Just talk tab A, slot B and pout a lot," she said, pushing me toward a closed door at the end of the hall.

"But what if he wants me to, you know… *play cards*?" I asked, lowering my voice.

Jasmine smirked, and I had a feeling this was some sort of divine revenge on her part. "Don't worry. Just ask him what he wants."

"But I-"

Jasmine cut me off, opening the door and shoving me in ahead of her. In the center of the room sat a large, canopied four-poster bed, covered in layers of pink and ruffles. In the center of which sat a brunette in her skivvies doing kissy faces at a camera mounted in the corner of the room. Beside the bed sat a computer screen with a bunch of cables running from the back of it. On the screen were lines of text written by someone named BigBoy78. I squinted and made out the words "you're so hot" and "take it off".

Oh boy.

"Anna," Jasmine said, playing to the camera. "I need you downstairs. Maddie is going to take over in here."

Anna did a seductive little wave to the corner, then followed Jasmine out the door.

"He's all yours," Jasmine said. And I could swear I heard her Barbie laugh as she shut the door.

I bit my lip. I stared at the camera. I did a feeble little one finger wave.

"Uh, hi."

A line of text appeared on the computer monitor to the right.

I have to go now.

"Wait!" I shouted at the camera. I looked down at my cell. Still silent. "Please wait, I… I'm new here. Just give me a chance, I swear I'm really, really good. Super sexy and all that."

I glanced at the monitor. Nothing. Crap.

"Um, I'm totally into talking about tab A. And slot B."

Still nothing. See, I knew I was no good at this stuff.

Channeling Dana, I did my best pouty face at the camera and let one sleeve of my dress slip down my shoulder. "So, big boy, what do you want?"

I swear to God if he told me to take it off, I was bolting. I nervously checked the monitor. And did a loud sigh of relief when text appeared.

Show me your feet.

My feet? Okay. Feet I could do.

I lifted up one pink pump-clad foot for inspection. "I know, the shoes totally clash with the dress. I originally had a pink sundress on but it kind of got caked. Then ripped. So, I'm clashing a little today."

I glanced at the monitor. No response. Had I lost him? Damnit, Felix, hurry up!

"Uh, want to see the other foot?" I asked. I lifted my left foot for inspection, crossing my ankles in the air.

Nice.

Oh, thank God. "Thanks. They're new."

Stuart Weitzman?

"Actually I designed them myself. See, I'm a shoe designer, and they're one of my few originals."

You're very talented.

"Thanks!" Okay, the guy couldn't be all bad if he knew a good pair of heels when he saw them.

Show me your toes.

"Oh. Well… okay." I let one pump drop to the floor and wiggled my half painted toenails at the camera. "I usually get a pedi down at the salon, but I was late for The Terror's party, so I only got one foot done. Sorry."

Take the other shoe off.

I complied, letting the other shoe drop to the floor. As long as we stuck to bare feet, I could do this. I glanced at my silent cell phone again. What was taking him so long?

Let me see your toes.

I leaned back on the bed, supporting myself on my elbows as I lifted both feet up in the air, wiggling my toes at the camera. "Like this?" I asked.

Beautiful.

"Thanks."

Now, suck your big toe.

Excuse me? I blinked at the screen.

A) Grooooosssss! B) Who'd wanna watch that? And C) Um… was that even possible? I mean, I'm not Gumby here.

"How about I just take my top off instead?" I offered, suddenly thinking stripping wasn't such a bad idea after all.

There was a pause. Then the words, *I've got to go* flashed on the screen.

"No, wait! Okay, I'll…" I paused, trying not to grimace. "…suck my big toe."

Do it.

Ugh. I closed my eyes, picturing Dusty's face. I was doing this for her. I'd failed her once; I wasn't going to let her killer get away with it. I would find the bastard. I would nail his ass to the wall.

I would suck the toe.

I took a deep breath and leaned forward as far as I could. But since the last time Dana had dragged me to yoga class I'd fallen flat on my face while doing a downward facing dog, my face came about six inches shy of my big toe.

"Hang on." I gave the camera the universal one finger "wait" signal. I scooched closer to the edge of the bed and curved my spine over into a ball, grabbing my right ankle with both hands and straining to reach it. I felt my leg start to cramp up as I attempted a human pretzel. I was close, if I could just roll forward a little more, just another half an inch…

Unfortunately, I rolled up so well that I rolled right off the bed. Head first. Landing with a thud on the pink carpeting. "Ow."

I stood up and rubbed my forehead, stomping feeling back into my legs. "Sorry," I told the camera. "I, uh, kinda fell. But I think I might have licked my toe. A little," I added hopefully.

I leaned over the bed and checked the monitor.

I have to go now.

"Wait, no! Let me try again. I can totally do this. I was this close," I protested, holding my thumb and index finger up.

But it was too late. A red line of text slashed across the screen, informing me that BigBoy78 had logged out of the system.

Shit, shit, shit! I grabbed my cell and quickly dialed Felix's number. He picked up on the first ring.

"Please tell me you got him?"

Felix chuckled. "Your head all right, love?"

"Fine." I rubbed at my forehead again where I could feel an imprint of the carpet. "Did you get the trace or not?"

"Yeah, we got him."

I did a sigh of relief. "Thank God. What took you so long?"

"I actually had him five minutes ago."

I narrowed my eyes at the phone. "Then why didn't you *call*?"

He chuckled again. "I was enjoying the show."

"I hate you."

"Yeah, well, you're going to love me after I give you his location."

"This better be good," I mumbled under my breath. I grabbed a pen from my purse and wrote the address Felix read off onto the back of my hand. It was a Hollywood zip code, though the street wasn't familiar. Felix pulled up map quest dot com while I waited; then he gave me directions from the 101.

Which would have been very helpful, I realized as I hung up, if I'd had a car.

Damn.

Jasmine opened the door to the bedroom. "You done in here? 'Cause we got another customer logging in."

I grabbed my purse and bolted for the door. No way did I want a repeat of that performance. "It's all yours."

Jasmine ushered Anna back into her pink room and shut the door behind her. "You get what you need?" she asked, turning to me.

"Yeah. The only problem is, now I need a car." I paused, doing my best puppy-dog eyes at her.

She planted both hands on her bony hips. "Well, don't look at me."

"Please, Jasmine," I pleaded. "I can make it worth your while."

Her eyes narrowed. "How worth my while?"

"Three months of ads in the *Informer*?"

She shook her head. "No way. Back cover ad. In color. And I drive. Nobody drives my baby but me."

I bit my lip, hoping Felix really was loaded. "Deal."

"Okay, where are we going?"

"Hollywood. But…" I paused, remembering the armed officer waiting outside for me. I had a feeling I'd been lucky to talk Officer Mustache into taking me here, a detour into Hollywood to confront a possible killer with a toe fetish was probably out of the question. Besides, I was pretty sure this was one of those "harebrained" things Ramirez had been talking about, and when Officer Mustache reported back, I was likely to be put under some sort of house arrest.

What I needed was a distraction.

I pulled my cell back out and hit number two on my speed dial.

Mom picked up on the first ring.

"Maddie? Are you okay? Oh lord, what's happened this time?"

I rolled my eyes. Geeze, give me a little credit, huh? "Nothing, Mom. I'm fine. I was just wondering what you were doing right now?"

"Mrs. Rosenblatt and I are at Molly's. We're helping her send out thank you notes. Why do you ask?"

"Are all the kids there, too? And Connor?"

"Yes."

Perfect! I almost felt sorry for Officer Mustache.

"Why, Maddie? What's going on?"

"Listen, I was wondering if you could do me a little favor? Could you pack all the kids into the car, Molly and Mrs. R, too, and drive them to my friend's house." I recited Jasmine's address.

I could hear Mom frowning through the phone. "What do you want us to do when we get there?"

"Oh, nothing. Just be yourselves."

CHAPTER FIFTEEN

Fifteen minutes later a gold minivan pulled up in front of Jasmine's house, and I watched from the window as the occupants burst out. Mom was first (in peg-legged white pants, an oversized DayGlo green T-shirt tied at her hip in a large knot, and penny loafers with no socks), then Molly (waddling due to her ever-growing belly encased in a huge maternity dress that looked like a tent with eyelets), all four of my cousin's kids (in various states of sticky mouth, sucking on leftover piñata candy as two of them wielded some sort of Nerf noodles and popped the unarmed one on the head), The Terror (blowing big, fat spit bubbles that dribbled down his chin onto his baby Gap sweatshirt as he wailed), and, last but not least, Mrs. Rosenblatt (in a bright orange and red muumuu and Birkenstocks). Oh yeah. And Pablo.

"*Squawk. Dontcha wish your girlfriend was a freak like me? Squawk. Yeah, dontcha?*"

"What the hell is that thing?" Jasmine asked beside me, gesturing to the cage dangling from Mrs. Rosenblatt's chubby hand.

"That is the best distraction ever."

I peeked between the curtains as Molly's kids ran circles around the lawn, Molly waddling after them and yelling at the munchkins to stop hitting their siblings. Connor wailed as he got whacked in the side of the head by a noodle. Mom picked up Connor, who promptly tried to wiggle out of her grip, doing the patented toddler back arch. Mrs. Rosenblatt told Pablo to stop singing, or he was going back to the salon in a teeny tiny body bag. Molly's oldest found a pile of doggy doo on the lawn and starting singing about doggies that made "hunks of stinky chunks." And above it all, Pablo screeched, "*A freak like me!*"

Officer Mustache didn't know where to look, his gaze ping-ponging between the players straight out of a madcap British comedy.

Some days I loved my family.

"Let's go." I grabbed Jasmine by the sleeve, and we slipped out the side door, making a beeline for the garage. Jasmine unlocked a tiny yellow Miata and hopped behind the wheel. No wonder she existed on a diet of vitamin water and Tic Tacs. Any bigger, and there's no way she would have fit in her toy car. I dove into the passenger seat and ducked down, crossing my fingers as she pulled out of the garage, backed into the street and punched it down the road. I waited for the sound of sirens to follow us. I held my breath, counting to four-Mississippi before I peeked my head up.

"Coast clear?"

"Yep." Jasmine nodded, her eyes shining. If I didn't know any better, I'd say she was enjoying this.

I pulled out my cell and dialed Mom's number, telling her thanks for the rescue, and I owed her one. The "one" being dinner at her house next week with her, Faux Dad, and my Irish Catholic grandmother. But, considering I'd just asked her to help me escape police custody, I figured it was a fair request. (Besides, my steady diet of Chinese take-out and Hamburger Helper was, I admit, getting a little old.)

We sped down the 101 into Hollywood, making a left on Cahuenga until we reached the address that Felix had given me. Jasmine killed the engine in front of a large, split-level ranch with a yard full of garden gnomes. The windows were covered in chintz curtains, and the front door was adorned with a big, heart-shaped wreath made of pink silk roses. Didn't exactly scream "murderer" in bright neon.

"You sure this is the right place?" Jasmine asked.

I looked down at my hand and doubled checked the address. Granted, after my great escape, I'd sweated some of the street name off, but the number was still visible enough. "This is it."

She shrugged. "I guess it takes all kinds."

I followed her up the rose flanked pathway to the front door, nerves starting to build. I admit the idea of coming face to face with a cold-blooded killer did more than a little to creep me out.

Not to mention the fact I'd just done a high heeled strip tease for him. I looked down at my pumps and blushed. If he made one reference to licking anything below the ankle, I was so out of here, killer or no.

Jasmine gave the bell a ring, and we waited while it echoed inside. Two beats later the door opened, and I got my first glimpse of BigBoy78.

My jaw dropped opened, and I stared in disbelief.

Deveroux Strong's frame filled the doorway, his broad shoulders clad in a baby blue sweater with skin-tight white, leather pants beneath. On his feet he wore alligator skin black ankle boots, and one diamond stud winked at me from his left earlobe.

"Hey, Maddie," he said, a big white smile flashing across his tanned face. Then he looked behind me and spotted Jasmine. At first his eyes went big as if he'd seen a ghost (or a fifty-foot billboard come to life); then his cheeks turned a red to rival Rudolph's shiny nose as he realized why we were here. "Oh."

"Yep, that's him. That's the guy I saw Veronika bring home," Jasmine said, jabbing me in the ribs.

Deveroux gave a fleeting glance to my pumps, then, if it were possible, blushed even deeper. "Uh, look, I can explain."

"You were dating Veronika?" I sputtered, finally finding my voice. Theories tumbled one over the other in my head, making me question whether we'd made a mistake after all.

Deveroux looked nervously from side to side. "Maybe you'd better come in."

I nodded, mutely following him into a neatly decorated living room, just a little on the floral side for my taste. Deveroux sat on an orange, hibiscus-printed sofa, set next to a lilac covered armchair, and gestured for Jasmine and me to take the petunia studded love seat. (Okay, a lot floral for my taste.) The only thing breaking up the garden of furniture was a small black TV set in the corner, tuned in to *Inside Edition*. I sank down onto the petunia seat, crossing my legs self consciously, as Dana's dress rode up my thigh.

"So, you're BigBoy78?" I asked.

Deveroux went red again, his blush spreading all the way to his blond roots. "Look, it's not what you think. I'm not into that porn stuff. I just… I just have a thing for feet."

"I noticed," I mumbled, tucking my heels underneath me.

"Specifically Veronika's feet?" Jasmine prodded. She leaned forward in her seat, her heavily lifted eyes intent on Deveroux's face. For how badly I'd had to bribe her to get here, she was really getting into this questioning-a-suspect thing. Any second now I feared she'd pull a spotlight and a Billy-club from her leather clutch.

He nibbled at his lip. "Yeah. Look, not that it makes any difference now, but Veronika and I were… well, kind of an item."

"Wait - I thought you were gay?"

Deveroux put one hand on his leather clad hip and tilted his frosted tips at me at me. "What makes you think I'm gay?"

Hmmm…

"Okay. So, you're not gay."

"No, I'm not," he said emphatically. Then picked at a stray piece of lint on his sweater. "That's just a vicious tabloid rumor."

"And you were dating Veronika?"

He nodded. "For the last four months. We met when she started working on *Magnolia Lane* and began dating soon after that."

"And soon after *that* started logging into my site to watch her," Jasmine piped up.

The blush worked itself into an all out five-alarm fire across his forehead. "Look, it's perfectly normal for a man to enjoy a woman's feet. Feet are the most beautiful part of a woman's body. Ancient cultures have revered women's feet for thousands of years. It's not weird!"

Not wanting to aggravate a potential killer, not to mention relive my moments as a foot whore, I changed the subject. "How serious were things between the two of you?"

"Very. We were both going to leave the show at the end of my contract. One more season. We were…" He paused, a watery look in his eyes, and sniffed hard. "We were going to get married."

"Married?" Jasmine spat out. "She never said anything like that to me. And she's got a six month lease!"

I shot her a look.

"Deveroux, did you know that Veronika was pregnant?" I asked.

He nodded his eyes tearing up in earnest. "She told me just last week. I was so excited. We were going to get married and move to Oregon. My sister's got a big place up there near the coast."

"Oregon?" Jasmine yelled. "Why that sneaky little…"

I gave her a quick shot to the ribs.

"So, Veronika was okay with leaving the show?"

Deveroux nodded. "It was her idea to move away. Away from all the Hollywood types. In case you hadn't noticed, the set can get kind of wild at times."

Understatement alert.

"Anyway," he continued, "she said she was coming into some money soon, and we could put a down payment on a place near my sister."

I narrowed my eyes. "Money?" I asked, remembering how little Dana said stand-ins made. "What kind of money?"

He shrugged. "I don't know. She wouldn't say. But she said she'd been working on something, and her investment was about to pay off."

"Investment? That's what she called it?"

He nodded.

I turned to Jasmine.

"Hey, don't look at me," she said. "My girls earn free room and board from me, but that's it."

I wondered. Veronika hadn't struck me as the kind to put her pennies into stocks and bonds. Granted I hadn't known her that well, but the fact she was playing strip go-fish for rent didn't speak to a bank account bursting with extra funds.

Which left one alternative.

Blackmail.

I worded my next question carefully. "Deveroux, was Veronika particularly close to anyone on the set? Anyone who might have shared, say, a secret with Veronika?"

His white-blonde eyebrows (perfectly waxed, I noticed. Wait til I told Felix this guy was straight!) drew together. "Well, she did have coffee with Kylie a couple of times."

My ears pricked up. Coffee? Or a confession where Kylie let slip a deep dark secret worth killing Veronika over? I had to admit, I had a hard time putting the perky cheerleader-esque Tina Rey in the role of homicidal maniac. But, stranger things had happened.

"But," Deveroux continued, "Veronika was really careful about keeping her personal life separate from her work. She was worried that if someone on the set found out she worked for the website, they'd fire her. I mean, despite the drama in the script, our core demographic is middle American housewives. It's one thing to have scandalous storylines, but an *actual* scandal like working for a porn site, well, that wouldn't fit the studio's image."

He turned to Jasmine as an after thought. "No offense."

She shrugged. "None taken. You paid for my last two PhotoFacials."

Deveroux blushed again.

"So, no one else she was particularly close to on the set?"

He shook his head. "Why do you ask?"

I hesitated to tell him my theory. But, then again, I was quickly running out of suspects, and at this point didn't have much to lose. "Do you think it's possible that Veronika may have been blackmailing someone? Maybe someone on the set?"

"No. No way!" Deveroux vehemently shook his head. Then he stopped. He did a little sigh and slumped his shoulders forward. "Maybe."

"And she never mentioned anything to you?" I asked again.

"No, just that she was coming into some money soon." His eyes got that watery look to them again. "You think that's what got her killed? I mean, we didn't have to move to Oregon. We could have stayed here."

I rose and gave him an awkward pat on the shoulder. "I'm sorry."

He nodded, sniffling loudly. "Excuse me, I need to find a tissue," he mumbled and slipped out of the room.

I sank back onto the sofa, my mind whirling with possibilities. If Veronika had been blackmailing someone on the set, it would have given them ample reason to want her dead. How easy would it have been for a blackmailer to lure Veronika to Mia's trailer under the guise of more money, then stage the death to look like Mia's stalker?

But it still didn't explain Dusty. Or Mia's threatening letters. Was it possible that it was all a coincidence? That Veronika really had just been in the wrong place at the wrong time? What if Veronika had been waiting to meet the blackmailer at Mia's trailer, but the stalker had gotten to her first? I had to admit, instead of explaining anything, this new development just added one more piece to the confusing puzzle that didn't seem to fit in anywhere.

I was flirting with that headache again when the television piped up from the corner.

"That's right, Tom, we've received breaking news about the Magnolia Lane Murders."

Jasmine and I both immediately turned our attention to the screen as a slim, African-American reporter came on, holding a microphone in front of her face. The backdrop of the Sunset Studio's Central Park, still cordoned off with crime scene tape, laid out behind her.

"We go now to Marcia Blanding at the scene," a voice just off camera said. *"Marcia?"*

The reporter sprang to life, lifting her microphone to her cherry painted mouth.

"Thank you, Peter. As you know, we've been following this story all morning, bringing you updates on the latest death on the set of the popular television show, Magnolia Lane.*"*

I winced as the camera moved left, showing a group of crime scene technicians in slick windbreakers combing the area.

"Now, it seems," Marcia went on, *"that star, Mia Carletto's, poisoned penman has struck again. We learned just moments ago from Miss Carletto herself that she has received another death threat. We come to you live from the impromptu press conference just outside her trailer on the Sunset Studios lot."*

I leaned forward in my seat, my eyes glued to the television as Deveroux wandered back into the room.

"I'm sorry, I just-"

"Shhhhh," I commanded, waving him off as Mia's face filled the screen.

Reporters surrounded her. To her right stood her publicist, a thin redheaded woman in a tailored black suit. To her left, the ominous presence of Ramirez, arms crossed over his pecs, his eyes ever watchful of the crowd pressing closer to Mia. For a second I had the tiniest prickle of guilt at giving my babysitter the slip, but it was quickly shoved to the background as Mia began to speak.

"Thank you all for coming," she said, her voice evenly modulated and booming over the assembled crowd.

"Are you all right?" one of the reporters shouted to her, shoving a Channel 2 microphone in her face.

Mia sighed loudly, her eyes downcast. *"Physically, I am unharmed. Though, emotionally, the day has* taken its toll on me."

"Where did you find the latest note?" a representative from Cable 12 asked.

"This morning I arrived on the set to find this note in my trailer, pinned to my pillow," Mia said, holding up a piece of plain, white stationary.

"What does it say?" shouted Channel 2 again.

Mia's bottom lip quivered momentarily. Then she cleared her throat, lifted her head, and began to read from the paper. *"Veronika and Dusty were only the beginning."* Her voice faltered, fear clearly evident on her pinched features as she continued. *"You've eluded me thus far, but no more. I will have you Mia Carletto. Make no mistake about it,"* she said, looking directly into the camera. *"You're next."*

A frenzy of flashbulbs went off, the reporters practically peeing their pants over this kind of news. I could see Ramirez's posture tense in the background as the clamoring mob of newshounds surged forward. Mia's publicist put an arm around her, ushering her back into the trailer as questions flew through the air one after another, ranging from "Are you hiring a bodyguard?" to "Who does your hair?"

"Mia knows how to work a crowd, doesn't she?" Deveroux asked, dabbing at the corner of his eye with a tissue.

I had to agree, the moment had been played for maximum effect. On the other hand, death threats did tend to be dramatic all on their own.

"I think she's had work done," Jasmine said, picking at a long, red fingernail. "Did you see her eyes? Wider than the aisles at Barney's."

I refrained from pointing out that Jasmine's own eyes weren't exactly a product of nature. Instead, I thanked Deveroux for his time (carefully making my feet as inconspicuous as possible), and left, taking the rose lined pathway back to Jasmine's Miata.

"Well, so much for Veronika's mystery man," Jasmine said, shifting the sports car into gear. "So, do we track down Kylie next, or what?"

I turned to her. "We?"

"What?" She gave me an innocent look and shrugged. "This *Charlie's Angels* thing is kind of fun."

I opened my mouth to protest but thought better of it. She did, after all, have the car.

"Okay, fine. Let's go question Kylie."

Luckily, I had it on good authority (*Star* magazine) that Kylie spent every Monday morning at the Kitson boutique on the trendy Robertson Boulevard. Twenty minutes later, Jasmine was circling the block to find parking, and I was scanning the racks for Kylie's perky blonde head. I spotted her holding a vintage "Little Miss Sunshine" T-shirt up to her ample chest in the mirror.

"Hi, Kylie! Wow, what a coincidence. You shop here too?" I grabbed a studded belt, trying to look like a casual shopper as she spun around.

It took a second for recognition to dawn in her eyes. "Oh, yeah. You're the new wardrobe girl, right?"

I nodded. "Uh-huh. Maddie."

"Riiiight. Sorry, I totally forgot your name. When I'm on the set, I tune stuff like that out. I have to be in a total concentration zone. You know, they expect me to have all my lines *memorized*? Like, every week." She turned back to her reflection. "What do you think of this shirt?"

"Very cute."

She wrinkled her ski-jump nose. "You think? I don't know. Is it too young?"

Considering Kylie still looked like she should be shopping in the kid's section, I decided that question was rhetorical. Instead, I got right to the point.

"So, I guess you heard about Dusty this morning?"

Kylie dropped the shirt and spun around. "Ohmigod, like, too totally sad, you know? I can't even believe someone could do that. Way random."

I hesitated to tell her just how un-random this was shaping up to be.

"I heard that you and Veronika were close. All of this must be so hard on you."

Again Kylie did the nose scrunching thing. "Um, sorta, I guess. We did lattes a couple of times. But she was kinda weird, you know"?

I cocked my head to the side, fingering a fur trimmed jacket. "Weird how?"

"Well, she just kept talking about this guy she was dating and how they were gonna get married and move to Oregon. Oregon of all places! I mean, I so did not get that fascination. There's, like, not even any cool malls there. And it's, like, totally rainy 'n' stuff. Way fubar if you ask me."

I watched as she picked up another T-shit. "Little Miss Giggles".

"So, um, was that all you and Veronika talked about?"

Kylie gave me a sidelong glance in the mirror. "I guess. Why?"

I picked up the belt again, trying to feign casual. "No reason. Just wondering if she might have confided something in you. Something that might help find who killed her."

Something sparked in the back of Kylie's eyes, and for a moment I thought I saw a glimmer of intelligence beyond her Tina Rey character cross her face. "Don't the police think Mia was the real target?"

"No one's really sure yet," I said, watching her carefully.

Kylie shrugged. "Well, Veronika didn't say anything to me about someone after her, if that's what you mean. Like I said, we just did lattes a couple of times. She wasn't like my BFF or anything." She turned back to her reflection. "Hey, what do you think about this top. Kitschy fun, or just passé?"

I handed her a pink T with a polka-dotted Chihuahua on the front. "Try this."

She grabbed it and held it up to her chest. "Too cute!"

"So, do have any idea why Veronika might have been in Mia's trailer that night?" I asked, switching gears.

Kylie shrugged. "I dunno. That wrinkle-faced police guy asked me that, too. All I can think is that maybe she was borrowing a script or something. I know Veronika was always losing her copy. She tried to borrow mine a couple weeks ago but I, like, totally needed it. I had, like, two whole pages to memorize!"

"Ouch."

"No doubt. Hey, wanna hand me that belt? I'm gonna go try some of these on," Kylie said, grabbing her pile of T-shirts.

I did. Then hung around the dressing rooms a while, but I figured I'd gotten all I was going to out of Miss Perk.

Jasmine was just pulling into a spot out front as I exited the boutique. I slipped into the passenger seat of the Miata. "Perfect timing."

"Are you done already?" Jasmine's face fell. (Well, as far as a facelift and chin implant would let it fall).

I nodded. "Either Kylie's too stupid or too smart to say anything useful."

"Damn." Jasmine pouted. "Okay, well where to next, Kate?"

I gave her a look. "Kate?"

Jasmine rolled her eyes at me. "Well, duh, if we're doing the Angels thing, I'm clearly Farrah, so you have to be either Jaclyn Smith or Kate Jackson. And, honey, you're no Jaclyn."

I gave her a dirty look. But, considering she had the car, didn't argue.

Only, the truth was, I wasn't really sure where to go next. The fact that Veronika may have been blackmailing someone on the set threw a whole new light on things. The only problem was that secrets ran through *Magnolia Lane* faster than a Malibu wildfire. Her victim-turned-killer could be any one of the cast. I wasn't even entirely ready to cross Kylie off my list. Sure, she seemed innocent enough, but I wasn't completely convinced that the perky ditz thing she had going on wasn't an act. I mean, who could really be *that* blonde?

And what about Dusty? What was her connection to all of this? I had a hard time picturing her and Veronika in cahoots. Dusty loved her job too much to jeopardize it that way. The girl had lived for fashion.

And then there were the letters. After this last one, it seemed clear they were somehow linked to the murders. But I couldn't for the life of me think how. Either he was the most bumbling killer ever, to have gotten the wrong target twice, or there was more going on here than I could figure. I swore, it was harder to follow than last season's love triangle between Tina Rey, the electrician, and that hooker they killed off in the supermarket after her secret love child with the neighbor who burned down Tina Rey's house and hit her dog with a Diaper Delivery truck.

"Let's go visit Margo," I finally decided, remembering the orange scarf.

"Good plan." Jasmine nodded. "I bet she's in this up to her eyeballs."

The only problem was that I had no idea where to look for her. "I don't exactly have her address," I confessed.

"No prob," Jasmine replied. "Easy enough to get that."

I raised an eyebrow at her. (And, since my beauty regimen included L'Oreal night cream in lieu of botulism injections, my eyebrow actually went up.) "You can?"

"Um, duh? Just pick up any map of the stars' homes. Margo's compound is always on there."

"Compound?" Since when did supporting TV actresses make the kind of cash to live in *compounds*?

Jasmine gave me a sidelong look. "Um, yeah. Margo Walton? She's freaking swimming in dough, that girl. She used to be a B movie actress back in the eighties, did, like, fifty of those high school sluts being chased by ax murderers flicks. She's still huge in Japan."

Considering Mom would have freaked if she caught my pre-teen self watching those kinds of movies, I had to admit, I'd never seen Margo outside of her Nurse Nan scrubs. I looked at Jasmine, wondering exactly how old she was. "You've seen her films?"

Jasmine nodded emphatically, doing a U-turn and heading back toward the 2. "Love 'em. I used to get this guy logging into the website from Japan, BigWu22. Dude was totally into that stuff. Wanted me to put on the leg warmers and tease my hair and everything. I totally channeled early Margo."

I looked up at the giant dyed red mass of hair moussed within an inch of its life atop Jasmine's head, wondering how on earth she could tease it any higher. Or balance on her chicken legs if she did.

Fifteen minutes later we were on Hollywood Boulevard, cruising past the Mann Chinese Theater and the Walk of Fame. "This guy looks good," Jasmine said, pulling the Miata up to a curb where an Indian guy in a lawn chair sat next to Groucho Marx's star, holding up a sign that read "Star Maps, $10." She jumped out and, after exchanging a few words and a few dollars with the guy, hopped back in the car.

"Bingo," she said, unfolding a blue, photocopied map. Since we were sitting in a Miata, the smallest car they make outside of the circus, the unfolded map filled the entire interior. I scanned the road lines for little red stars indicating the houses of Hollywood's most famous residents. I resisted the urge to suggest a detour when I saw Orlando Bloom only lived a few blocks away.

"Right there!" Jasmine shouted, pointing a red nail at a spot in Bel Air. Two inches north of Sunset were the printed words "Margo Walton."

I loathed to admit it. Jasmine had done good.

She put the car in gear and shot out into traffic, weaving in and out of the lanes as she took Sunset west to the 405. Unfortunately, the traffic gods were not with us today and, as soon as we hit the freeway, we were stuck in a virtual parking lot.

"Shit," Jasmine swore and flipped on the radio, cruising through stations until she found one promising a traffic report. Apparently a high-speed chase had gone through earlier, and police were still cleaning up the tack strips and mangled cop cars that had resulted.

I slunk down in my seat, watching the smog layer hover over the city as we inched forward. My stomach growled, reminding me I hadn't filled it since that cup of coffee this morning.

"Got anything to eat in here?" I asked, opening the glove box. "A snickers bar, candy, anything?"

Jasmine gave me a look like I'd suggested she was smuggling dead bodies in the trunk. "Candy? You think I got this body harboring candy bars in my glove box?"

"Oh puh-lease. We both know you got that body from Doctor 90210."

Jasmine gasped. "I did not!"

I gave her a get-real look.

She bit the inside of her cheek. "Okay, fine. I've had a *little* work done."

I snorted. But refrained from comment as my stomach did another unholy moan. "Look, this traffic isn't letting up. Let's pull off somewhere and wait it out. Preferably somewhere with a drive-thru. I'm starving."

Jasmine shoved her purse at me. "I think there's a couple of Tic Tacs in there."

I opened her red, leather clutch and rummaged through a collection of lipstick, compacts, and concealer that rivaled even mine until my fingers wrapped around a case of green Tic Tacs. I ate one. Then another. I popped a handful of them in my mouth and crunched loudly.

"I'm still hungry."

Jasmine rolled her eyes. "Fine. I'll pull off at the next exit." I swore she shot my mid-section a look that said I could do with a *little* work, too, but I ignored her, downing another handful of Tic Tacs instead.

Ten minutes later we inched our way onto the off-ramp. One thing that can't be beat about L.A. living, you're never more than two blocks away from a Big Mac and fries. My stomach did one more groan (this one I'm pretty sure was of glee) as Jasmine parked next to the Dumpster in front of the Golden Arches. I led the way inside and ordered a Quarter Pounder with cheese and large fries from the pimply kid behind the counter. Oh, and a strawberry shake. And an apple pie.

Jasmine looked down her sculpted nose at me and ordered bottled water and a side salad – no dressing. Apparently she wasn't scheduled for another lipo round for another six months.

We ate in silence, mostly because I was scarfing down my food with an appreciation that would make Ronald McDonald proud. It only took ten minutes, and we were back out in the parking lot. Me rubbing my full belly with the kind of satisfaction that only an apple pie chaser can provide. Personally, though, I still thought Jasmine looked a little hungry.

I was about to offer her the last Tic Tac when a loud pinging sound erupted from the Dumpster next to us.

I jumped, Jasmine and I both doing mirrored "What the…?" looks.

"What was that?" she asked, her red hair whipping around her face as she scanned the parking lot.

"I dunno."

Then I heard it again, closer to me this time, and accompanied by a little spark as something whizzed off the metal side of the Dumpster.

A voice yelled from across the parking lot. "You bitch!"

I looked up.

And froze.

Oh. Shit.

Running toward me, long black hair flapping behind her like a cape, silver gun straight armed in her right hand, was Isabel.

Chapter Sixteen

"You stupid fucking bitch!" she screamed. Another bullet ricocheted off the Dumpster. Jasmine and I instinctively ducked, trying to make ourselves as tiny as possible behind the Miata. Which, since it was designed for midgets, wasn't nearly tiny enough.

"You are so mine now," Isabel screamed, her voice growing closer.

"Holy shit," Jasmine yelled. She scuttled around the car and dove behind the Dumpster.

Second good idea Jasmine had had that day.

I joined her, my knees scraping against the ketchup-stained asphalt as another shot pinged off the metal side.

"You ruined everything, you dumb bitch! Snake won't even talk to me because of you. I'm going to fucking kill you!"

"Gee, you're popular," Jasmine hissed, covering her head with both of her skinny arms.

"I'm not good with relationships. So sue me."

Ping, ping, ping. Two more bullets bounced off the Dumpster, adrenalin shooting through me with each one, as I heard Isabel pause to reload.

I ripped my purse off my shoulder, digging for my cell to call in the cavalry. But of course, with my hands shaking worse than the Northridge Quake, that was easier said than done.

Ping, ping, ping.

"Jesus Christ, call nine-one-one," Jasmine shouted, rolling into a tight ball beside me. "This chick is crazy."

No kidding. I dumped my purse upside down, spilling the contents onto the ground just as I heard the door of the McDonalds open.

"Hey, what's going on out here?" I heard the pimply kid ask, his voice cracking.

"None of your goddamned business, pizza face!"

Two more shots rang out, one of them followed by the sound of shattering glass and a car alarm wailing pitifully.

"My car!" Jasmine moaned beside me.

"Holly crap, call the cops!" the pimply kid screamed, ducking back into the restaurant.

I finally spied my cell phone. But, considering the nearest cop car was probably a good twelve blocks away, and Isabel was twelve feet, I had a sinking feeling I knew which one would get here first. I'd already been held at gunpoint once by Isabel. Quite honestly, not an experience I was dying to repeat.

So, instead of reaching for my cell, I wrapped my fingers around the little silver canister sitting on the asphalt next to my tampons and lip gloss. Mrs. Rosenblatt's special stash of pepper spray.

I pulled the top off, stuck my finger over the trigger, and took a deep fortifying breath that smelled a little of stale French fries, then jumped out from behind the Dumpster.

Isabel was standing over Jasmine's car, systematically shooting out all the windows. What was it with this chick and cars?

"Hey Isabel!" I shouted.

She turned to face me, her eyes big, pupils the size of silver dollars. The girl seriously needed a double dose of Xanax.

I straight-armed the pepper spray in front of me, aiming it right at Isabel's face, and pulled the trigger.

Which, I realized, would have been totally effective if I'd been standing the suggested four to six feet from my target. Unfortunately, Isabel was a good ten away. A fine stream of liquid shot out from my canister… and dribbled harmlessly down on the Miata's tires.

Uh-oh.

Isabel pointed the gun at me. "You stupid bitch, now you're going to pay!"

I looked down at the useless canister in my hand. On pure instinct, I threw it in her direction.

If I'd actually tried out for the softball team in high school instead of just *telling* my mother I was going to try-outs and *actually* sneaking underneath the bleachers with Jason Pratt, I might have had something resembling aim, maybe even enough to pull a cool Lucy Liu move and knock the gun out of her hand. But, considering Jason Pratt was the best kisser in all of ninth grade, not to mention the spitting image of Luke Perry, circa 1991, my aim sucked.

The canister bounced on the ground, landing at Isabel's feet.

She laughed. "You are so girly."

Crap. Damn you and your magical tongue, Jason!

Only, my curse at the French-kissing god of ninth grade was cut short as a hissing sound erupted from the canister. Both Isabel and I looked at each other. Then down. Just in time to see the canister explode, covering Isabel head to toe in cayenne pepper water.

"Ahhh!" She screamed, dropping the gun and clawing at her eyes. "I'm on fire!"

Thank you, Mrs. Rosenblatt.

Sirens erupted in the background, the signal that Pimple Boy had, indeed, called the cops. Isabel pulled her hands away from her swollen eyes just long enough to scoop up her gun before bolting in the opposite direction.

"Don't think I'm through with you, bitch!" she yelled, slipping into another no-doubt stolen SUV at the end of the lot. This one a red MDX with fuzzy dice hanging from the rearview mirror. I watched her wild hair flying out the window as she turned the corner, disappearing behind the Tip Top Dry Cleaners.

"Come on." I grabbed Jasmine by the arm, hauling her skinny butt off the ground. "We have to go."

Jasmine was shaking, and I wasn't entirely sure I didn't see a wet stain peeking through her Brazilians. "Is she gone?"

I nodded. "Uh-huh. And we have to be, too." The only thing worse than being shot at by Isabel would be The Wrath of Ramirez if he caught me here, sans babysitter.

I shoved Jasmine into the passenger seat, hopped behind the wheel, hastily brushing broken glass off the seat, and put the Miata into reverse, squealing out of the parking lot just as two cop cars, lights blazing, rounded the corner.

Jasmine looked pale in the seat beside me. So pale that her foundation stood out on her cheeks like poster paint. I wasn't entirely sure she wasn't about to hurl.

"Are you okay?" I asked.

Jasmine turned and did her best Evil Barbie, squinting her eyes and hissing through her teeth. "Okay? Okay?! No, I'm not *okay*. I just got shot at!"

"Yeah, I know. I hate it when that happens."

"I changed my mind," she said, pink slowly seeping back into her skin, "I so don't want to be an Angel."

* * *

We rode the rest of the way into Bel Air in silence, Jasmine periodically wincing and re-paling as wind ripped through her shot out windows. Me periodically looking in the rearview for SUVs driven by crack heads.

Luckily, none appeared, and twenty minutes later we were sitting outside the gated home of Margo Walton.

I hit the intercom button and waited as a man's deep voice buzzed over the speaker.

"Yes?"

"Hi, I'm Maddie Springer. I work with Margo."

Nothing.

"I, uh, wanted to see if I could talk with her?"

I waited as he did the strong, silent routine again.

"Please?"

Finally, "Hang on a minute."

He clicked off, and I let the Miata idle, hoping Margo was in a chatty mood. I tried to peek around the wrought iron gates, but all I could see from here was a winding, gravel-lined drive leading into a grove of strategically placed oak trees, planted, no doubt, specifically to keep nosey people like me guessing.

"How much do you think a place like this costs?" I asked.

Jasmine shrugged. "I dunno. Ten mil?"

I shook my head, marveling at the thought that a woman worth ten million dollars in prime California real estate would show up to work wearing plastic Crocs. I guess money can't buy fashion sense.

Just when I was beginning to think the gatekeeper had forgotten about us, the intercom buzzed to life again. "All right, you can go on through."

As if by magic the heavy iron gates in front of us slid back, allowing entry. I put the car in gear, tires crunching as we wound toward the center of the property. The drive was flanked by long expanses of green lawn, punctuated here and there by blooming flowerbeds and the occasional fountain with a naked Greek god spurting water from completely inappropriate body parts.

Finally the drive ended in a roundabout in front of an enormous plantation style home. Immediately I thought of *Gone With the Wind*, but to my knowledge Bel Air wasn't known for its historic cotton roots. Large white columns flanked the brick steps leading to an oversized wooden door. Ornate moldings covered the cornices, and a long, white balcony stretched the entire length of the upper floors.

It was official. I lived in the crappiest place in all of L.A.

I parked the dwarfed Miata near the front steps and stared up at the building.

"How many B movies did you say she made?"

"At least fifty in the U.S. Maybe more overseas. I heard she even had a short stint as a German pop star in the late nineties."

And here I thought I knew everything there was to know about my favorite TV stars.

"So…" Jasmine said, her eyes darting to the imposing front door, "you really think Margo might have done it? Killed two women?"

I shrugged. "Maybe."

Jasmine's throat bobbed up and down, a little of that pasty look returning to her cheeks. "Know what? Maybe I'll just wait in the car."

"Suit yourself." I opened the door and hopped out, my heels crunching on the white gravel leading up to the steps. I rang the bell and heard elegant chimes echo throughout the home. Two beats later the door was opened by a young, Asian woman in a gray uniform.

"Hi, I'm Maddie Springer?" I said. Only it sounded more like a question. I'll admit, growing up around Beverly Hills, I wasn't easily intimidated by wealth. But being faced with a real live uniformed maid right of out a Merchant Ivory film, was something I wasn't accustomed to. I nervously tugged at my hooker outfit.

The woman was obviously a pro, and if she wondered why a woman in spandex and clashing pumps, driving a Miata that looked like it belonged to Bonnie and Clyde, was standing on her employer's doorstep, she didn't show it. Instead, she did a slight nod of her head and motioned for me to come in. "Please follow me," she said in softly accented English.

I did, as she led the way down a narrow hallway to her right. I'm glad she had her back to me as we walked because I was pretty sure I was staring with an intensity that bordered on rude as I took in Margo's décor.

It was like I had walked into a Hollywood museum. Every square inch of wall space was occupied by large, framed movie posters. Most of which had either the words "sorority," "slasher" or both in the title. I recognized a younger version of Margo, minus the overzealous facelift, gracing half of them. Most were films I didn't recognize; some were even done in foreign languages – Japanese, German, Spanish.

As the maid led me into a large room at the back of the house, the feeling of being in a showplace increased when I noticed that everything was encased in plastic. And I mean *everything*. The sofas were wrapped in the kind of covering seen on my Irish Catholic grandmother's virgin living room set she purchased at Sears in 1957. Plastic display cases took up every available surface, displaying things like vases, jewelry, teacups, and even a stuffed ferret. Along a black lacquered mantel sat a collection of trophies – one of which I picked out as a Golden Globe. I took a step closer. Best Supporting Actress in a Drama. 1997. Ouch. Been a while since Margo had appeared on the big screen.

"Miss Margo will be right with you," the woman told me, then disappeared back the way she had come.

I took the opportunity to browse the museum. Of course, the first stop was the ferret. (What can I say? I'm curious like that.) A brass nameplate on the case said: Mr. Bobo, from *Sorority Strangler 7.* I looked at Mr. Bobo, permanently suspended in mid leap inside his plastic tomb. Creepy.

I moved on to the next case, which held a huge pair of ruby colored earrings. The case read: Worn by 'Magdalena' in *The Slasher Co-Ed Returns.* The rest of the cases were similarly marked, all holding memorabilia, it seemed, from Margo's various film efforts. I paused next to a case from *The Campus Killer,* which held a pair of black, silk pumps, embroidered with little emerald butterflies down the sides.

"Gorgeous, aren't they?"

I snapped my head up to see that Margo had entered the room.

"I wore those as Eleanor Swift, sophomore at UCLA and the Campus Killer's third victim."

I nodded. "They're beautiful." Personally, I thought it was a shame they were stuck behind plastic. Shoes like those deserved to be worn. Fleetingly, I wondered what size they were…

"My death scene in that one was superbly written. The killer slit me across the throat right here." She made a line from ear to ear with her forefinger. "God, I was cleaning fake dye out of my hair for a week, there was so much blood. Did you see that one?" Margo asked

I shook my head. "No, sorry. I must have missed it."

Margo shrugged. "Oh well, it was a straight-to-video. Great reviews in Sweden, though. Please, sit," she said, indicating a low loveseat.

I did, my spandex dress slipping awkwardly on the plastic surface.

Margo sat opposite me. She was dressed in a maroon skirt, black blouse and black, sheer stockings that swooshed together as she crossed one leg over the other. Though, I was pleased to see a pair of classic black pumps on her feet and not the rubber Crocs.

"So, you wanted to talk to me?" she asked. She pulled a slim, silver cigarette case from a drawer beside her and flipped it open.

"Yes, I was wondering if I could ask you a few questions about the show."

"Sure." She offered the case to me. I shook my head, and she shrugged again, pulling out a long, slim clove cigarette. "What do you want to know?"

"I suppose you saw Mia's press conference this morning?"

Margo snorted. "Who didn't? That woman is the biggest media whore I've ever seen. And I've been around," she added, gesturing to her treasure trove of B-movie credits. "I know whores."

"I take it you're not that fond of Mia?"

"Hell no." Margo punctuated this by stabbing the unlit cigarette in my direction. "She's a first rate bitch, that woman."

"Because of the comment she made about your age the other day?"

Margo gave a sharp bark of laughter. "Oh, honey, we go back way farther than that."

"How far?" I asked, leaning forward.

"I was the one who first discovered her."

"Oh?"

Margo nodded. "She was doing this terrible actor's playhouse production in North Hollywood. I was there with my second husband, Randolph Amsted, the director of *Dorm Demons*?" She paused, looking expectantly at me as if I should know him.

I nodded, playing along.

"Anyway, the play was awful, but Mia, I could tell she had something. She was driven. She *made* the audience pay attention to her. I convinced Randolph to put her in his next picture. You know, just something small, like a bit part. He did, and she used that as the springboard to television. Of course," Margo added, a bitter note to her voice, "*Magnolia Lane* has been her big breakout."

"I heard that Mia was originally cast in the role of Nurse Nan," I said watching her reaction.

Her blue eyes whipped around to me. "Who told you that?"

"Uh..." I shrugged non-commitally. "Not sure. I guess I just heard it... around."

Margo narrowed her eyes at me, and for a second I feared I was going to get thrown out of the B-Movie Museum. But finally she just leaned back on her sofa with a little plastic burp. "I was the one who suggested her to the producers in the first place. She was supposed to be *my* supporting actress. But, being Mia of course, she went behind my back and convinced them that she would be a better fit to play opposite Ricky." Margo barked out a sharp laugh. "Please. I've had lovers half his age."

I refrained from commenting on Margo's math. Ricky didn't look a day over thirty, and if Margo had fifteen year old fans, I was a rocket scientist.

"So, Mia got the role of Ashley, and you got the supporting role?" I prodded.

Margo lit her cigarette, blowing a fine stream of smoke toward the ceiling. "At least on the small screen." She looked at me, her eyes twinkling. "Did you know that FOX has picked up the film rights? There's going to be a *Magnolia Lane* movie, staring yours truly."

My heart leapt into my throat, and my internal TV junkie did a happy squeal. "Really? Ohmigod – too cool!"

Margo smiled smugly. "Oh yeah. 'Cool' all right. Even cooler? I'm the executive producer. The movie was not only going to be my return to film, but also my revenge on that little tramp." She took another long drag. "I was writing Mia out of the film."

"Writing her out?" I asked. "But isn't she the star of the show?"

Uh-oh. The second the words left my mouth, I regretted them. Margo froze, cigarette halfway to her lips, and gave me a death look.

"There are other inhabitants of *Magnolia Lane*, you know," she barked out. "Tina Rey and the electrician was the hot item in the ratings last season. And my lines have doubled since Blake went into that coma."

"Right. Of course. Sorry." Though I personally couldn't imagine a *Magnolia Lane* without Mia. I mean, Blake in a coma and Nurse Nan hovering over him a story did not make. Where was the drama in that?

"Anyway," she went on, "that was going to be my revenge on the backstabbing bitch."

"*Was*?" I asked, honing in on the word. "Did something change?"

Margo stood up, slashing her cigarette in the air. "Mia found out about the film and pitched a royal fit! Suddenly the whole project's on hold. And now with the letters and these murders, backers are talking about pulling out altogether. All because of that overrated prima donna."

I waited while Margo took a long drag of her cigarette, exhaling vigorously before she sank down into the loveseat opposite me, the plastic casing crackling beneath her frame. "I swear to God, if that wacko writing the letters offs Mia next, I'll die a happy woman."

I watched Margo's nostrils flare in and out, thanks to the aggressive facelift, the only part of her face that held any expression. The bad blood between the two actresses ran deep, that much was clear. Deep enough for Margo to kill two innocent victims just to get to Mia? I wasn't sure. But if the treasure trove of artifacts filling her home was any indication, Margo took her films seriously. Mia sabotaging her comeback to the big screen just might be enough to put Margo over the edge.

I was about to ask Margo how well she had known Veronika when the maid came into the room again.

"Excuse me, Miss," she said softly addressing me.

I turned. "Yes?"

"There's a woman out front. She told me to say…" The maid blushed. "To get your 'fanny' outside. She's on the night shift tonight, and if you don't hurry the," she paused again, "'heck' up she'll take off without you."

Any other time, I would have sent a return message that Porn Star Barbie could go to "heck." But, unfortunately, she was my only ride.

I rose, painfully peeling my exposed thighs off the plastic couch, and thanked Margo for seeing me.

"Anytime, honey," she said, blowing smoke out through her nostrils. "My door is always open for a bitch session about Mia."

* * *

Jasmine drove through the evening traffic back toward West Hills, having composed herself enough by now that instead of freaked, the set of her bony jaw just looked pissed off. She was silent, no doubt using all her brainpower to mentally add up how much it was going to cost to have her baby fixed. I took the opportunity to check my voicemail. Just one message. I keyed in my pin number and got an earful of Ramirez's growl.

"I'm at your place, Maddie. I couldn't help but notice that neither you nor my officer is here. Where the hell are you Maddie?" he asked, his voice growing louder with each word. "I got a call about a woman shooting at a blonde in a McDonald's parking lot. You wouldn't happen to know anything about that, would you?" Then the slam of his receiver hanging up echoed through my ears as the message clicked over.

Needless to say, I didn't call him back.

I looked out the window. The sky was turning dusky pink and blue as the sun sank behind the hills. It was clear that I couldn't go home tonight without risking a) a pissed off cop with a pair of handcuffs, or b) a pissed off crack head with a gun. Ditto Ramirez's place. Despite his invitation this morning, I had a feeling he wouldn't be all smiles and sunshine to see me right now.

I hit speed dial and called Dana's number.

No answer on her cell, and Daisy Duke informed me that she hadn't been home all day. Great.

I looked across the console at Jasmine. If I bribed her with an above-the-fold mention, I could probably spend the night in her den of iniquity, but the idea of strangers touching their tab A while watching me sleep was creepier than a stuffed ferret.

Which left me with only one place to go.

I bit my lip.

"Hey, Jasmine, do you think you could drop me off someplace?"

She did an exasperated sigh and looked at her dash clock. "If it's on the way. Where?"

I took a deep breath, hoping the slime didn't rub off as I gave Jasmine Felix's address in the Hollywood Hills.

CHAPTER SEVENTEEN

The sun was long gone by the time we climbed the last ridge to Felix's monument to modern architecture, the sky a deep blue by now, almost dark enough to see stars if the ever present sheen of city lights didn't blind them out. The night air had chilled considerably, and Jasmine and I were doing a teeth chattering duet as wind whipped through her non-existent windows.

"I swear I'll pay for these," I stammered, feeling my lips turn blue.

"Damn straight you will! Are we almost there?"

If I didn't know better, I'd say Jasmine was anxious to get rid of me.

"A couple more turns," I responded.

Jasmine mumbled something under her breath (I caught the words "blonde" and "pain in the ass") and cranked the wheel to the right as she wound further upward. Finally the trees broke, and Felix's glass structure came into view.

"Wow," Jasmine said. "Who is this guy? And more importantly, what does he like to watch? I could retire on a perv this rich."

I ignored her comment as, at the moment, the important question on my mind was would he put up a slightly snarky shoe designer on the run from the cops for a night?

"You can let me out here," I said as she pulled into the drive.

Jasmine shot me a look, and for a second I could see her desire to meet Mr. Mega-bucks warring with her desire to be Maddie-free. For a second. Personally, I think it was the shot-out windows that put her over the edge.

"Yeah, fine. And don't think I won't send you the bill for the car!" she reminded me as I grabbed my purse and got out. I scarcely had the passenger door shut again before she had the car in reverse, peeling out of the drive and back down the hill.

I climbed the steps to Felix's front door, crossing my fingers he was home. I gave a sharp rap and waited two beats while footsteps approached from inside.

Felix opened the door and stared at me.

"Maddie?"

I gave him a one finger wave. "Hi. So, um, I need another favor."

His eyes crinkled at the corners. "Lovely to see you, too. What, me? I'm just fine, thanks for asking, love."

If I'd had any energy left I me, I might have felt bad. "Sorry. It's been a long day. I hate getting shot at."

At the word "shot" Felix's face immediately lost it's mocking hint, his eyebrows drawing together in a tight line. "Again? Are you okay?"

"Yeah, I'm fine. She's got terrible aim. Can I come in?"

Felix stepped back. "Of course. I was just making some cappuccino." He gave me a quick (sort of) up and down. "You look like you could use one."

He motioned for me to follow him as he led the way down a hallway and into a kitchen massive enough to make Rachel Ray jealous. He proceeded to flip on a cappuccino machine the size of a Buick and pull two coffee mugs down as I sat at the granite counter and relayed to him the entire events of the day, starting with his gun getting confiscated (to which he asked if I knew how much that thing had cost him. Cheapskate.) and ending with the Mickey D's shoot out and my conversation with Margo. By the time I was done, we were both downing steaming mugs of cappuccino, and Felix's forehead was permanently etched in a frown. No doubt from trying to take mental notes on every detail for the *Informer*'s headline tomorrow: Blonde Fugitive Spotted Eating Massive Amounts Of Apple Pie While Getting Shot At. By Bigfoot. (Hey, they were the *Informer*. They took a little artistic license with their facts.)

"So, you think Margo did it?"

I rested my chin in both hands. "Maybe. I don't know. But with Mia getting another note today, it sounds like whoever it is isn't satisfied yet. I mean, if Veronika was a mistake, and Dusty was just in the wrong place at the wrong time, maybe whoever is after Mia will try again."

"Personally, I'd say it sounds like she deserves it. Is there anyone she hasn't screwed?"

I shrugged. "Beats me."

"So, what's our next move, Miss Marple?"

"Who?"

He shot me a lopsided grin. "Never mind."

"Well, I don't know about you, but my next move is sleep. Which reminds me…" I trailed off, biting my lip. "I was kind of hoping that maybe I could stay here tonight?"

Felix raised one eloquent eyebrow at me.

But I didn't give him a chance to say no, jumping right into the speech I'd mentally practiced on the way here. "See, my place isn't safe, what with Isabel running around, and it's still kind of trashed, and I can't go to Ramirez's because, even forgetting the fact that I don't have a key, he left a really pissed off message about the whole escaping the babysitter thing, and he probably wouldn't open the door for me anyway, and Dana's not home, probably at SA, and Jasmine has cameras all over the ceiling, and, well, you were my last hope."

"It's always lovely to know I'm at the bottom of your list, Maddie."

I ignored his sarcasm. "Please?" I pleaded, doing my best pathetic voice. Which, considering the day I'd had, wasn't too hard to fake.

He paused, his face unreadable. Then finally said, "I'm not sure that's a good idea."

"Come on. I'm sorry about the whole Deveroux-is-gay story. I promise I'll make it up to you. Please, please, pretty please?"

Felix looked at me over his mug. He bit the inside of his cheek and narrowed his eyes. I could see emotions at war behind his blue eyes, but I wouldn't venture to guess what they were.

Finally he relented. "All right, you win. Guest room's upstairs. First door on the left."

I was so relieved I actually jumped off my stool and hugged him.

For a half a second he went completely rigid. Then his arms circled around my waist. Lightly. As if he was almost afraid to touch me. Odd as it may sound, it actually felt kind of nice. His rough cheek pressed against mine, and I felt myself inhaling deeply the scents of expensive cologne and warm cappuccino.

"Thanks." I lifted my face to give him a quick peck on the cheek.

And that's when it happened. Somehow, his head turned. And instead of my lips coming up against stubbled cheek, they were suddenly on his lips. Soft lips. Lips that tasted like imported coffee. And they were moving. Slowly, brushing over mine, warm breath whispering as they skimmed my bottom lip.

I think I made a little sighing noise.

And just like that they were gone.

I realized I had my eyes closed and opened them to find him two steps away, his chest rising and falling heavily, his eyes locked onto my mouth.

I blinked. What had just happened?

"Felix, I-" I started.

But he cut me off, his voice husky and thick with an emotion I didn't *want* to guess at, as he turned his back to me and quickly grabbed both of our mugs, taking them to the stainless sink. "Guest room's the first door on the left. Goodnight."

I stood there watching his back for a full two seconds before I managed a feeble, "Goodnight," myself and followed the stairs to the first door on the right.

Which turned out to be a bathroom, because, of course, Felix had said "left," not "right". So sue me if I wasn't totally paying attention at that point. I'd just been kissed by Tabloid Boy.

And worse yet, I'd liked it.

* * *

I was on a beach. A white, sandy beach filled with palm trees and tropical breezes. The sound of the ocean roared behind me, the scent of salt water filling my nostrils as warm sun soaked into my skin. I was probably going to get a sunburn, but I didn't care. It all felt too good.

I was wearing the itty bitty blue bikini I saw on sale at Nordstrom's last week, and lying on a soft lounge chair. I looked over to the side and saw another chair beside me. I was just wondering whose chair it was when he walked up. Shirtless. I think I drooled a little as Ramirez stood over me, his bronzed chest glistening in the afternoon sun, pecs rippling as he sank down beside me.

"Hi, beautiful," he said, his voice low and deep and accented with that unmistakable undertone of pure sex. He trained his dark eyes on me and slowly leaned in.

I closed my eyes as his lips brushed mine, letting myself melt beneath his touch. It was a slow kiss, long and sensual, as lazy as the sounds of the ocean crashing around us. I never wanted it to end. By the time our lips finally did part I was panting, my entire body burning for more. I slowly opened my eyes.

And saw Felix's face hovering above mine.

* * *

I screamed, sitting straight up in bed. I took deep breaths (In… out. In… out.) My gaze whipped around the room. I was in a low, sleek bed. Blonde woods, piled high with a white goose down comforter and fat pillows. The walls were painted a stark white, splashed with abstract paintings in deep burgundies and greens. Hardwood floors with plush white rugs and the windows were covered in light, flowing curtains, gently swaying in the breeze.

It took a few minutes before a) I stopped panting and b) I remembered where I was. Felix's house.

I did a groan and fell back on the pillows, covering my face with my hands. Had that really happened last night? What was wrong with me? Felix of all people. He was dirt, slime, scum. There was nothing redeemable about Felix.

Never mind the fact that just yesterday I'd been waking up in a different guy's bed. A guy who was supposed to be my boyfriend. Oh God, had I cheated on my boyfriend? Was a kiss cheating? Was I cheater? What would Ramirez say? I had a vision of him punching that clown.

And groaned again.

It had been the gunshots. The peril. The long day. The endless fights with Ramirez. Mercury in retrograde! That was all, right? I mean, it's not as if I *wanted* to kiss Felix. Besides, it was just a kiss. And an accidental one at that! He turned his head. I hadn't even meant to kiss him. I hadn't even enjoyed it!

Much.

I popped out of bed, still in the spandex monster, and grabbed my pumps in one hand, purse in the other. I made a feeble attempt at smoothing my bed-head as I gingerly stuck my head out the door, peeking into the hallway. No sign of life. Good.

I slowly padded barefoot down the stairs, hoping to slip out before Felix woke.

No such luck. As I rounded the corner I spied him in the kitchen, in much the same place I'd left him last night.

He was standing at the counter, this morning's copy of the *Informer* spread out in front of him. Khaki Dockers hugged his frame and, despite the fact that I'd almost convinced myself The Kiss hadn't happened, I felt myself blush as my gaze strayed to his Magnum territory.

I cleared my throat.

Felix glanced up briefly. "Morning. Coffee's in the machine. Cups in the cupboard above." Then returned to his paper.

I set my purse and pumps on a stool. "Thanks. Uh, about last night..."

Felix looked up and gave me a blank look. "Yes?"

"Um, I mean, I just wanted you to know that... I mean accidents happen and... You know, Mercury in retrograde makes people do strange things and... Well, it's not like I..."

I searched his blue eyes, but nothing stared back at me. No trace of emotion or the awkwardness that had me verbally tap dancing all over his hardwood floor.

"Did you have something to say, Maddie?"

I bit my lip again. "No."

"Hmm." He grabbed his coffee cup and took a long sip. "You know, you've got a serious case of bed-head."

See? Scum.

I stuck my tongue out at his back as I poured myself a cup of coffee from the stainless machine in the corner. I was just taking my first heavenly sip when my cell rang from my purse.

I crossed the kitchen to flip it open just before voicemail picked up.

"Hello?"

"Hey, Maddie," came Dana's voice. "I got your messages last night. You okay?" I heard her stifle a yawn as she asked.

"Yeah. Fine. Sorta." I sat down and filled her in on the previous day's events as I sipped my way through my steaming cup. "By the way," I asked as I finished, "where were you last night? Your roommate said you were out all day."

Dana stifled another yawn. "Oh, you know, just kinda busy." I heard her stretching.

"SA?"

There was a pause. "Um… yeah. Sure. SA. So, where did you end up spending the night?"

"Uh…" I looked across the kitchen. "My mom's." I cringed. Dana was my best friend. The last time I'd actually lied to her had been when I'd seen her tenth grade boyfriend, Eddie Van Houton, kissing a cheerleader beneath the bleachers after fifth period. As much as I'd known the truth would hurt worse, I'd hated lying to her then. So I had no idea what made me do it now.

"Yep, me and Mom, all night long."

Felix looked up and gave me the raised eyebrow thing. I blushed, ducking my head down.

"Oh. Okay," Dana replied. "Oh, hey, listen. The reason I was calling is I just got some totally good news from my agent this morning."

"Oh yeah?" I said, only too glad to change the subject. "Do tell."

"Okay, drum roll please. Tadadadadada," she said, drawing out the suspense. "Guess who is the one and only Mia Carletto's new stand-in on *Magnolia Lane*?"

I froze. "No."

"Yes! Can you believe it? How lucky am I?"

"Lucky?! You do realize that the last person to hold this job is dead, right?"

Dana waved me off with a pft sound between her teeth. "Oh, come on, Maddie, what are the chances of that happening twice?"

I refrained from pointing out that it already had – with Dusty.

"I'm going to be a permanent member of the cast of *Magnolia Lane*. Like, how totally cool is that?"

Considering the last person to fill this role had wound up strangled with a pair of support hose, "cool" wasn't exactly the word I'd choose.

"Dana, please don't do it."

"What? Why not?"

I bit my lip. "What about the letter Mia got yesterday? This guy isn't giving up. And if Mia really is the target, and he tries again… well, I just don't want you in the way."

"Don't worry, Maddie, there's, like, tons of security there now."

Right. Which hadn't helped Dusty at all. "Dana, I don't think this is a good idea."

"The AD said I might even be able to speak a line now and then. A line, Maddie! You know how much SAG base pay for one line on *Magnolia Lane* is?"

"Dana, I know this might be a good career move, but-"

"Good? It's the best thing that's happened to me since I got that walk-on part in the Brad Pitt movie. I'll be a permanent member of the cast, Maddie. This is huge!"

So was the feeling of dread, slowly building up in the pit of my stomach. "Dana please-"

"Holy crap! Is it really seven o'clock? Wow, I've got to go." She stifled another yawn. "Gotta be on set by eight. They can't start blocking scenes with out a stand-in. Wish me luck, Mads!"

"Dana, wait!" I called into the receiver. But she was already gone.

I stared at my cell, my heart racing, my stomach churning. Probably Dana would be fine. Probably I was overreacting. Probably the police presence on set was huge, and whoever the killer was, he wouldn't be able to get within ten feet of Dana.

Probably.

"So, I'm your mother now?" Felix asked, folding his paper.

"What? Oh, sorry. I had to tell her something."

"And you didn't want to tell her you came begging at my doorstep in the dead of night?"

"I wasn't begging." Much. "And ten o'clock is hardly the dead of night."

Felix shrugged. "Hey, that's okay. If you want to keep our torrid affair a secret from your friends, be my guest."

I opened my mouth to protest (It was an accident!), when I saw the teasing twinkle in Felix's blue eyes.

"Jerk."

"Sticks and stones, love. Sticks and stones."

Felix downed the bottom of his coffee cup. "I've got to go check in with my editor. There are clean towels in the guest bath," he called over his shoulder as he sauntered out of the room.

I twirled the dregs of coffee in my cup, that ball of dread still sitting like a lead weight in my stomach. By taking the stand-in job, my best friend had just effectively labeled herself killer bait. If someone was really intent on going after Mia, that meant anyone close to her was in harm's way. It wasn't like this guy was picky, he'd already gotten rid of two innocent victims. I paused. Well, okay, maybe if Veronika had been blackmailing someone, she wasn't entirely innocent, but I was pretty sure she didn't deserve death by control tops.

Any way you looked at it, Dana was throwing herself right into the thick of it.

Alone.

I set my cup down on the counter. Right next to Felix's keys and wallet. The wallet was leather, looked expensive. The keys were attached to a ring that had a 99 cent plastic fish dangling from it. Total Felix.

I reached out and slid one finger down the soft leather siding of the wallet. Hmm… I wondered…

With a quick glance over my shoulder, I flicked it open. Yep, right there, stuck into the billfold, was Felix's press pass. His golden ticket that could get him in just about anywhere.

Even the *Magnolia Lane* set.

I bit my lip. I glanced over my shoulder again. I could faintly hear Felix on the phone with his editor, arguing about word count and column placement.

I took a deep breath. Then hopped off the stool, grabbing my purse with one hand and Felix's wallet and keys with the other.

That's it. He was so never letting me sleep over again.

* * *

My hands were shaking as I stuck the keys into Felix's battered Dodge Neon. I turned the ignition, wincing at the loud sound erupting through the quiet morning. I glanced at the front door, expecting to see an irate Felix come running from it any second. Nothing. I quickly backed out and pulled down the street, my eyes glued to the rearview mirror. Nothing. I did a small sigh of relief. Maddie: 1. Tabloid Boy: 0.

I know, I was a terrible person for stealing Felix's car, especially after he made me cappuccino and let me stay over. I consoled my guilty conscience by telling myself I'd make it up to him, that I'd feed him the exclusive of the century once I made sure Dana was safe.

And, by the time I came down out of the hills, I had formed the beginnings of a plan to do just that. To not only get Dana out of harm's way, but to get a killer behind bars, as well. Step number one was to get inside the studios.

While I hadn't officially been fired as wardrobe assistant, I had a feeling that after the whole carrying-a-gun-onto-studio-property thing, my name was on Bug Eyed Billy's "do not allow entry" list. (Not to mention the fact that if Ramirez caught me on set he'd likely throw me in the back of a squad car faster than you could say purple Prada pumps.) Luckily, I knew for a fact that Felix's name *was* on Billy's list. All I had to do was convince Bug Eyed Billy and Queen Latifah that I was not the crazy blonde with the habit of setting off their metal detector, but a crack tabloid journalist with the *L.A. Informer*. Which meant I needed to change my look and I needed it quick.

There was only one person I knew that carried a virtual wardrobe around in his trunk, not to mention a fully stocked make-up kit. I floored the accelerator as I pointed my stolen car in the direction of Fernando's.

* * *

"Maddie, dahling!" Marco dropped the fishing net he was draping over the reception desk and attacked me with air kisses as I walked through the doors of the salon.

Followed closely by Pablo's greeting. "*Squawk! Oops, I did it again. Squawk*!"

Marco shot the bird a dirty look. "No Britney. That's the rule. I told you no, Britney."

I'm not sure, but I thought I saw the bird spit in Marco's direction.

I tippy-toed over to his desk, doing a pseudo whisper. "Is Mom here?"

Marco shook his head. "Nope. Your mama isn't due until three, when she has a bikini wax scheduled for Mrs. R.

I did an internal shudder. Okay, I admit, it was so big, some of it carried over externally.

"And Ralph?"

"*Fernando*," Marco chided, "is doing a cut and color for Mrs. Lohan." He leaned in close. "Lindsay's mom."

I nodded, looking to the back of the salon where I saw Faux Dad running his scissors through the wet locks of a slim, forty-something blonde.

"Good. Because I need a favor."

Marco clapped his hands together. "Are we on a case?" His eyes twinkled with that same *Charlie's Angels* look I was coming to know and dread. But, considering it was Dana's tush on the line, I plowed ahead, explaining my need for anonymity.

"Oh, dahling, I've got just the thing! Follow me!"

Marco skipped out from behind the white washed desk, motioning one of the nail girls to cover for him. I followed him into the back, giving Faux Dad a cursory wave as I passed his station.

As I made my way through the rich and not-so-famous clients, I could have sworn I saw a woman point at my shoes and whisper behind her hand to the lady in the next beehive dryer over. I couldn't help a little swell of pride. The first Maddie originals, and already people were talking.

I followed Marco into one of the back rooms where he pulled out a black duffel bag. "I'm going clubbing later with this adorable boy I met in NoHo last weekend. Lucky for you, I brought a couple of outfits to choose from.

And, lucky for me, Marco and I were approximately the same size. Unluckily, his taste tended toward leather, leather and more leather. (Studded with gold, of course.) He held up a pair of black, leather pants and a red leather jacket to match. I cringed.

"Um, don't you have anything a little less conspicuous?"

Marco looked pained. "Dahling, I don't dress to blend!"

As well I knew. "Okay, okay. What else do you have?"

He rummaged around and pulled out a see-through, mesh shirt in hot pink and a pair of white stretch pants.

"I'll take the leather."

I stuffed myself into the extremely non-breathable leather outfit, topping it off with a white T-shirt that read, "Fernando's Beverly Hills", a pair of big, black sunglasses and, thanks to a quick rinse, brunette hair.

And my pink heels. (There was no way I was fitting into Marco's size twelve loafers.)

I looked in the full-length mirror hanging at the front of the salon.

"Well, what do you think?" I asked.

"Exquisite," Marco said, clasping his hands together.

"Not bad," the nail girl agreed.

"*Squawk! Hit me baby one more time*!"

CHAPTER EIGHTEEN

By the time I arrived at the studio, the line to get through security had diminished to something slightly less than a Monday morning at Starbucks. I waited impatiently, tapping my foot as I inched forward, all the while keeping my head down and trying to look small and inconspicuous.

Finally I made it to the front, watching Queen Latifah take inordinate pleasure in wanding an overweight PA.

Bug Eyed Billy looked up from his clipboard.

"Name?" he asked, eyeing me carefully.

I did a nervous throat clearing thing and held my breath as I handed over my stolen press pass.

He glanced at it. Then up at me. Then back at the pass.

"Felix Dunn?" he asked, narrowing his eyes behind his coke bottle glasses. "You're Felix?"

I nodded. "Uh-huh. That's me!" My voice suddenly sounded helium laced. I cleared my throat again.

"Felix sounds like a man's name," Billy said, glancing back at the pass.

"It's, uh… French. It's pronounced, 'Fe-lay.'"

He narrowed his eyes again. "Fe-lay?"

I nodded, mentally crossing my fingers. "Yep."

"Like a Fe-lay o' fish?"

"Uh… yeah." I nervously glanced from side to side, sure that at any moment someone would stand up and yell, "Fake!"

"And you're with the *L.A. Informer*?"

"Yes?" Which might have been more convincing if I hadn't phrased it as a question. I bit my lip, tasting Raspberry Perfection lip gloss as I nervously shifted from one pink pump clad foot to the other.

Billy grunted. "Hmph." He flipped through his list, his myopic squint searching for a "Fe-lay." I held my breath, resisting the urge to peek over his shoulder.

Finally he checked off an entry and handed the press pass back to me. "Okay, you're cleared. Go on through."

I did an internal sigh of relief so loud it echoed inside my brain. I took off my earrings and belt and pulled my stolen keys out of my pocket, depositing them all in a plastic tub to ride through the x-ray machine. I did a silent prayer to the gods of false disguises and stepped through the plastic archway.

Beep.

Oh hell! I froze. What, what, what? I chewed my lip again, sure that panic was written all over my face.

Latifah glanced down. I think I heard her stifle a snicker. "Those your shoes?"

I looked down at my pink heels. "Yes, why?"

No disguising the snicker this time. "Nothin'."

"Yeah, I know they clash with the red jacket."

"Uh-huh. Well, maybe you wanna put them on the belt, there, honey. You know… take 'em off. Take 'em <u>all</u> off." She snorted again and glanced at Billy. He was grinning, too.

"Uh… o-kay." I slipped my shoes off and threw them into a plastic tub to ride through the machine.

I stepped back through again.

Silence. Blessed silence!

I gave Latifah a little wave, keeping my head low, and grabbed my belongings, just barely resisting the urge to sprint through the lot.

Step one, accomplished.

On to phase two.

* * *

Ten minutes later I was slinking around the corner of stage 6G, carefully watching for any sign of a) Steinman (lest he draft me for wardrobe duty), b) Ramirez (lest he notice me on wardrobe duty and slap a pair of handcuffs on me), or c) Dana (whom I desperately needed to get to before either a or b happened).

I entered the warehouse, keeping close to the walls and hoping I blended into the background as I slunk toward the soundstage. I picked my way over wires and ropes duct taped to the ground, thinking inconspicuous thoughts as I passed the craft services area. Luckily, no one tried to stop me. Though, I did notice a couple of PA's looking at my shoes as I scuttled past. I think one even snickered a, "Hot stuff," as I walked by. Okay, now I was starting to get a little self-conscious. Yes, they clash. I get it!

I was almost to the soundstage when a familiar voice hailed me from the wings.

"Hey, Maddie."

I had a mini heart attack, spinning around so fast I feared whiplash. I breathed a sigh of relief when I saw who it was.

"Hi, Ricky."

"What are you doing here? That big cop said you weren't allowed on the set any more."

I cringed. Oh yeah, handcuffs were definitely in my future.

"I'm just here to see Dana. Know where she is?"

"Sure. She's blocking out the next scene. Ashley and Chad are having make-up sex today. Apparently he doesn't care who the baby's daddy is after all."

The wonders of television.

"Thanks," I said, turning to go.

"Hey, did that woman ever find you?" Ricky called.

I paused. "What woman?"

"There was this woman looking for you earlier. She didn't leave her name but she had, like, really long black hair. And she seemed a little high strung."

Oh. Crap.

Isabel.

"She was here?" I squeaked out, sounding way too like Minnie Mouse for my liking. I had no idea how she got onto the lot, but knowing she was anywhere in the vicinity of my person made my skin instantly break out in goose bumps.

Ricky nodded. "Yeah. Hey, you okay? You look kinda pale."

I gulped down a dry lump in my throat. "Yeah, sure, fine. When was she here? What did she say?"

Ricky scrunched up his face like he was thinking really hard. "Um, it was earlier this morning, right after I got in. I told her I wasn't sure you'd be here, but she just said she'd hang around and 'catch up to you.'"

Oh boy.

I mentally added one more name to the list of people that I so did not want to run into today. In fact, I moved her name right up to the tippy top of the list. I debated calling Ramirez and telling him that Isabel was lurking somewhere on studio property. But that would mean telling him I was lurking on studio property, and me in the back of his squad car wasn't going to help Dana any.

So, instead, I mumbled, "Thanks," to Ricky and made a beeline for the soundstage.

I spotted Dana right away. She was lying in Ashley Culver's bed, dressed in a peach colored tube top and tight briefs that almost exactly matched her skin tone. Unless you squinted, it looked like she was in the buff. Which, it seemed, was the idea, as Steinman directed her though a series of seductive poses, all the while shouting about the white balance and back lighting.

Long extensions had been added to her hair, so that Ashley's curly blonde locks now fell over Dana's shoulders. Her make-up was done to perfectly match Mia's skin tone and I think she was even wearing green contacts. The dread I'd been feeling all morning kicked up a notch. Even I might have mistaken Dana for Mia.

Then again, it was perfect for what I was planning.

I waited behind an unused camera crane while Steinman blocked out the rest of the scene, Dana beaming and making kissy faces at the camera the entire time. Never mind that the cameras weren't on, Dana was milking her fifteen minutes for all it was worth.

Finally Steinman signaled one of the PA's in a headset to go get Mia for the real deal.

Dana slipped on a pair of flip-flops and a robe before stepping off the soundstage. I grabbed her arm almost immediately, dragging her into the shadows.

"What the-" she started.

I did an instant shooshing motion, holding an index finger up to my lips.

"Maddie!" she whispered. "What are you doing here?" She scrunched up her nose. "And what's with the hair?" she asked, fingering my newly brown tresses.

"It's a disguise."

"Totally good idea," she said, nodding sagely. "'Cause if Ramirez catches you here, you're toast."

"You've seen him?" There was Minnie Mouse again.

Dana nodded. "Yeah, and I'm pretty sure he used the words, 'arrest' and 'blonde' in the same sentence. He gave me the total third degree about where you were. I told him that you were at your mom's, and I think he's on his way over there now."

I cringed as an image of Ramirez interrogating Mom popped into my head. Though, I wasn't sure which one I felt more sorry for.

On the upside, having Ramirez out of the way for a couple of hours made things that much easier.

"Listen, I've got a plan," I said, dragging Dana behind the crane as a pair of grips walked by. I quickly filled her in on the idea that had been cooking in the back of my head all morning. And, yes, I'll admit it was just a wee bit on the "harebrained" side, but that didn't mean it wouldn't work.

All I needed to implement it was one more person.

Mia.

* * *

I realized that Mia was the key to all of this and the only person on the set that I hadn't talked to yet. And, unfortunately, I needed her help if we were going to pull this off. I know Mia wasn't exactly known around the set as the helpful type, but I had a feeling that if anyone was eager to get rid of Mr. Poisoned Pen, it was her.

Dana and I watched from the wings while Mia and Ricky wiggled under the sheets of Ashley's bed, pausing every few minutes for Mia to complain about Ricky's hands skimming inappropriate places or the camera not zooming in on her good side. Finally Steinman was satisfied (or fed up with Mia) and yelled, "Scene," breaking for lunch. Poor Ricky looked infinitely relieved.

Dana and I gave Mia a three-count head start to her trailer, before slipping out the back.

I was happy to see Ramirez was still nowhere in sight (Thank you, Mom!) as we tippy-toed between the corrugated metal trailers, passing Ricky's, Blake's, and the one marked "Talent" before coming to Mia's. Dana rapped two knuckles on the metal door.

"Yes?" came the sharp reply from inside.

"Wardrobe," I called.

"Oh for God's sakes," I heard her respond, her voice growing louder as she moved toward the door. "We just finished the last scene." The door popped open and Mia stood glaring at me. She was wrapped up in a red, silk robe that contrasted sharply with her pale skin. Her lips were painted a red to match, as if lipstick was the first thing she'd thought of putting on when she return to her trailer. Her feet were bare, and her enviable blonde curls framed a face that was etched in a deep scowl.

"Who are you?" she demanded. "I have my own wardrobe person, you know?"

"Right. Um, listen, could we come in for just a minute?"

She put both hands on her slim hips narrowing her eyes at me. "Why?"

I glanced nervously over my shoulder. I wasn't sure how long Mom could keep Ramirez occupied, but I had a feeling even she had her limits. "I need to talk to you about your stalker."

Mia blew a short puff of air through her ruby red lips. "What, you trying to sell a story to the tabloids? Think you can get a quote from me or something?"

"No, no. Nothing like that. I…" I paused, not sure how to voice my idea without sounding like a bad Scooby Doo episode.

But Dana jumped right in. "She has a plan to catch the killer."

Gee, thanks, Shaggy.

Mia arched one slim, professionally shaped eyebrow at me. "So you're a wardrobe assistant *and* a detective?"

"Look, can I please just come in for a minute to talk?"

I could tell she still had her doubts, but luckily her curiosity won out over skepticism. She stepped aside, silently allowing us entry. We navigated the two metal steps and quickly shut the door behind us.

"So?" Mia sank down into one of her velvet covered sofas, arms draped casually over the back in a practiced pose straight out of a Marlene Dietrich movie. "What do you want from me?"

I gingerly perched on the sofa opposite, glancing out the brocade covered windows to make sure the coast was still clear. Just a couple of grips smoking cigarettes. So far, no Bad Cop.

So far.

"Maddie has been helping the police investigate the murders," Dana started.

"Really?" Mia eye's roved my person, taking in the leather and clashing heels. "*You're* working with the police?"

"Uh, well, sort of." I shot Dana a look. "Loosely."

"We've already questioned tons of suspects and narrowed it down to someone on the set," Dana continued.

"I'm not surprised," Mia snorted. "They're all jealous of me. Any one of them could want me out of the picture."

"So you think the killer really is after you?" I asked.

"Of course! Veronika was just a stand-in. Who'd bother with her?"

I paused, wondering if I should mention Veronika's extracurricular activities on the set. But I figured at this point, what did I have to lose?

"We think Veronika may have had a little side business going on. Blackmail."

Mia raised both eyebrows and gasped out loud. "Blackmail? Who on earth was she blackmailing?"

I shrugged. "We're not sure."

"But we'll find out," Dana piped up beside me. "Maddie's a totally good detective."

Mia turned to me. "Oh?"

"Um, well…"

"Don't be so modest." Dana chucked me on the shoulder. "She's helped the police lots of times before. And we always get our man. Right?"

Mia's lips quirked up, seeming truly amused at this. "Just like the Mounties, huh?"

I cleared my throat. "Anyway, we have a small favor to ask. We think we might be able to find the identity of your stalker if we catch him in the act, so to speak."

She narrowed her eyes. "What do you mean?"

"In the act of trying to harm you," Dana supplied.

"You want to use me as bait?" Mia's voice rose to a level of shrill just slightly below dog whistle.

"No, no," I reassured her. "He'll only think it's you."

"I'm the bait," Dana said proudly.

Mia gave her a slow up and down and made a face. "You seriously think someone would mistake you for me?"

"They mistook Veronika for you," I reminded her.

She sucked in her cheeks, thinking this over. "What do you need me to do?"

I felt my stomach lurch. Maybe at the relief of getting her cooperation (no small hurdle, as the last week had taught me), or maybe at the thought that we were actually going to go through with this Lucy and Ethel scheme.

"All we need you to do is stay away from your trailer tonight."

Mia frowned. "Why?"

"I'll pretend I'm you," Dana chimed in, "and after we wrap, go into the trailer, seemingly alone. Only Maddie will be watching from the bushes, ready to call for help as soon as the killer appears. But, if he sees two of us, well, he'll know I'm a fake. So we need you to stay out of sight."

"Can you do that?" I asked.

Mia nodded, slowly. "All right. You really think this will work?" she asked, watching me carefully under her sculpted brows.

I took a deep breath. "I hope so."

* * *

The rest of the day passed in slow motion as I hid out in the "Talent" trailer, drinking coffee, playing solitaire on the tiny laptop computer, and feeling the bundle of nerves in my stomach escalate higher than the price tag on a pair of Blahnik originals. I diligently ignored the piling messages on my voicemail from Felix, all of them promising bodily harm if anything happened to his Neon, and none of them using language I could repeat in polite company. But they paled in comparison to the escalating threats on my machine from Ramirez. He went from a peeved, "Where the hell are you?" last night to this afternoon's growling, "Goddammit, Maddie call me, or I swear to God I'm going to…" and then it kind of trailed off into Spanish curse words. I almost felt bad. I almost gave in and dialed his number. Almost. If he had any inkling I was within ten feet of the set, he'd probably cuff me to a radiator somewhere and throw away the key.

So, instead, I kept a close eye on the windows, watching for any sign of Bad Cop or his buddies in blue. None. Though my heart leapt into my throat when I saw a swish of black hair disappear into Blake's trailer. I think I forgot to breathe for two full minutes until Kylie skipped out, wearing the black wig for her scene as Tina Rey's evil twin sister from Baltimore.

By the time the sky was beginning to turn a dusky blue, I was nursing my fifth cup of coffee, and my nerves were strung tighter than Felix's wallet.

"Hey," Dana said, popping her head in the door.

I yelped, spilling coffee on my wrist. "Geeze, you scared me."

"Oops, sorry. Next time I'll knock."

I wiped at the coffee with a napkin. "You finished?"

Dana nodded, stifling a yawn. "Yep, we're done blocking. Ricky and Mia are shooting their last scene, then we're a wrap."

And Operation Bait was a go. I felt those nerves do another flip and sipped at my drink.

Dana stretched and yawned into her hand. "Man, I am beat. Any more of that left?" she asked gesturing to my cup.

"I'll make a new pot. Stand-in work more tiring than you thought?" I asked, slipping a filter into the Mr. Coffee in the tiny kitchenette.

Dana nodded. "It's exhausting. Plus I had kind of a late night last night."

"At SA?"

"What?"

"Sexaholics Anonymous? That's where you were last night, right?"

"Oh. Uh, yeah. Right."

I paused, scoop of French Roast hovering over the basket. "You were at SA last night, right?"

Dana shifted on the sofa and did a nervous laugh. "Where else would I be?"

"Oh, no. Don't tell me, that extra with the cute butt? The PA with the van? Please tell me it's not a grip?"

"No! Geeze, none of the above. I'm celibate, remember?"

I narrowed my eyes at her. "Just promise me one thing. Promise me that this new stand-in job of yours is not the product of you sleeping over at the shifty eyed AD's house."

"Maddie, please!" For the first time in her life, I think I saw Dana blush.

Yikes. This was more serious than I'd thought.

I was about to further lecture my best friend on just what Therapist Max would have to say about all this, when the trailer door burst open again.

I jumped, spilling coffee grinds onto the counter.

Maybe I should switch to decaf.

"Oh, sorry, I didn't know anyone was in here," Deveroux said, stepping into the trailer. Then he took one look at my pink heels and blushed like a schoolgirl.

"Oh, you're wearing them again."

I stepped around the counter, obscuring his view. "Long story. I didn't have time to change."

Deveroux sat down on the sofa beside Dana. "Maddie, I want you to know that I am so, so sorry."

I raised an eyebrow at him. "For?"

He shook his head. "I don't know how it happened. Usually those websites are so discrete. I don't know how this clip got out."

"Clip?" My internal radar pricked up. "What clip?"

He looked down toward my feet again. "You know, from yesterday. I have no idea how it got out."

"Wait-" I held up a hand, crossing the room to face him. "What do you mean, 'got out?'"

Dana looked down at my shoes. "Ohmigod! I didn't put it together before. It's you!"

"*What's* me?" Okay, now I was starting to worry.

"The YouTube clip!" Dana yelled, bouncing up and down. "It's all over the internet, this girl doing a foot strip-tease. Ohmigod, you're, like, famous!"

Mental forehead smack.

Dana popped up from the sofa and grabbed the laptop, closing my solitaire game. After a couple of clicks, she opened a browser window and typed in the address of the internet video sharing site. I watched in horror as she clicked a clip entitled "High Heels Seduction," and the soundtrack to a *Debbie Does Dallas*-esque film played over a scene in a pink, fluffy bedroom. A scene featuring a pair of pink, leather ankle strap, rhinestone buckled, high heels. On my feet!

"Oh. My. God. I'm going to kill her!"

"Who?" Dana asked.

"Jasmine! She must have put that video up on the internet." I was supremely thankful she'd edited out my face, though the idea of internet pervs getting their rocks off to my pink pumps still squicked me out beyond belief. "How many people have viewed this?" I asked, frantically trying to see if there was a delete button anywhere. No such luck.

Deveroux (who was turning a little flushed as he watched the screen) looked at the counter in the corner. "Only three hundred thousand."

"Only?" I smacked my forehead with the heel of my palm. No wonder I'd been getting shoe snickers all day. If this was some sort of retribution for getting Jasmine's windows shot out, we were so even after this.

"Great. I have sunk to a whole new low."

Deveroux made a low groaning sound.

"Stop watching that!" I flipped the laptop screen shut. Then tucked my feet back under me.

The trailer door opened again (this time I was too pissed off to jump) and a PA stuck his head in.

"Steinman just called a wrap. We're done for the day," he said, before ducking back out as his headset crackled to life.

Dana and I looked at each other, images of strangling Porn Star Barbie fading as she voiced my thoughts.

"I think that's my cue."

"You sure you want to do this?" I asked, that bundle of nerves returning full force.

"Of course!" She grinned. "Wish me luck, Mads."

"Good luck, Ethel."

"Who?"

"Never mind."

* * *

The air was eerily still for how chaotic it had been just hours ago, cranes, props and trailers casting odd shadows along the outside walls of stage 6G. I hugged the walkie-talkie that I'd "borrowed" earlier from a PA as he left. (Borrowed. That was my story, and I was sticking to it. Okay, so I slipped it out of his bag when he wasn't looking, but I fully intended to return it once the night was over.) One press of a button, and a yell of a code two-fifteen, and security would be swarming from all directions. As well I knew.

Sill, my heart was beating against my rib cage so hard I feared I might crack something as I crouched behind a golf cart, watching the door to Mia's trailer. Dana had gone in an hour ago, pausing on the step with her back turned to anyone who may have been watching. Giving them ample time to realize she was inside, alone and vulnerable.

Again my stomach clenched, and I wondered if this was really such a hot idea. But the truth was, I was tired of being chased, tired of being scared, and most of all, just plain tired of wearing other people's clothes. What I wouldn't give to be able to go home and throw on a pair of my own jeans. And a pair of heels that hadn't starred in internet porn.

The last grip had just filtered out of 6G, but already my feet were starting to go numb from all the crouching. I thanked the weather gods that the night was clear and not too cold as I hugged Marco's leather jacket against me.

And then I heard it. Footsteps.

I froze, adrenalin surging through my veins so hard I was sure that it was audible. I held my breath, watching the door to Mia's trailer as they grew closer. Closer. Then stopped.

Damn.

From behind the cart I could clearly see the door to Mia's trailer, but I had to admit that without giving away my hiding place, my vision was limited to just that. Where had the footsteps come from? And, more importantly, where had they stopped?

I bit my lip, willing myself to be silent as I strained against the night air to hear more.

Nothing.

I did a one-Mississippi, two-Mississippi count, then, ever so slowly so as not to rustle my leather pants, stretched my legs and craned my neck to peek around the hood of the golf cart.

That's when I saw him.

A dark figure, all in black, wearing baggy clothes with a low baseball cap pulled down over his eyes.

I sat back down, my pulse hammering in my ears, my fingers fumbling with the walkie-talkie. I hit the talk button. But nothing happened. Damn. I hit it again, listening for the telltale static that it was working, my eyes whipping wildly from it to the door of Mia's trailer. No dark, menacing figure filling the doorway.

Yet.

"Come on, come on," I whispered, banging it against my hand.

Then it crackled to life.

I was so relived I almost cried out. I hit the talk button, static filling the silence, and was about to tell them that we had a serious code two-fifteen and needed back up, like, now!

But I never got the chance.

Just as my finger hit the button, something thick and rough wrapped around my throat, pulling tight.

Choking off my air.

CHAPTER NINETEEN

Instinctively, I dropped the walkie-talkie, my hands flying up to my neck. I gasped for breath. In vain, I might add, as the pressure on my throat tightened. I tried to call out, but no sound. Just a sickening gurgle of air being squeezed out of my lungs.

I fought to keep the world from going fuzzy, my vision blurring as the pressure behind my eyes built, stronger and stronger until I thought they'd bulge right out of my head. I kicked my legs wildly, coming up against a whole lot of empty space. My lungs burned, my stomach spasming, begging for oxygen. The lot began to fade from my vision, a big black nothingness slowly wrapping around my brain. In another two seconds, I knew I'd be a goner. I had to do something. Fast.

I closed my eyes, summoning up what strength I had left, and channeled Dana, doing the one move I'd remembered from the Aerobic Kickboxing class she dragged me to last fall. I moved my leg back in a swift motion, kicking back like a donkey in the region I hoped contained my attacker's family jewels.

I heard a soft grunt behind me, his grip loosening momentarily. That was all I needed. I clawed at the strap around my neck, pulling just enough slack to slip it over my head. I bolted forward, tripping on my heels in the attempt. Marco's leather pants scratched against the pavement as I fell on all fours, scraping the palms of my hands. But I barely felt it. My entire body so grateful for air that I was taking huge, thirsty gulps of the stuff as I scrambled back up to my feet and took off running like a shot.

But apparently my kickboxing was a little rusty, as my attacker was quickly on my heels. I heard his footsteps echoing through the near empty lot behind me. But I didn't turn around to look. I couldn't. I was too freaked out. He was gaining on me. No small surprise considering that my lungs still felt like I'd been inhaling Tabasco sauce.

I bolted past 6G, weaving through the maze of warehouses until I turned a corner and found myself in New York. The city streets were eerily still in the nighttime, dark in a way the real New York never was. I barreled through the Bronx and Manhattan, turning a corner and finding myself in San Francisco. I tripped once on the hilly terrain, but quickly scrambled to my feet as the steady pounding of footsteps behind grew closer.

I barreled on, turning the corner and curving back down a hill lined with fake Victorians. My throat hurt, my head hurt, my thighs burned, my entire body protesting that this was the hardest workout I'd had since Dana made me try a Billy Blanks Tae Bo video with her. I'd almost died of exhaustion then.

Only this time if I pooped out, I really would be dead.

I surged forward, running on pure adrenalin. I hit the bottom of the hill and rounded another corner into the Central Park section of the lot. I could feel him gaining on me, my heart racing as I wove between the trees. He was so close I could hear his breath coming hard and fast behind me, warning me that an out of shape shoe designer was no match for a determined killer.

And then I saw it. The metal detector.

I saw the little red light blinking over the archway, indicating it was still turned on. I prayed to God it was hooked up to a remote monitor somewhere in the security office. If I could make it to the metal detector, my shoes were sure to set it off – hadn't they always? – and security would come running. I surged forward, new hope spurring me on. I felt my legs pumping so hard it was like running on overcooked spaghetti. My arms were shooting back and forth like pistons, my entire body leaning forward, urging me on despite the ever present footsteps hovering just behind me.

I was so close, only a few more feet. I could see the gate beyond the metal detector, closed and locked now, of course. A sole overhead lamp illuminated the ugly plastic frame. Only right now, it looked like heaven to me.

I closed my eyes and pumped with all my might, visualizing myself as Flo Jo, crossing the Olympic finish line. I was close, I could make it…

Though, on my steady diet of Top Ramen and take-out, it was clear I was no Olympic athlete. And, as I felt a hand clamp down on my shoulder, it became clear I wasn't going to make my finish line.

I felt his hot breath on my neck as he spun me around. Hard.

"Uhn." The force threw me to the ground. I landed on my butt, facing the menacing figure in black. I crab walked backward, whimpering as he hovered above me.

Then he stepped into the light and my breath caught in my throat, my paralyzing fear for a moment converted into pure shock.

"You!" I found myself saying, like some victim in a bad detective film.

She snorted, her perfectly manicured brows drawing together over familiar green eyes. "Surprised?" Mia asked. Then threw her head back and laughed, tendrils of blonde hair escaping from the cap on her head. "Some detective you are, huh?"

I shook my head. "I… I don't understand."

"That's not surprising; you're not exactly a rocket scientist."

Hey!

I ripped my gaze from her eyes, wide and slightly unbalanced I now noticed, and traveled down to her hands. One was twisting a brown, leather belt. The other held a gun.

I gulped.

"You killed Veronika?" I squeaked out.

"Don't pass judgment on me, you little twit," she said, pointing the gun at my nose. "If you saw what Veronika was doing, you wouldn't think she was such an innocent victim. She was blackmailing someone all right. Me!"

My head was spinning, partly from the lack of oxygen, but mostly with bits and pieces of information that had been swirling in my brain for days. And suddenly, as if by magic, they were falling into place.

"It was about the letters all along," I said.

Mia grinned, showing off two rows of perfectly bleached teeth. They seemed to glow in the moonlight, giving her face an eerie otherworldly look. If it was possible, she creeped me out even more.

"Yes, it was about the letters."

"Only…" I paused, letting things fall into place, "Veronika didn't write them. You did."

For a moment her creepy smile faltered. Apparently I wasn't playing role of "dumb blonde" to her satisfaction. "It was all Blake's fault. I was trailing in the ratings because of his stupid nerves. The man couldn't even give a goddamned red carpet interview without breaking into a sweat and stuttering like Porky Pig. And then that bitch, Margo, goes and tries to write me out of the film script. Me! Can you believe it? I'm the fucking star of the show. So, I decided I needed more screen time. If the writers weren't going to give it to me, I'd just have to write myself a new part."

"Like the victim of a stalker fan?" I glanced behind Mia. Where was this extra security everyone kept talking about? If I could keep her talking long enough, surely someone would see us, right?

"Why not? Do you know how much fan mail I get every single day?" She snorted. "Five times as much as that Margo, I'll tell you. So, I started sending some to myself. Increasingly obsessive. Then they start arriving daily, threatening my life." She smiled again, and I was reminded of a wolf grinning down at its prey.

I shuddered. I hated being prey.

"You wouldn't believe how the media ate that story up," she continued, eyes shining like a fever victim. "You know, I hit the cover of *Star, People*, and *US Weekly* all in the same week?"

"So what went wrong?" I glanced over Mia's shoulder. Come on, come on, what was the hold up?

"Veronika, that's what." Her smile disappeared, her jaw setting into a hard angle as she stared at a point just beyond my head. "That nosey bitch. One day I come into my trailer and who do I find there but nosey Veronika. Lost her copy of the shooting schedule and wanted to borrow mine. Or so she said.

She found one of my letters. Half finished. She may have been a nosey little bitch, but she wasn't stupid. She put two and two together and realized I'd fabricated the entire story for the press."

"And she threatened to go public if you didn't pay her off?"

Mia nodded, her cap bobbing up and down. "Greedy bitch. She wanted half a mil."

Which would have seemed like a fortune to Veronika. Only, according to *Entertainment Tonight*, Mia made at least that per episode.

"Why didn't you just pay her off?"

Mia's face distorted, her lips curling back to bare her wolfish teeth at me. "Because that wasn't the way I planned it. Being a blackmail victim was not in my script. Blackmail is dirty and deceitful. I'm the fucking star of this show! No one drags me to that level."

O-kay.

Eccentric artist didn't even begin to describe the kind of crazy that was going on here.

Mia took a step toward me, her eyes flashing, the gun catching the light as it glinted my direction.

I winced, feeling my throat tighten up.

"So you killed her?" I squeaked out, stalling for time.

"Minor rewrite. But a good one, don't you think? The perfect opportunity to escalate my stalker into a full blown, above-the-fold murder story. I told her to meet me in my trailer after the wrap, and I'd give her what she wanted. Greedy little thing actually thought I was going to pay her off. Ha!" Mia laughed out loud, a short bark that held little humor. "So, I handed her the money, and while she was busy counting it, I came up behind her and strangled her with a pair of pantyhose I'd taken from wardrobe earlier that day."

The final piece of the puzzle clicked in my brain. "Dusty saw you take the pantyhose."

Mia frowned, obviously peeved that I'd skipped ahead in the script. "Yes. At the time I told her I'd run my first pair. But after she found Veronika, it became clear that Dusty wasn't as stupid as she looked. She confronted me. Told me she was going to the cops with what she saw. Maybe the cops would have believed her, maybe not. But I couldn't take that chance. Not when the press was eating this story up. I had a Barbara Walters interview scheduled! So, I had to write Dusty out of the picture."

The way Mia referred to killing Dusty, as if she'd simply dropped a character from her little show, made me sick to my stomach.

"So you killed her, too?"

Mia smirked. "I used Margo's scarf to try to throw suspicion on her. Nice plot twist, huh?"

I glanced behind Mia's shoulder again. Nothing. No sign of security. No sign of anyone.

I felt my heart clench in my chest as Mia took another step toward me, and I realized I was truly on my own here. Maybe if I could just slowly inch backward toward that metal detector…

"What are you doing?" Mia took a step forward, shoving the gun my face.

I froze. "Nothing."

She snarled at me. "Then stop moving! I don't want to have to shoot you. It's supposed to be strangulation. Don't make me ruin your scene."

I gulped. And just barely avoided those five cups of coffee sitting in my bladder from staining Marco's leather pants.

"So, what happens next?" I asked. Not that I really wanted to know. I was pretty sure that this was the point in the script where Mia went for an R rating by adding some gratuitous violence via one badly dressed blonde. But I figured the longer I kept her talking, the longer I had to come up with some brilliant plan to get away. (Yes, I was aware that as plans went, so far mine had backfired miserably.)

"Next," Mia said, taking a menacing step forward, "the nosey new wardrobe assistant is found dead by the back gate. The *Magnolia Lane* strangler strikes again."

Mia's wide eyes suddenly went calm as she took a step toward me, and I realized it was now or never. Unless I wanted to be found with black and blue marks on my neck that would really clash with my red leather and porn shoes, I had to move.

I watched Mia take one more step, closing the gap between us. I took a deep breath, closed my eyes, and said a silent prayer.

Then, in one swift movement that would make my mother's tabby cat jealous, I pushed off the ground and lunged at her throat.

She screeched, thrown off balance, and staggered back a step as my weight slammed into her anorexic build. Had she been the one wearing three inch heels, she might have fallen backward, giving me the upper hand. Unfortunately, she was wearing sturdy work boots, and I was the one in the three inch heels. She quickly regained her footing, dropping the belt to grab a handful of my hair instead.

I screamed. Loudly. It was one thing to catch a hair or two in a zipper, quite another to have an entire handful yanked from the roots. With visions of bald spots dancing in my head, I retaliated, my fingernails clawing at her face.

Her turn to scream. "Not my face, you bitch!"

She stomped on my foot with one of her boots, crushing my toes. I yelped, then knocked her cap off her head and grabbed a handful of blonde locks.

Yes, I admit it, we were in an all out catfight. If this had been MTV, we'd be in the money. Only the winner of this catfight didn't get their own reality special and label of Celebrity Bitch Queen. The winner got to walk away alive. The loser… well, I didn't even want to think about the loser. Mostly because as Mia shifted and I felt that gun barrel poking my ribs I had a bad feeling it might be me.

I grabbed her wrist and focused everything I had on pointing that gun anywhere but at my person. I danced her backward toward the metal detector. She resisted, pulling the other way. We tugged and pulled back and forth, moving closer and closer. One more little inch and…

Beep, Beep, Beep!

The thing went off, echoing through the air and, I hoped, making little red lights dance across Bug Eyed Billy's monitor at the security office.

Mia dropped her hands, momentarily stunned before she realized what had happened.

"You stupid bitch! Look what you did!"

I let go of her and took another step back, setting off the machine again.

"Stop it! Stop walking back and forth!"

She straight-armed the gun in front of her, and I froze.

"You ruined everything! This was the perfect episode," she screamed. If she'd sounded crazy before, she looked it now, her hair sticking out on one side, red scratches down the side of her face, and her eyes big and wide, burning with an emotion only Freud could identify.

"That's it," she said, taking one giant stride closer, "I'll have to go with the alternate ending."

My breath stopped as she cocked the gun, the sickening click echoing through the air. Suddenly time stood still. Each beat of my heart thumping in my chest like a drum, blood rushing in my ears, the scenery going fuzzy until all I could see was the barrel of Mia's gun. Big chicken that I was, I closed my eyes and felt hot tears build as I braced myself for the sound of a bullet thundering through the chamber.

And then it happened. The gun went off.

I sucked in a breath…

Then slowly let it out. What do you know – I wasn't dead. One more breath in and out. Yep, still living.

I flipped my eyes open.

And saw Mia lying on the pavement in front of me, her eyes wide and unseeing, a big red stain pooling around her blonde curls.

Bile rose in my throat, and I would have screamed if I'd been able to find my voice.

"I told you I'd catch up to you!"

I looked up.

Oh. Hell.

It hadn't been Mia's gun going off.

It was Isabel's.

Black hair flapped behind her like a cape, long, fishnet clad legs pumping toward me. Gun pointed out in front of her as two more cracks filled the air, bullets pinging off the side of the metal detector that started beeping like a car alarm again.

Mental forehead smack. Was I the only person in L.A. not packing?

"You shot her!" I yelled, ducking behind the metal detector.

"You're next, bitch!"

I held my hands out in front of me to ward her off. "Look, Isabel, I didn't have anything to do with your boyfriend…"

"Snake hates me, and it's all your fault!" Two more shots rang out.

"I'm sure you're better off without him."

"What do you know, blondie?" Another bullet pining off the side of the metal detector.

"Have you thought about couples therapy? I saw this *Dr. Phil* episode the other day about rage in relationships…"

But, luckily, I didn't have to go any further.

Out of the corner of my eye, I saw a blue streak race across the lot and go flying at Isabel like a linebacker, tackling her to the ground with a thud.

I watched, relief thudding through me, as Queen Latifah pinned Isabel beneath her considerable bulk, one hand on her walkie-talkie as she yelled, "I've got a two-fifteen here! Requesting backup! I repeat, a two-fifteen!"

CHAPTER TWENTY

Five security golf carts surrounded the scene, dozens of uniformed officers and security personnel wrapping bright yellow crime scene tape around the dark red puddle staining the asphalt. Three huge spotlights, courtesy of the lighting department, shone enough wattage down on the scene to make it feel like noon instead of midnight. And me, sitting on the edge of the medic's van, wrapped in an ugly green blanket, serious amounts of mascara streaked down my cheeks as I watched the medical examiner wheel Mia's lifeless body away.

After the studio security guards had swarmed from every direction toward Isabel's kicking and screaming body, the rest of the evening had kind of blurred together. Isabel had been handcuffed and dragged away by three security guards, shouting obscenities the whole way. A medic had arrived on scene and scooped my crumpled, crying self off the ground and into a van where he'd examined me head to toe and pronounced a slight case of shock. (Understatement alert.) Then the LAPD had arrived in full force, followed closely by the media. I searched the flashbulbs and camera crews for a glimpse of Felix. True to my word, he'd been the first call I'd made once security had arrived on the scene. He'd been so excited about the story, he hadn't even cursed at me (much) for taking his car. Instead, he'd yelled something about evening editions and calling a cab. But if he was here now, he was lost in the crowd of paparazzi.

I did, however, spy Detective Prune Face making his way onto the scene, along with two other plainclothes detectives wearing gun bulges and grim expressions on their faces. No sign of Ramirez.

I wasn't quite sure whether that made me glad or not. On the one hand, the thought of his big arms around me was comforting enough to downgrade my shivers from a 7.2 to mild aftershocks. On the other, I could only imagine the lecture I'd be getting once he saw the outcome of harebrained scheme number three thousand gone awry. If, that is, he was still even speaking to me.

"Maddie!" I looked up to see Dana rushing toward me, her fake blonde locks flapping behind her. A uniform stopped her at the crime scene tape, but after a couple of nods from Prune Face, he let her through.

"Ohmigoooooood! Are you okaaaaaay?" Dana grabbed me in a rib crusher hug.

"Ouch."

"Oh, sorry." She stepped back. "What happened to your hair?"

I cringed, gingerly lifting a hand to my head. "Mia ripped out a chunk. It's bad isn't it?"

Dana was such a good friend, she didn't even answer that. "God, I'm so glad you're okay!" she said instead, diving in for another hug. "I was so worried about you. I waited and waited in the trailer, but no one showed up. And I got totally bored, so I, like, booted up Mia's computer to surf YouTube some more. And guess what I found?! Letters, Maddie. Just like the ones she said she'd been getting. Know what I think? I think maybe Mia's been writing them all along."

Does my friend have good timing or what?

"Anyway," she continued, "I peeked my head out the door to tell you, but you were, like, totally gone. I was so totally worried about you!"

She gave me another rib crusher. But, honestly, this time, I didn't even mind.

"Uh-oh." Dana stepped back.

"Uh-oh?"

"Trouble at three o'clock."

I turned my head to the left.

"No, *three* o'clock." Dana grabbed my chin and tilted my head right.

Detective Prune Face was talking with the latest plainclothes to appear on the set. He was dressed in worn-in-the-right-places jeans and a muscle hugging T-shirt, and wore a day old growth of stubble on his dimpled chin. Along with a tired expression that said he'd been out chasing down one errant blonde all night.

Ramirez looked up and caught my eye, his jaw going tense.

I did a little dry gulp. Uh-oh.

"Um, I'll just be over here if you need me…" Dana trailed off, wisely giving Bad Cop a wide berth as he made a beeline toward the medic van. If my legs weren't still in a jelly state, I might have joined her. As it was, I just hugged my green blanket a little tighter as his imposing form stopped in front of me.

"I'm so, so sorry," I squeaked out, my voice doing the caught-in-the-cookie-jar thing. "I so didn't mean for this to happen; I was just going to call security, that's all. And I'm so, so sorry about ditching Officer Mustache, but Dana was here all alone, and she's my best friend, and she looked so much like Mia, and then there was another letter, and I was sure he was going after her again; only then he turned out to be the she that he was going after and-"

But I didn't get any farther. Ramirez leaned in and covered my lips with his. Roughly. Possessively. His hands grabbing my shoulders, pulling me to him with a fierceness I'd only seen in Carey Grant movies.

By the time he came up for air, my legs weren't the only part of me turning to jelly.

"Oh," I sighed.

Ramirez looked down at me, his eyes dark, a frown hovering over his brows. "You're going to be the death of me, you know that, right?" he rasped out.

"I'm so amazingly sorry. For everything. But, get this - Mia was the one writing the letters all along!"

"I know."

I cocked my head to the side. "You know?"

Ramirez nodded. "I just came from the crime lab where SID has been analyzing the envelopes Mia's letters arrived in. The only DNA found in the saliva on the seal was a match to the sample we took from Mia's lipstick."

Mental forehead smack. "So you already knew that Mia was the killer?"

"We had enough to question her as a suspect." He glanced at the red stain on the asphalt. "At least that would have been our next step."

"I'm so, so sorry," I apologized again. "If it's any consolation, she totally confessed to me before Isabel shot her." I paused. "Hey, how did Isabel get on the lot anyway?"

Ramirez scrubbed a hand over his face, as if the evening had taken more out of him than he was willing to admit. "Apparently she stole a stunt car they were going to use for a chase scene in that new police drama. She hijacked the driver outside the studio and security let her drive the damn thing right onto the lot." He paused, narrowing his eyes at me. "Apparently security doesn't check credentials as closely as they should, *Fe-lay*."

I bit my lip. "Sorry about that. Seriously, mega-sorry. And you have every right to be angry."

He shook his head at me. "Angry? Jesus, Maddie, I've been worried sick. I was all over L.A. county looking for you last night. Do you have any idea how scared I was that something had happened to you? That Isabel had tracked you down?"

My heart clenched in my chest. "You were worried?"

"Of course I was worried. Dammit, Maddie, I don't know how you do it, but you're a walking time bomb. You get taken hostage, receive death threats, get your place ransacked, your car rammed into, appear in internet porn-"

"Oh, you heard about that, huh?" I felt myself go red.

Ramirez raised an eyebrow at me, but continued. "-impersonate a member of the press, sneak onto studio property, and managed to get yourself attacked by not one, but two killers in one night."

"You forgot the grand theft auto," I mumbled, remembering Felix's multiple messages.

Ramirez raised the other eyebrow. "Excuse me?"

"Uh…"

But luckily I didn't have to answer as he put two hands in front of him. "Wait. Never mind. I don't want to know."

Thank God. Because I so didn't want to tell him.

"All I want to know right now," Ramirez continued as he took a step closer, "is that you're all right."

I opened my mouth to speak, but he put an index finger over my lips. "Don't talk. Just nod."

I shut my mouth. And nodded.

"And that you're done chasing killers and pissing off junkies?"

I nodded again.

"And that I won't be getting any more calls on my police scanner that my girlfriend has just suffered an attempted murder."

I paused. Then nodded, slowly.

"And," he said, leaning in so close that his body pressed against mine, "that you're coming home with me."

Heat pooled south of my belly button and I did a long, low shiver.

And nodded.

* * *

"Nurse Nan, please tell me it isn't true!"

"I'm afraid so, Chad. We did everything we could to save her, but Ashley... she died on the table."

"No!"

"I'm so sorry. But after losing the baby, well, she just wasn't strong enough. She knew this radical new womb transplant surgery was risky. I'm sorry, Chad, there was nothing we could do."

"I... I can't believe it. I don't know how I'll ever go on without her. She was my entire life."

"I know it's hard, Chad, but we have to be strong."

"Hold me, Nurse Nan!"

Dana and I watched as Nurse Nan and Chad fell into an embrace that even the casual watcher could see was leading to a June-December romance for sweeps week.

"He is so freaking hot." Dana popped a pretzel (fat free, salt free, and made with organic rice flour, of course) in her mouth and crunched down hard.

"I can't believe how easily they wrote Ashley out of the story. You think they'll bring in a new actress?"

Neither of us had gone back to the set after my last late night encounter with Mia. Dana had been let go because, with Mia gone, they obviously didn't need a look-alike for her anymore. Steinman had asked me to return as assistant wardrobe, but the moment I'd gotten home I'd had about a hundred messages on my machine. In between the usual newspapers calling for a story there had been Tot Trots saying I had, in fact, gotten the My Little Pony contract. But what had really put me over the edge was the call from a trendy Beverly Hills boutique saying customers had come in looking for the "High Heels Seduction" shoe, and where could they order a few dozen? Okay, so infamy may just have an upside after all. I was still a far cry from Milan, but, thanks to Jasmine, having a fall line of my own wasn't completely outside of reality.

Dana shrugged. "I dunno. But if they are, my agent so better get me an audition. I kinda miss that set."

"Seriously?" I asked around a mouthful of pretzel (full fat, extra salt and chocolate dipped. What can I say? Old habits die hard.).

Dana nodded and sighed, her eyes doing a wistful faraway thing. "Anyway, what are you up to tonight?"

I grinned. "Ramirez is coming over."

She raised an eyebrow. "*More* make-up sex? What are you two, rabbits?"

"I wish. Actually, I promised Mom that I'd come over for dinner. Ramirez agreed to be a buffer."

"Oh. Bummer."

"But… if I'm lucky he might sleep over after."

Dana grinned. "Niiiiice."

"And, I promise I'll give you all the juicy details tomorrow. I know how you sexually sober gals live vicariously."

Dana's grin faded. "Oh. Right. Um, about that…"

"Yes?"

She chewed at her lower lip. "I, uh, well, I kinda have a confession to make."

I smirked. "I thought so. Spill it, sister. Who's the new guy?"

Dana glanced at the TV screen where Chad and Nurse Nan were still grabbing each other like teenagers. "Um, well, you remember how nice Ricky was about letting me borrow his car and how sweet that whole monogamy thing was…"

"No. Way. You're dating Chad!?"

Dana nodded. "I'm so sorry, Maddie. It just kind of happened. I was helping him with his lines, and next thing I know we're in his bedroom, and my panties are across the room. I wanted to tell you, but you seemed so proud of me over the whole SA thing. I just felt like I was letting you down. Honestly, I haven't seen Therapist Max in over a week. And I gave all my chips back. I guess I'm just not a celibacy kind of girl. Think you can forgive me?"

"Are you kidding? You're dating one of *People Magazine*'s sexiest men alive! You go, girl."

"Aw, thanks, Mads."

"Just promise me one thing."

"Anything."

"If he asks you to go to the Emmys with him, you have to sneak me into the after parties."

Dana grinned. "Done."

"Nurse Nan, come quickly."

Dana and I turned our attention to the screen where a man in a white coat was hailing Nurse Nan from down the hospital corridor.

"What is it, doctor?"
"It's Mr. Culver."
"Ashley's husband? What's happened to him?"
"He… he's waking up from his coma!"

* * *

Two hours later I was popping one last chocolate covered pretzel into my mouth as I took a final turn in front of the mirror. The short, black DKNY dress I'd picked out at the mall earlier was a perfect compliment to my three inch, strappy emerald slingbacks. It was cut low in the front, high on the thigh and draped like silk with half the wrinkle. As a concession to the faint purple marks still gracing my neck, I slipped a loosely knotted emerald scarf around my throat and topped it all off with a pair of dangling silver earrings.

I was just adding a swipe of Raspberry Perfection when I heard a knock at the door.

"Coming," I called, capping my lip gloss and crossing my studio in three quick strides.

I peeked through the hole and got that familiar rush in my belly as two chocolate brown eyes peered back at me above a growth of sexy day-old stubble.

Grinning like an idiot I undid the security chain and opened the door to let him in.

Ramirez hovered in the doorway, leaning his broad shoulders against the frame. He crossed his arms over his chest, that black panther peeking out beneath the hem of his shirt as it strained against his larger-than-life biceps. His tongue darted out to lick his lower lip as he gave me a slow up and down and did that low growl thing in the back of his throat.

"You like?" I asked, doing a slow turn for him.

The corners of his mouth tugged up until that deceptively boyish dimple made an appearance in his left cheek.

"Oh yeah. I like."

"Good. 'Cause we've gotta go. And Mom invited Molly, Stan and the kids over, too, so if we're late, we're going to have to sit next to Connor, and I am so not getting mashed potatoes flung at this dress."

I grabbed my purse and moved to walk out the door. But Ramirez caught my arm.

"Hang on."

I paused. "Yes?"

He leaned in close. I could smell the mingling scents of leather, aftershave, and pure guy as his lips gently skimmed over mine. It was just the slightest of touches, but it made my insides quiver.

Okay, so maybe I could spare a couple of minutes…

But before I could follow through with that thought, Ramirez pulled away.

He took a step back, his eyes intense on me, some emotion building behind them that I couldn't read. He wiped one hand across his jaw and shifted back onto his other foot. "Listen, Maddie, there's something I need to say before we go. Something I *want* to say."

"Okay…" I waited.

Ramirez did another foot shift. He bit the inside of his cheeks. He did some more intense staring. If it was anyone but Bad Cop, I'd say he almost looked nervous.

"Are you okay? I mean, if you want to sit down or something we could…"

But I trailed off as Ramirez took a step closer to me and pulled something out of his jacket pocket. Something small. Something round.

Something in a jeweler's box.

I froze, my heart forgetting to beat as I stared at a *ring box* in his hands.

Oh. My. God.

"Maddie, these past few days have made me crazy. Not knowing where you were was the scariest thing that's ever happened to me. It made me realize, I don't ever want to not know where you are again."

And suddenly my heart was beating again. Way, way too fast. Holy shit! Was he proposing!? I felt my breath shoving in and out of my lungs double speed and feared I was hyperventilating. I so was not prepared for this. I mean, marriage? To Bad Cop? He was the love 'em and leave 'em type. The bad boy who made your heart go pitter-patter then rode off into the sunset type. He was the I-carry-a-gun-and-I'll-handcuff-you-to-the-bed-for-a-night-of-really-kinky-sex type. People like Faux Dad and Mrs. Rosenblatt got married. Not people like Bad Cop.

Right?

Right?!

"Look, I know we've had our moments lately. And, I realize I can be a bit of a jerk at times. But not knowing where you were that one night almost drove me crazy."

That one night. Right. The one I'd spent at Felix's house. Sitting in Felix's kitchen. Drinking Felix's cappuccino.

Kissing Felix's lips.

Ohmigod, I'd kissed Felix! I couldn't say "yes" to Ramirez now. What about that kiss? What would he say? I mean, it *had* been an accident. It didn't mean anything. It was all a big mistake. A misunderstanding. Yes, that's what it was, a misunderstanding.

I realized that the panic pounding in my ears was so loud it had drowned Ramirez out. I gave myself a mental shake, willing my heart to stop drag racing.

"…all I'm saying is that I don't want to keep you out anymore." Ramirez made a move to open the case.

Instinctively, I slapped a hand over his. "Wait, Jack. I…" I took a deep breath. Here goes nothing. "There's… there's something you should know."

Ramirez looked down at me. His eyes dark and sincere, filled with emotion that this time I didn't have to guess at. It was plain as day. It was the most tender look I had ever seen from him. My throat suddenly closed up, and I couldn't breathe.

"Just, let me say this first, okay?" he asked, covering my hand with his and extracting the box.

I bit my lip. Oh lord, I was going to cry. I was going to bawl like a baby.

And I was pretty sure that if he got down on one knee, I was going to have a heart attack.

"Maddie…"

Oh God, this was it. This was the moment. My stomach churned, those chocolate covered pretzels threatening to make a repeat appearance.

"I want you to have this."

Ramirez opened the jewelry box.

I took a deep fortifying breath, willed my stomach to stand still, and looked inside.

To find a key.

What the…?

"It's a key to my house." Ramirez pulled it out of the box and dangled it from his index finger. "I want you to have your own key. That is, if you still want it?"

A key.

I let out a big breath, emotion draining from me. Whether it was relief or disappointment I wasn't yet ready to examine. But on the upside, I was pretty sure it wasn't a heart attack.

Ramirez opened my hand and pressed the key into my palm. He'd had a copy made onto a pink, metal key with little red lipstick kisses all over it. Very cute. Kinda sassy. Very… me, I realized.

I guess Bad Cop did know me after all.

"Thanks," I said, thoroughly meaning it.

Ramirez leaned in and planted a soft kiss on my forehead. "You're welcome," he whispered. "Is that a 'yes?'"

I gulped down a dry lump in my throat. I would tell him about that accidental kiss. Later. Possibly when I knew he wasn't armed. But not now. Not in the middle of this perfect proposal of almost cohabitating or at least sleeping over without notice.

"Yes."

Ramirez's grin was so big twin dimples popped out on his cheeks. "Good. Now, let's get to your mom's before The Terror drools on every available seat."

I grabbed my purse, slipping my new pink key inside. Somehow it felt a little heavier. Fuller. Actually, it felt kind of nice. Like I had a little piece of Ramirez with me everywhere I went now.

I bit back a big goofy grin.

"By the way," Ramirez said, his lips close to my ear as I closed the door behind us, "I do expect you to use that key tonight."

My stomach flipped, sending a shiver right down to my toes.

Oh, boy.

ABOUT THE AUTHOR

Gemma Halliday is the author of the *High Heels Mysteries*, the *Hollywood Headlines Mysteries,* and the *Deadly Cool* series of young adult books. Gemma's books have received numerous awards, including a Golden Heart, a National Reader's Choice award and three RITA nominations. She currently lives in the San Francisco Bay Area where she is hard at work on several new projects.

To learn more about Gemma, visit her online at www.GemmaHalliday.com

JAICO PUBLISHING HOUSE

Elevate Your Life. Transform Your World.

ESTABLISHED IN 1946, Jaico Publishing House is home to world-transforming authors such as Sri Sri Paramahansa Yogananda, Osho, The Dalai Lama, Sri Sri Ravi Shankar, Robin Sharma, Deepak Chopra, Jack Canfield, Eknath Easwaran, Devdutt Pattanaik, Khushwant Singh, John Maxwell, Brian Tracy and Stephen Hawking.

Our late founder Mr. Jaman Shah first established Jaico as a book distribution company. Sensing that independence was around the corner, he aptly named his company Jaico ('Jai' means victory in Hindi). In order to service the significant demand for affordable books in a developing nation, Mr. Shah initiated Jaico's own publications. Jaico was India's first publisher of paperback books in the English language.

While self-help, religion and philosophy, mind/body/spirit, and business titles form the cornerstone of our non-fiction list, we publish an exciting range of travel, current affairs, biography, and popular science books as well. Our renewed focus on popular fiction is evident in our new titles by a host of fresh young talent from India and abroad. Jaico's recently established Translations Division translates selected English content into nine regional languages.

Jaico's Higher Education Division (HED) is recognized for its student-friendly textbooks in Business Management and Engineering which are in use countrywide.

In addition to being a publisher and distributor of its own titles, Jaico is a major national distributor of books of leading international and Indian publishers. With its headquarters in Mumbai, Jaico has branches and sales offices in Ahmedabad, Bangalore, Bhopal, Bhubaneswar, Chennai, Delhi, Hyderabad, Kolkata and Lucknow.

SINCE 1946